Chance of a Lifetime

BARBARA KAYE

Harlequin Books

TORONTO • NEW YORK • LONDON
AMSTERDAM • PARIS • SYDNEY • HAMBURG
STOCKHOLM • ATHENS • TOKYO • MILAN

Published April 1991

ISBN 0-373-70449-6

CHANCE OF A LIFETIME

Kirsten felt nothing but pure bliss

She wiggled deeper in his lap, unwittingly eliciting an elemental response in Grady that caused him to feel strangled. "If you thought it might happen, even would happen, I confess I didn't. I didn't see how it was possible for two people to come together after so many years and feel so much for each other," she confessed dreamily. "It seemed pretty farfetched. I told myself I was only taking the haven you offered, but . . . I love you, Grady. Just like before."

The knot in the pit of Grady's stomach tightened. "Do you remember 'before' now?"

"Quite a bit, yes."

"It was magic, wasn't it?"

"I seem to recall that . . . yes, it was magic."

He stood with her still cradled in his arms. "Let's see what we can do about finding some of that magic now. . . ."

ABOUT THE AUTHOR

Barbara Kaye is justifiably proud of the
Hamilton House trilogy—the pinnacle of her
Harlequin career thus far. Newfound fans will
be glad to know that Barbara, a veteran
Superromance author who lives in Oklahoma
with her husband, is already hard at work on
future Supers!

NOTE:
If you missed the first two books of this
trilogy, *Choice of a Lifetime* and
Challenge of a Lifetime (#411 and #433),
you may order them from
Harlequin Reader Service.
In the U.S.:   P.O. Box 1397, Buffalo, NY
                14240-1397
In Canada: P.O. Box 603, Fort Erie, Ont.
                L2A 5X3

PROLOGUE

DAVID O'CONNOR was fifteen when he discovered that his mother had lied to him. His real father had not died in Vietnam, after all.

The discovery came about innocently—the result of a school assignment. Each student in David's American history class had been asked to choose a state and write a paper about some significant event that had occurred there within the past hundred years. David had chosen Mississippi because of the civil rights movement and because it was where his mother had grown up. He'd known she had many boxes of memorabilia stored in her sitting room closet, and he'd hoped to find some information in them that couldn't be found in books.

It was Sunday afternoon, and he was alone except for the servants. His mother, Kirsten, and his stepfather, Travis Garrison Patrick IV, had gone to one of the countless social functions they were required to attend as full-fledged members of North Shore society. David climbed the stairs to the small room that was his mother's private retreat. A large picture window allowed the pretty, feminine room to be flooded with light. From there he could look out over Long Island Sound and see the Connecticut shore in the distance. Opening the closet door, he poked through the dozens of boxes on the top shelf until he found what he was looking for.

His mother had not left Mississippi until late 1975, and he'd thought he might be lucky enough to find some newspapers dating from the sixties. What he found in the boxes, however, were the predictable things: old letters, loose photographs, a program from a high school prom, another from his mother's high school graduation. The photographs fascinated the boy, particularly the ones of his pretty, dark-haired mother when she was a teenager. But unfortunately, there was nothing in the boxes that would help with his assignment.

He was closing one of the boxes when he spied a yellowed envelope pushed to one corner. The return address was that of the county clerk's office in Jackson, Mississippi. Opening it, David found two legal documents. That struck him as strange since his stepfather kept all their important papers in his study's safe. The first of the documents was the certificate of marriage between Kirsten Janice Marshall and Grady Carter O'Connor on March 11, 1970, in Jackson. David stared at it with a wistful smile, regretting once again that he'd never known his father or seen anything but a dim snapshot of him. From his mother he had learned that Grady O'Connor had left for Vietnam six months after their wedding, before she'd known she was pregnant, and he'd died there. David had always admired his mom for carrying on and taking care of him until she'd met and married wealthy Travis Patrick.

Then he opened the second document, and the world stopped spinning for a minute. He had to read it twice before he fully assimilated its meaning. Kirsten Marshall O'Connor had divorced Grady O'Connor in October 1974, more than three years after his supposed death. David was stunned. Why had his mother lied to him?

He was forced to wait until the following day, when Travis wasn't at home, to ask her. He found her alone in Travis's study. Without preliminaries, he handed her the divorce papers, watched her shocked expression and asked, "My real father isn't dead, is he?"

For a minute Kirsten looked as though she might faint. The color drained from her face, and she clutched a nearby table for support. The confrontation she once had dreaded so much had come with frightening suddenness. "N-no," she stammered. "Not to my knowledge."

"Why did you tell me he was?" David asked accusingly.

"Because that's what Travis told his family when we got married," Kirsten said. It sounded feeble and was.

"And you went along with it?"

"You know how the Patricks are." Kirsten had a tissue in her hand; she began twisting it around and around until it was a tight paper rope. "You're smart, David, and I know you're aware that Travis's family doesn't exactly approve of me. In fact, he openly defied them when he married me. If a lie was part of the deal...well, I didn't have too much trouble with that...not then. I trusted Travis to do what was best for all of us."

David gulped. "I want to know what happened to my father."

"What good will that do?"

"Please tell me."

Kirsten heaved a struggled sigh. She was woefully unprepared for this and not at all sure how to handle it. With the truth, she supposed. "Your father's plane was shot down not long after he arrived in Vietnam. The crew was captured and spent over three years as prisoners. I had no word from or about him all that time."

She paused. She'd always regretted the lie, but it had been told before she'd known anything about it. Years ago she had lived in fear that Grady would try to contact them, but that hadn't happened, and the lie had become second nature. Sometimes she forgot it was a lie.

"Did he ever come home?" David asked.

Kirsten nodded. "Yes, when the POWs finally were released. You weren't quite three. It was a very difficult time...for all of us. Prison had been hard on Grady. Of course, it was hard on all of them, but more so on Grady because he had grown up in an orphanage. He couldn't stand being confined."

To call those days merely "difficult" did not describe them adequately. Grady had returned from the war a disturbed, moody, irritable man. He suffered migraines, nightmares and a variety of ailments brought on by years of malnourishment. He was stunned to discover he was a father, and he found he was married to a woman he no longer knew. He had left behind a rather shy, unsophisticated bride; he came home to an independent working mother who was accustomed to being in charge. The presence of a noisy, lively toddler in the house got on his nerves, so Kirsten had seen to it that David spent more and more time with her mother. Father and son simply never got to know each other. The marriage, she could see in retrospect, had been doomed from the moment Grady stepped off the plane. When he left to return to duty, he'd told her to get a divorce.

Kirsten did not think she had ever regretted their decision to part. They had been strangers, and Grady, at the time, had needed something she hadn't been able to give him. As soon as the divorce was final, she accepted a new job at a Gulf Coast resort that the Patricks owned. There she had met Travis, who was spending the winter on the sunny coast. When they were married, they bought her mother a condominium in Palm Beach and settled down in the Long Island mansion. All ties to Jackson and Mississippi had been severed. Now this.

"So what happened when he came home? Did you just . . . leave?"

"No, I wasn't the one who left. Grady was."

"Tell me something about him," David urged her. "What was he like?"

"Oh, David, so much time has passed, and I really didn't know him very well. We were together such a short time."

"You must remember something."

"Well, I . . . I seem to remember that he was this dashing pilot who was a lot of fun and very handsome." The Grady she'd married was nothing like the gaunt, moody stranger who had returned home later.

"How did you meet him?"

"At a Halloween dance in Jackson. He was on leave and visiting a buddy who was a friend of mine. I'd known him exactly five months when I married him." Kirsten was surprised that the memories brought on such a feeling of sadness. She rarely thought of Grady anymore, but she suddenly wished she knew what had happened to him, if he'd ever again found peace. "Now, David, no more."

She fervently hoped that would be the end of it, so she couldn't have been more appalled when David said, "I . . . think I'd like to find him."

Kirsten looked at her son in horror. "Oh, darling, no! What purpose would that serve?"

David shrugged. "I don't know. It just seems like I should at least know where he is."

Kirsten shook her head vigorously. "Even if there was a sound reason for finding him, I wouldn't have the slightest idea where to begin. He must be forty-six now and probably has a family. Why throw his life into a tailspin?"

"He might like knowing me," David persisted stubbornly.

"He never tried to contact us," Kirsten reminded him.

"There might have been reasons for that. Or maybe he did try and couldn't find us. You left Jackson, then left Mississippi. So did Grandma. He might have tried."

"No, no, please, David. Forget this. You can't begin to imagine the harm you might do." Kirsten was genuinely shaken. "I don't understand this, really I don't. Haven't you been happy with your life here? I'm afraid this would hurt Travis deeply."

"This doesn't have anything to do with Travis. He's been great, but he isn't my father."

"He is in all the important ways. He's the one who went to Parents' Day at school and attended all those Little League games. He's the one who paid the orthodontist and paced the floor when you were sick. He's the one who raised you—and raised you in great comfort and luxury, I might add. You're very fortunate, son. Please, just forget about finding Grady. It's impossible.''

David opened his mouth to say something, then closed it. He conceded that he was powerless. He was only fifteen. What could he do without his mother's help? But he wouldn't be fifteen forever. He stared at the floor another minute before leaving the room without a word. Kirsten sank into a chair, feeling oddly exhausted.

KIRSTEN NEVER TOLD Travis that David had discovered the truth about Grady, and David didn't mention the matter again. At fifteen, life was too full and exciting to dwell on something that had happened years ago. New friends, hobbies and interests seemed to crop up every week. So the years passed, and Kirsten conveniently convinced herself that he had put the notion of finding his father out of his mind.

She couldn't have been more wrong.

CHAPTER ONE

Four Years Later

SHORTLY AFTER COMPLETING his freshman year at Harvard, David made a fateful decision: he wasn't going back in the fall. He found himself in the midst of the most uncertain time of his life. The things he had thought he wanted to do when he was sixteen no longer held appeal. Though his grades the previous year had been superlative, they hadn't brought him the feeling of accomplishment he had expected. Majoring in business bored him, yet nothing had come along to take its place. He was restless, edgy, at an impasse. He was going to sit out the fall term.

He fully expected his mother to be dismayed over the decision, and Kirsten didn't disappoint him. "David! But going to Harvard is what you've wanted all your life."

"No, it's what you and Travis wanted. Just give me some time to decide what it is I really want to do. It seems so pointless to spend so much money and to sit in classes all day when I don't have a goal."

"You can get the basics out of the way. It's always easier to stay with something than to get back to it."

Actually, for some time now, Kirsten had felt a vague uneasiness about David's attitude toward college. He had always been an enthusiastic student, but one did not have to be an astute observer to know that no longer was the case. Most of her questions about school were answered with little more than a shrug. However, she didn't easily accept his decision, and they had many conversations about it that summer. Yet, when the fall term began, David stayed home. Kirsten told herself that such periods of doubt were normal for young people. She refused to entertain the notion that her once brilliant student simply was burned out on academics. Privately, she thought that a semester of idleness would leave him so bored he would be raring to go when the spring term began.

David, however, rarely thought about college. He had something else altogether on his mind. Although he had never mentioned Grady O'Connor to his mother again, he had never forgotten. If anything, he had become obsessed with the idea of locating his father, and he had done some homework. Now it was time to tell his mother what he planned to do.

The news hit Kirsten like a thunderbolt. If she had thought about it at all, which she hadn't, she would have sworn David had abandoned the notion of finding Grady. The four years since his discovery of those documents had been busy, productive . . . and the previous one, immensely sad. Travis's untimely death from a heart attack had grieved Kirsten deeply. He had been only sixty and thought to be in perfect health, so his death couldn't have been a greater shock. For many weeks after the funeral, she had sequestered herself inside the house, seeing almost no one but David and the servants, and during that time, mother and son had grown even closer. She couldn't believe she hadn't known he still was thinking about Grady.

"Oh, David, not that again! Why?"

"I'm sorry if it upsets you, Mom, but I've never given up on finding him. There wasn't much I could do about it when I was fifteen, but now I want to try."

"I wish you wouldn't," Kirsten said. Then, as she faced an implacable expression she'd never before seen on her son's face, something incredible happened. A face she thought she didn't remember at all flashed through her mind, as clearly as if she'd last seen it yesterday. Her eyes raked her son from head to foot. David was just shy of six foot, tawny haired, green eyed, and he had an ingratiating smile. *My God,* she thought, *he's going to look exactly like Grady did when I met him!*

"I'm sorry," David said again, "but I have to try. It may take years. I may never find him, but I have to try."

"I hope you remember that none of the Patricks know I'm divorced."

"Give me some credit. And I don't know why you let what the Patricks think bug you so much."

Kirsten bristled. That was a sore point with her because it was too true. She did allow the Patricks to bother her. "Don't change the subject, David."

"Mom, I don't intend shouting this from the rooftops, and I won't cause any trouble for my father. If he has a family and doesn't want to have anything to do with me, I'll butt out. But maybe he'll write me a letter and tell me something about himself... provided I find him."

Kirsten sighed, shaken. "Just where do you plan to begin this...this quest?"

"With the Air Force. I'm going to contact the Personnel Center in Texas. They'll have his address and phone number at the time of his discharge. And if he didn't get out—if he's still in the service—it'll be a piece of cake.''

"How do you know all this?''

"Do you remember Tim Larsen from school? He has an uncle who's a retired Air Force colonel. He told me how to do it.''

So there it was; he had already begun. After David left the room, Kirsten paced nervously, overcome with a sense of foreboding. She wondered why she hadn't put her foot down, forbidden him to pursue this, but being realistic, she knew the best she could do was postpone the search. David had grown up. He had been away from home for an entire school year, and she was astonished at just how much that one year had changed him. He was so much more mature than he'd been a year ago, so much more independent, and thanks to the trust Travis had left him, her son was secure in the knowledge that he'd never want for money. A young man like that could do just about anything he set out to do, and David was determined to find Grady. She didn't really understand the burning need, but she had to accept its existence.

Kirsten went into the sunny solarium adjacent to the study, hoping the cheerful room with its bright colors would lift her spirits. So much of the twenty-room mansion was almost gloomy in its formality. The first time she saw it she had thought of Wuthering Heights, and it still reminded her of England's great manor houses. There was little she could do about the decor since the house didn't belong to her. It, like all the other Patrick houses, was owned by the Patrick Institute, and as such, was considered community property. To do more than add a few personal mementos or knickknacks required family consensus, so Kirsten didn't bother. She enjoyed the solarium, Travis's cozy study and her upstairs bedroom suite, but she merely endured the rest of the museumlike house.

Hardly a week passed that someone didn't remind her that four generations of Patricks had lived and died in the place. The family's traditions were deeply rooted in the past and were firm and unyielding. Though Kirsten's marriage had been a satisfying one, neither she nor David had ever felt they truly belonged with the illustrious Patrick clan. Travis had told her many times she was being ridiculous. "You belong because you are my wife and David is your son," he would say. "Try not to take this bunch too seriously, sweetheart. Remember, the founder of this dynasty was once jailed for horse theft." Yet, the feeling had persisted, and since Travis's death she had felt more excluded than ever.

Her acquaintances would have been astonished to learn that Kirsten ever felt she didn't belong anywhere she chose to. As her forty-second birthday approached, her raven-haired beauty was more breathtaking than ever. Her poise and bearing seemed inborn. Her very presence telegraphed a subliminal message of wealth and privilege, so much so that most of her friends had long forgotten her humble beginnings. She had a gaggle of servants to do her bidding. She and Travis had had use of a home in Palm Beach, another in Vail and a Park Avenue apartment they had kept stocked for evenings when they were in the city late. She wore clothes by Bill Blass and Mary Mc-Fadden, jewelry by Harry Winston, and her picture appeared in *W* with humdrum frequency.

Few people knew how hard she had worked to become the woman she was. All she'd had going for her when she'd come to Long Island from Mississippi were her beauty, a working-class sense of propriety and an older, sophisticated husband to guide her. With the single-minded determination of a scholar seeking an advanced degree, she had studied the manners and mores of the very rich and eventually had found her way through the maze of dos and don'ts. Still, years later, the staid and proper Patricks continued to withhold their unequivocal seal of approval.

There was, however, an exception in the family. Pivoting, Kirsten went into the study to make a phone call. She needed to talk to someone, and when that need came over her, there was one person she always turned to: her sister-in-law, Denise. She dialed and waited. A maid answered and summoned her mistress. Then Denise's voice came on the line.

"Hello."

"I need to talk to you," Kirsten said.

"There or here?"

"It doesn't matter."

There was a pause. "Did Maddie bake today?" Denise asked, referring to Kirsten's cook.

"Maddie bakes every day. It's her hobby."

"Then I'll be right over."

It didn't take long since all of Travis's family lived within spitting distance of one another. Less than twenty minutes later, the two women were seated in the solarium, having coffee and freshly baked croissants. Denise was a bubbly, upbeat extrovert, a refreshing change from most of the Patrick women, whose smiles were more practiced than genuine. Kirsten knew no one she liked as much as she liked her sister-in-law. She admired her gumption and sense of self-worth.

It had been eight years since Denise had shocked her family by filing for a divorce from a husband who was a compulsive philanderer. The situation had been sticky since the husband had been thoroughly integrated into the family's various enterprises, and he had refused to step aside without a healthy financial settlement. Many of the Patricks had begged Denise to adopt a "boys will be boys" attitude toward her husband's dalliances, but she had refused. In the end, the divorce had cost the family a million dollars and considerable embarrassment, thanks to the husband's penchant for talking to the press. For a time Denise had been all but ostracized by most of the family, partly because of the divorce but mostly because she had made waves. Patrick women were forgiven for being many things—snobs, neurotics, hypochondriacs, alcoholics—but not for being wave makers.

The ostracism hadn't lasted long, however, because Denise possessed all the qualities that the Patricks and their ilk most admired in a woman. She was a fashion plate, an accomplished fund-raiser and a superb hostess. But it was her sister-in-law's delightfully droll sense of humor about being a Patrick that had endeared her to Kirsten. The woman took neither herself nor her privileged class seriously. Moreover, her loyalty had been proved time and time again. Denise knew what the word *friend* meant. And she was the only person in the entire family who knew the truth about David's father.

"So, what's up?" Denise asked. "Why the summons?"

"Do you remember when David discovered the truth about his real father?"

"Uh-huh. I certainly remember how upset you were."

Yes, Kirsten had been totally upset yet filled with the need to talk about it. She had, as usual, turned to Denise, as she was doing now. "Well, he's started in on it again," she told her friend. "He wants to find Grady, and this time I'm afraid he's determined."

"Can he do it? Find his father, I mean."

"I have no idea. My first guess was no, but David's pretty smart. He's going to start with the Air Force, which is exactly where he should start."

Denise thought about that. "What do you think will happen if he does find him?"

"Lord, I can't begin to imagine. Grady's probably married and has a family. David's sudden appearance might be the last thing he wants. Remember, he never tried to contact us, and I don't think we were all that hard to find. It seemed to me that he just wanted to forget us and start all over again. When I last saw him, he was an emotional wreck. Maybe he never got over that. If he doesn't want to see David, will David be hurt? I just . . . don't know. I'd give anything if David would drop it, but he's not going to."

"Kids!" Denise exclaimed. "You never know what they're going to come up with next. Even the good ones like David can be such a pain at times. Now me, I'm blessed with a couple of self-serving monsters who are a pain all the time." She paused and frowned. "Are you worried that my family will get wind of this?"

"Not really. David's aware of the situation, and I trust him to be discreet."

"Well, Kirsten, maybe he *should* find his natural father, at least open some avenues of communication. If, heaven forbid, he should ever get sick and the doctors need the medical histories of both parents, you ought to know how to get in touch with Grady. You read about that sort of thing all the time."

Kirsten chewed her bottom lip, prompting Denise to touch her hand in a sympathetic gesture. "I'm a few years older than you are, and if there's one thing I've learned it's that most things work out for the best in the long run. David's got a good head on his shoulders. He's not apt to do anything foolish."

"I hope you're right."

A minute of silence passed. Then Denise glanced around the room and out the window at the spacious grounds. "This house is so huge, just like mine. Sometimes I'd love to pack up and move into a nice apartment somewhere. Wouldn't you?"

"Oh, I guess I've thought about it once or twice, but this is home and has been for a long time," Kirsten said.

Denise was glad Kirsten was blissfully unaware of the family's feelings about having her in the house. In spite of Travis's wishes, which were made clear in his will, the rest of them wanted her out. At the last gathering of the clan, Denise's parents and her younger brother, Roger, had stated flatly that they didn't recognize Kirsten's right to occupy a house that had been home to four generations of Patricks. Traditionally, this house belonged to the oldest Patrick son, and that was now Roger. They were going to make a move soon, Denise was sure of it, and she hoped she could lend Kirsten moral support if nothing else. She herself had been a thorn in her family's collective side so long that the thought of another battle royal didn't dismay her in the least.

It would have dismayed Kirsten terribly had she known of the undercurrents of hostility running through the family, but her thoughts were solely focused on David's desire to find Grady. She tried to think of some positive aspects of a meeting or exchange of correspondence between them, but nothing much came to her. All she could foresee was discomfort, embarrassment, disappointment and, perhaps, rejection.

Denise watched the worry lines crease Kirsten's forehead. "Don't let this bother you so much. There's a very good chance David won't be able to find his father. If a lot of time goes by without results, his enthusiasm is bound to wane."

"I'd like to think so, but David has this quality about him that's . . . Call it tenacity or dogged determination or plain pigheadedness, but I have this gut feeling that if Grady's alive and living in North America—no, make that the Western Hemisphere—David's going to find him."

HE DID, but it didn't turn out to be as fast or as easy as his friend's uncle had led him to believe. After having gotten the man's advice, David had returned to the sitting room many times to sift through the boxes, looking for anything about his father that was Air Force related. He'd finally found an envelope containing stubs from the government checks his mother had received while he was a POW. That had given him his father's Social Security number. Armed with that information, he was ready to contact the Air Force.

First he called directory assistance in San Antonio. Once he had the appropriate personnel center's number, he dialed it, stated his mission and was connected with the worldwide locator. The friendly man on the other end of the line took the wind out of his sails fast. "Sorry, we're not allowed to give out that information."

"But, sir... I have this friend whose uncle is a retired colonel, and he told me you would. He said he'd done it many times when he was in the service, that that's what you people are there for."

"I know. We used to do it, but your friend's uncle must have retired some time ago. The Privacy Act prohibits it now."

David couldn't believe it. He absolutely wouldn't accept that he had reached a dead end, not after all the excitement that had been building for days. "It's vitally important that I find Mr. O'Connor. Isn't there anything else I can do?"

"Yes, there's one thing. You can write your letter to Mr. O'Connor and mail it to us, requesting that we forward it. We'll see that it's sent to his last known address. If it's returned to us, we'll send it back to you. That's the best we can do."

David's spirits plummeted, but he took down the address the man gave him and thanked him. Though he'd hoped for more, he couldn't stop now. After a great deal of thought, he sat down and composed a letter to Grady O'Connor, tore that one up and wrote another. Something short and to the point. He wanted to make it easy for his father to tear it up and forget it, if indeed his reaction to receiving it was negative. Then David personally went to the post office to mail it.

The minute the letter was in the mail drop, however, he began to experience anxieties and doubts that weren't entirely alien to him. For years he'd envisioned taking the first step toward finding his father, but now he asked himself exactly what he hoped to accomplish by finding Grady O'Connor. The man, after all, had made no attempt to find him. His mother might have been right all along. Maybe it was best to let sleeping dogs lie. He might find out things he was better off knowing nothing about.

During the past four years, he often had experienced feelings heaped upon feelings, confusion and curiosity being the most prevalent. And a certain amount of resentment—that was directed far more toward his mother than the father he didn't know. However, he found it impossible to stay mad at Kirsten for very long, and not once had he considered abandoning his quest. Now he wondered.

Confusion resurfaced. How would he honestly feel if his father wanted to have nothing to do with him? He didn't know. He thought he was prepared for anything, but how could he predict his reaction if that actually happened?

Worse, what if the letter came back? Would he drop it then? He'd waited so long, thought about it constantly of late, and at last he'd begun. He didn't think he could ever forget about it. Uncertainty warred with curiosity.

But curiosity eventually won out. He wanted to find his father, if only to exchange a few words with him. If Grady O'Connor no longer was at the address the Air Force had for him, hopefully someone there would have a forwarding address for him. If not, if the letter came back to him, he'd decide what to do next. He'd heard there were people who specialized in finding missing persons. He might consider that.

In the meantime, all he could do was wait . . . and wait. The days dragged interminably. The letter was all

David could think about, and it was going into the hands of people who didn't give a flip whether or not he ever found Grady O'Connor. The knowledge made him feel strange and helpless.

Kirsten watched her son and worried. All she knew was that David had written a letter to Grady and had sent it to the Personnel Center for forwarding. Given all the years that had passed, she couldn't help but suspect the search would prove futile. And it was so important to David. Too important. After six days he began hounding the mailbox. She wondered which would be worse—a returned letter or nothing at all.

Finally she had to talk to him about it. "David, if the letter comes back to you undeliverable, what are you going to do?"

"I don't know."

"But you aren't going to drop it?"

"I . . . don't think I can now, Mom."

Kirsten sighed. She had been afraid of that. "All right, suppose you do hear from Grady. Suppose he finally gets your letter and answers it. What then?"

David shrugged. "I . . . I guess I'd like to meet him someday, if he wants to. But the idea also scares me."

"Scares you? Why?"

"I guess in my mind, he's become sort of unknow-able . . . distant. I have to remind myself that he's only a person. And, too, I find myself wondering . . . what if he doesn't like me?"

"Don't be absurd. Of course he'll like you. Best ask yourself what if you don't like him."

"I have." David gave her a rueful smile. "That scares me, too."

Dear God, Kirsten thought once again, *why didn't I put a stop to this before it could go so far?*

THE LETTER WAS FORWARDED from the Personnel Center five days after David mailed it. The forwarding address was an apartment house in Jackson, where Grady O'Connor had lived for several months after leaving the service. Beth Harrison, the resident manager, came across the letter as she was putting the day's mail in the residents' boxes. It had been so many years since Grady had lived here that she had gotten totally out of touch with him. Her first impulse was to mark it "Address Unknown" and send it back.

But something stopped her. Someone was going to the trouble of tracking Grady down through the Air Force, and to Beth's mind, that meant the letter was important. She'd forwarded mail to him for quite a while after he moved out; if she put on her thinking cap, she ought to be able to remember where she'd sent it.

The name of the town came to her right away. Culver, a small place about an hour's drive from Jackson. When Grady had moved out, he'd been excited about his new job, a position with a very large company. It was the name of the company that had Beth stumped. She did remember that it owned restaurants, a lot of them. One was located in Jackson, as a matter of fact.

When Beth finished with the mail, she went into her office and opened her telephone directory to the Yellow Pages. With luck, her faulty memory would be jogged. She found what she was looking for. Hamilton House, that was it. That was the name of the company Grady had gone to work for. There probably was a box number, which she didn't have, but surely in a town the size of Culver, simply addressing the letter to Grady in care of a big company like that would be enough . . . provided he was still there. Now all she had to do was phone the post office and get Culver's zip code.

Normally Beth would not have gone to so much trouble to forward a letter. Tenants came and went, and if she had no forwarding address, mail was simply returned to sender. But she had been unusually fond of Grady. He was one of the few true gentlemen she had ever met, something of a loner who had been more given to long walks and quiet evenings than to partying. No complainer, that was for sure. She only wished she had more tenants like him.

CHAPTER TWO

GRADY O'CONNOR HALTED his Jeep Cherokee at the first of the town's four stoplights and waved at Jerry Jackson, who was seated on the bench in front of Drummond's Hardware. The vehicle's windows were rolled down, so Grady called out, "How's it going, Jerry?"

"Not too bad, Grady. How's it with you?"

"Can't complain."

The light changed and Grady drove on, stopping again at the red at the next corner. The lights were timed so that it was virtually impossible to drive through town without stopping at least once—a safety measure designed to discourage speeders, claimed the mayor and the police chief, but Grady suspected it was an effort to encourage travelers passing through to stop and spend a few dollars in the small community.

Peering idly through the windshield, he spotted Annette Taylor, who worked at the bank. She waved and called, "How's it going, Grady?"

"Not too bad, Annette. How's it with you?"

"Can't complain."

Grady continued on when the light turned green. Culver, Mississippi, was a sleepy southern belle of a town whose commercial district comprised no more than six square blocks. Robert E. Lee Avenue was the main thoroughfare. The rest of the north-south streets were named after United States presidents, and the whole town petered out around Coolidge Street.

There were those who claimed there hadn't been enough changes in Culver during the past twenty-five years to fill up one column in a Jackson newspaper, but Grady thought they did the town an injustice. Years earlier, when Hamilton House, Incorporated— the town's leading employer and Grady's bailiwick— had expanded its nearby agricultural operation, the town had experienced a brief spurt of growth. New businesses had sprung up on both sides of Lee Avenue—restaurants, a new motel, even a few bars. They had been built mainly to serve the needs of the men who drove Hamilton House's refrigerated eighteen-wheelers through town on a regular basis. And most of the old businesses had undergone face-lifts to keep up with the times. One such establishment was Slick's Café, Grady's first destination of the morning.

The breakfast rush was over, and Slick's was almost deserted. Two men wearing caps with the Caterpillar logo on the front sat at the counter, drinking coffee and talking to Slick. Grady waved to the proprietor but did not break stride as he made his way toward a booth in front of the window. He was an athletically built man who moved with fluid grace and a shoulders-back straightness that was a holdover from his Air Force days. His hair was tawny, and he sported a golden tan since he never stayed indoors if he could go out. His hazel eyes were direct and decisive. His everyday working attire consisted of starched khakis like the ones he now wore, and in hot weather they were changed at least once a day. He was in excellent physical condition for a man of forty-six; there wasn't a superfluous ounce of flesh on his five-eleven frame.

He had been in Culver fourteen years and was considered a community leader, a solid citizen, the first to contribute to a variety of charities and the staunchest supporter the Culver High Tigers had. He projected an air of self-confidence, but that had been hard won, as had his peace of mind. Everybody who knew him liked him, but no one claimed to know him really well. Grady, they said, was just too "unknowable." He led the most private of private lives, and if there was a woman in it, nobody knew who she was.

He slid into the booth and signaled to Loretta, the waitress, who poured a cup of coffee and brought it to him. "'Mornin', Grady," she greeted him. "How's it going?"

"Not too bad, Loretta. How's it with you?"

"Can't complain."

"How's your mother?"

"Doin' much better, thanks. The doc gave her some new medicine that seems to be working. Oops, got me another customer. I'll be back in a jiff." The waitress hurried away.

Grady sat sipping his coffee in silence for a few minutes, until he was joined by Slick's wife, Rosemary. She slid in to sit across from him. "Hi, Grady. How's it going?"

"Well, Rosie, I just feel awful," he said with a grin. "I seem to have this pain running from my hip down..."

Rosemary rolled her eyes. "Sorry I asked. Boy, it's been a hot summer!"

"I don't remember many cool ones."

"True. Do you think the earth really is getting warmer, like they say?"

Grady shrugged. "Beats me. But the man in charge of my fields thinks so."

"What's that called?"

"The greenhouse effect."

"Yeah." Rosemary pondered that, then dismissed it. "Well, they say we'll have our first touch of fall next week. Anything new and exciting in your life?"

"Not a thing."

"Sounds like my life. Oh, look, there's Alice Howard," Rosemary said, indicating a pretty redhead walking along the sidewalk past the window. "Is it true she and Claude Brown are having an affair?"

"Good Lord, Rosie, I don't know."

"Sure you do. Guys always know these things."

"Sorry. You've come to the wrong guy." Actually, Grady did know that the school teacher and the banker were having an affair, but as far as he was concerned, that was none of his business. He did not know if Alice and Claude wanted to keep their alliance a secret, but if they did, he reflected, they would do well to conduct the affair somewhere other than Culver. Very little occurred in the community that wasn't common knowledge.

Rosemary looked disappointed. "Well, it must be true. I heard it at the beauty shop."

Grady grinned. "I think if I were head of the FBI, I'd station an agent in every beauty shop in the country."

Loretta returned to the booth and scooted in beside Rosemary. "Are we any nearer getting the hospital's new birthing center?" she asked Grady.

He shook his head. "Afraid not. Folks are reluctant to part with their money these days. We've raised maybe a fourth of what we need."

"That's a shame. I thought it sounded so neat to be able to labor, deliver and recover all in the same room. I guess Doc Morrison's disappointed."

"What we need to do," Rosemary said, "is to throw some kind of big bash that will bring in folks from all the towns around here."

"But what?" Grady asked. "We've had chili cook-offs, spaghetti suppers, a softball tournament."

"No, I'm talking something really big."

"Believe me, I'm open to suggestions, ladies."

Rosemary rubbed her chin thoughtfully. "You know, if Elton Woodruff would let the moths out of his wallet, he could build that center and not even notice any money was gone. Instead he sends his kid on a world cruise as a wedding present."

Loretta sighed. "When I got married, my dad gave us a hundred bucks and wished us well."

Grady smiled over the rim of his coffee cup. This was what passed for meaningful conversation in Culver, and he loved it. It was so delightfully banal.

The tinkling of the bell over the door heralded the arrival of another customer, so Loretta was on her feet again, and Rosemary left to man the cash register. All in all, Grady spent twenty-five minutes in the café, and during that time half a dozen people stopped to have a word with him. It was his custom to "make the rounds" at least twice a week, more often if possible. He usually stopped at Slick's first, more to see and be seen than for the coffee. Then he ran errands and went to the bank. Finally he stopped at the post office to collect the mail. He felt it was politic to be seen around town, to shake as many hands and slap as many backs as he could. When people saw him they thought of Hamilton House, and he never wanted the citizens to forget just how important the company was to the local economy.

He had grown to like Culver and its slow tempo, but that had taken some time. When he'd first come to the community he had taken a look around, groaned resignedly and imagined staying three or four years, just long enough to impress the powers that be at the home office in Dallas, then moving upward and on. He'd moved upward, all right, but he'd done it in Culver. Without consciously setting out to do so, he had convinced Vanessa Hamilton, the company's cofounder and C.E.O. that the agricultural operation was every bit as important to Hamilton House as any of the other divisions. The result was, to the astonishment of many people within the corporation, he had been promoted to vice president and now seemed destined to remain in Culver until he retired.

Once his rounds had been made, Grady tossed the stack of mail onto the passenger seat of the Cherokee and drove back to the imposing compound south of town where he lived and worked. Nestled in the verdant Mississippi countryside, Hamilton House's agricultural operation was an impressive sight. What first caught the eye was the beautifully landscaped entrance with its huge brick arch. Driving through, one followed a two-lane paved road that meandered through hundreds of acres of prime farmland. The three-story building on the right was the processing plant where the restaurants' famous sauces and salad dressings were bottled for retail sale, a sideline Grady had suggested to Vanessa ten years ago and one that had been successful beyond even his expectations.

On the left were the seemingly endless fields of vegetable gardens that grew practically every warm weather crop indigenous to North America, all destined for Hamilton House kitchens. During Mississippi's short winters, mammoth greenhouses were employed to keep the food coming. Supplying fifty-two restaurants with fresh produce was no easy task, but Grady's fields and smaller ones in California and Texas's Rio Grande Valley got the job done.

Immediately past the fields was a low-slung, buff brick building that housed executive offices, and on beyond that was a scene that looked straight out of a science fiction movie—miles and miles of giant tanks where thousands upon thousands of pounds of grain-fed catfish and trout were raised for rapid shipment to the restaurants all over the country. That was another of Grady's innovations that had further endeared him to Vanessa. Not only did the aquaculture operation assure plenty of fresh fish, it supplied it far more economically than previous methods ever could.

Sometimes Grady liked nothing better than to get in the Cherokee and just drive through the compound, basking in the feeling of personal achievement. He often thought about how everything that had happened to him since meeting Vanessa seemed to be due at least in part to Divine Providence—or incredible good luck. Being hired by Hamilton House in the first place, just when the agricultural operation was being expanded, had been a case of being in the right place at the right time. The suggestions he had made that had so impressed Vanessa now seemed inspired. His rise in the corporate ranks had been nothing short of meteoric, and he had accomplished it without having to wear a coat and tie and sit in an office all day. It bothered him not at all that the other vice presidents fondly referred to him as "the farmer." Vanessa liked him, and she counted. After some rotten years, first in the orphanage, then in that damned prison camp, life had turned benevolent. Even the thing that had haunted him for so many years—the boy he didn't know who was his son—no longer invaded his thoughts so insidiously. Many years ago he had made a decision, and it must have been the right one. If not, deep down in his heart he knew Kirsten somehow would have gotten in touch with him.

Grady maneuvered the Cherokee into his private parking space at the side of the office building. Carrying the mail, he entered the building through a side door that led directly to his office. Inside, he punched the intercom to let his secretary know he had arrived. Then he sank into his comfortable swivel chair and began sifting through the mail.

Halfway through the stack he encountered a small envelope addressed to him in a bold, squarish handwriting. Opening it, he found still another envelope addressed to him in care of the Air Force Personnel Center. It, in turn, had been forwarded to the old apartment house in Jackson. He guessed Beth had sent it on to him. Who on earth would be trying to contact him through the Air Force? He had no service contacts left. Frowning, Grady turned the envelope over in his hand, read the return address on the flap, and for a minute his heart seemed to stop beating. A lot of years had passed, but he'd never forgotten that address.

Slumping in his chair, he opened the envelope and withdrew the letter. It had been written on plain, expensive stationery and was dated nine days ago.

Dear Sir,
I didn't know how I should address you. Mr. O'Connor seemed too formal, but Dad didn't seem right, either. I hope my getting in touch with you after all this time doesn't present a problem for you. I would have done this years ago, but for a long time I thought you had died in Vietnam. When I found out that wasn't so, I wasn't sure how to go about finding you. Someone suggested starting with the Air Force. They promised to forward this. It's a long shot, admittedly, but I hope this reaches you eventually.

I'm nineteen now. Last May I completed my freshman year at Harvard, but since I haven't decided exactly what I want to do, I'm taking a semester off. Mom and I live alone now. My stepfather died of a heart attack last year. My grandmother died in Florida four years ago. You knew her, didn't you? We have a house on Long Island's North Shore. From my bedroom window I can look across the sound and see Connecticut.

Unless you prefer not to, I'd like for you to write and tell me something about yourself. Mom has reminded me that you probably have a family and would be embarrassed by my popping up suddenly. If that's true, you can tear this up, and no one will ever know about it. If I don't hear from you, I won't try to get in touch with you again.

I'm enclosing my yearbook picture. It's not very good, but it will give you some idea what I look like.

Sincerely,
David Marshall O'Connor

Grady studied the photograph for the longest time. His eyes stung and he swallowed away the gigantic lump that had formed in his throat. That face! The resemblance was unmistakable. His flesh and blood!

He reread the letter twice before refolding it and putting it back in its envelope. Stuffing it into his shirt pocket, he rubbed his eyes and was startled to find tears in them. It had been a very long time since there had been tears in those eyes. The last time was on a bleak January day on Long Island, when he'd watched a young boy being chauffeured through iron gates and had made the decision to turn around and take the next plane back to Jackson. At the time, Grady had been so sure he was doing the right thing—the only thing—but had it been a mistake? He could have been exercising his parental rights all these years.

He was touched beyond words that David had gone to the trouble to locate him.

Getting up from his chair, he picked up the mail and carried it to the outer office, where he dumped it on his secretary's desk. "Take care of this, Phyllis. If you need me, I'll be home."

Phyllis Graves shot him a peculiar look. Like most longtime secretaries, she was sensitive to every nuance of her boss's voice. "Is anything wrong?" she asked.

"No, everything's fine." A minute later he was back in the Cherokee, heading home. At the point where the paved road curved and headed back to the entrance, a dirt path veered to the east and led to a rock and cedar house nestled in a grove of trees, a house that had been built to Grady's personal specifications. The high-ceilinged, open floor plan made it seem more spacious than it was, and the blinds on the many windows seldom were closed. He could not abide tight spaces, and he always wanted to be able to see outdoors. There, in the comfortable and familiar privacy of his own home, he read David's letter again.

Why had Kirsten lied to the boy? Grady wondered. She must have if David had thought his father died in the war. Had it been her final attempt to exorcise him and their marriage from her life and make a fresh start? Or had the lie somehow been linked to that high-powered family she'd married into?

What difference did it make? For years he had agonized over his decision not to try to see his son, but maybe he had done the right thing. If everyone in Kirsten's new life had thought him dead, he could have ruined that life by showing up. And God knows, he hadn't had much to offer anyone in January, 1976, when he'd made the fateful decision. All the good things had come along afterward. Now he led a life of ease and order.

Perhaps his life had become *too* calm. It had been several years since he'd been involved with one woman, and that relationship had sputtered to an indifferent end, without heartbreak or resentment on either side. He had no problems at work. Vanessa ran a tight, efficient ship and demanded that her vice presidents do the same. He played golf occasionally, and he was always available to the city fathers with his time and money for various worthy causes, but he couldn't say that anything but his work was a riveting interest. He didn't covet wealth and power. He was already making more money than he ever thought he would, and power only brought on problems. Maybe his son's letter was another message from Divine Providence. His life needed a kick in the seat of the pants.

So what did he do about it? David had made it easy for him. Just ignore the letter and he wouldn't be contacted again. It didn't sound as though Kirsten was enthusiastic about any sort of reunion. Maybe he should just drop it.

But that was only an idle thought. Grady knew there was no way he could do that. He wanted to see his son, and being honest, he thought it would be nice to see Kirsten again, too. He'd call and ask if he could visit them. Simple as that. She was a widow now, so there wasn't bound to be any problem with a reunion. There had been a time when just thinking about Kirsten could make him pant. If it hadn't been for that goddam war, they might have built something wonderful together.

KIRSTEN FOLDED her hands primly in her lap and regarded the distinguished gentleman seated in the chair opposite hers. Her father-in-law, Travis Garrison Patrick III, commonly referred to as T.G., was a formidable man of eighty-three years, a perfect example of the head of a family with old money. Through the Patrick Institute, he wielded enormous financial power in the form of endowments, foundations and trusts. The dynasty, founded on a real estate fortune, now reached into banking, insurance, aviation, the arts and politics.

Yet the controlling passions of his life were not money and power but family and traditions. His older son's two marriages had disappointed him greatly. The first, to a woman with an outstanding social position, had produced no offspring, and the second...

It was enough to say that Kirsten's background had prevented her from ever becoming a true Patrick. T.G. could only thank God there had been no issue from that union. If Travis and Kirsten had produced an heir, particularly if they had produced Travis Garrison Patrick V, his present task would have been impossible.

He also thanked God that his own father had placed the family's considerable real estate holdings under the institute's ownership. That had been done for tax purposes, but now it seemed a stroke of genius and foresight. Had Travis owned this house, he no doubt would have left it to Kirsten, for he had been absolutely besotted with his young wife. Travis's will had requested that she be allowed to live in it as long as she wished; that, however, was only a request, not legally binding. As it was, Travis had left his stepson a healthy trust fund, and his young wife had received his thirteen percent share of the vast Patrick fortune. It would remain hers for life unless she chose to remarry. In that case, the family would buy back her share.

That rankled. Not only did that keep Kirsten tied in with the family, it made her a very wealthy woman. T.G. couldn't shake the notion that she had no right to such enormous riches, just as she had no right to the Patrick name or to admission into their exclusive social circle. Far too many of their friends openly accepted the woman, forgetting her modest background. It was his intention to someday ease her out of that ridiculous inheritance, then out of North Shore society altogether. Anyone who thought he couldn't do that was unaware of the scope of his power. But that was for the future. Today he had an immediate mission.

Good manners, which the Patricks possessed in abundance, had dictated that the family leave Kirsten in peace for a respectable period following Travis's death, but now that almost a year had passed, it was T.G.'s unpleasant duty to ask her and her son to vacate the house at the earliest convenient moment. The mansion, after all, was an integral part of the Patrick legacy. It was only right that his younger son, Roger, live in it.

T.G.'s request was so couched in gentle words that it took some time for Kirsten to understand what was being asked of her. When she finally realized that the family wanted her to quit the premises, she simply stared at T.G. a minute, immobilized by rage, thunderstruck by their gall.

And she was peevishly miffed, too, that the family had come to her before she could go to them. Only the night before she had mulled over the possibility of moving. It was far, far more house than she wanted or needed. She and Travis had often thrown lavish parties, but now she imagined her entertaining would be limited to small affairs for close friends. There were a lot of arguments in favor of her giving up the stiffly formal house.

But not once had it occurred to her that she would be asked to leave it, not when Travis's will had stated that the house was to be hers for as long as she chose to live in it. Now, no matter how skillfully she handled this, it would always seem that she had been evicted.

"I hadn't planned to make any drastic changes right away, Mr. Patrick," Kirsten said coolly. She had never called her father-in-law anything but Mr. Patrick, and he had never requested that she do otherwise.

"Yes, yes, I can understand that," T.G. said, clearing his throat. "Moving can be such a chore. I didn't mean to imply that there was a rush. I thought perhaps...sometime after the first of the year."

Suddenly Kirsten recalled the spate of visits from various members of the Travis's family: his mother, Evelyn, only the day before; his brother, Roger, last week; and Roger's wife, Constance, the week before that. These were people who did not customarily call on her. Were they checking up on the house? On her? Were they afraid she might be squirreling away some family heirlooms? Sadly, she conceded that she had never ceased being "that woman from Mississippi" in their eyes—simply an employee who had lured Travis with her youth and beauty, no one to be taken seriously. Kirsten lifted her chin slightly higher and fixed T.G. with a steely stare. For a minute the silence was ponderous. The distant ringing of the telephone was the only sound to be heard.

She was certain she had never seen T.G. look uncomfortable, but he did at that moment. Murmuring something about keeping an appointment, he got to his feet. Kirsten walked with him to the front door, and as he was preparing to leave, the elderly gentleman turned to her. "You know, my dear, the family would be more than happy to have you use the Palm Beach house or the one in Vail for an extended period, if you like."

"Thank you, but I've become used to living in New York." She had no intention of making this easy for him.

"Yes, well... as you wish. Good day."

Kirsten was seething when she closed the door. This would kill Travis, she thought. His family was trying to shuttle her off to Florida or Colorado, somewhere nicely out of the way. She had the distinct feeling she had just been told to get out of Dodge by sundown.

She was still smarting when David bounded down the stairs and almost collided with her. "Mom," he whispered furtively, "is Mr. Patrick gone?"

"Yes."

David's voice rose. "My father's on the phone!"

Kirsten's eyes widened. "Grady? Good heavens, he got the letter!"

"Yes. It had to be forwarded twice, but he got it. He wants to talk to you. He wants to ask you something."

Kirsten placed a hand over her suddenly racing heart. It hadn't occurred to her that Grady might telephone David. At best she'd imagined her son would receive a letter, but then, she had no idea what he'd said in his letter to his father. David hadn't offered to show it to her, and she hadn't asked. Never would she have thought that Grady would want to talk to her.

The nearest telephone was in Travis's study. She walked briskly down the hall, David hard on her heels, but as she stepped into the room, she turned. "Let me speak to him in private, David."

"Come on, Mom."

"Just for a minute. This is very delicate for me."

David shrugged. "Okay, but don't hang up without letting me talk to him again."

Kirsten closed the door behind her, took a deep breath and walked to the desk, where she lifted the receiver. "H-hello."

"Kirsten? This is Grady."

How odd, she thought. *I expected to recognize his voice. He could be anyone.* "Hello, Grady. How are you?"

Strange, Grady thought, *she doesn't sound familiar at all.* She still spoke with some Mississippi softening her words, but he thought he detected some Yankee there, too. "I'm fine, thanks. Surprised but pleased to get David's letter."

"Were you? Pleased, I mean. I . . . wasn't sure he should do it . . . if it turned out to be an embarrassment for your family or something."

"It couldn't very well be that since I have no family. I never remarried."

"Oh . . . well, I . . . Where are you living now?"

"Not far from Jackson. Believe it or not, I'm a corporate vice president."

"How wonderful. You've done well."

"You sound surprised."

"No, no, I . . . didn't mean it that way."

There was a pause. "Kirsten, I want to ask a favor of you. Would you object if I came to see David? Just for a day or two."

"Oh . . ." Come here? That really caught her off guard. Kirsten immediately thought of the Patricks and the way they had been hovering lately. If her memory hadn't failed her, if David really did favor Grady as much as she thought he did, she didn't want her in-laws to see father and son together. Though

Travis could no longer be hurt, she didn't want him caught in a lie.

"Kirsten?"

She rounded the desk to sink into its big chair. "Well, Grady, I don't object in the way you might think, but... It's just that my husband's family doesn't know I was ever divorced. Do you understand?"

"I figured something like that because of the lie about my dying in Vietnam."

Kirsten expelled a labored breath. "So David told you about that, did he?"

"Not in so many words, but why else would he have thought I was dead?"

"Yes, I...maybe someday I can explain that to you. I know there's no excuse for it, but—"

"No explanation necessary. It's water under the bridge. But I would like to see David, and he wants to see me. Can't something be arranged?"

Kirsten rubbed her temple with her free hand. "I suppose we could pass you off as some long-lost relative or... No, that's not such a good idea. A lot of time has passed, but if I remember correctly, you and David look an awful lot alike."

"I know. He sent me a picture. Please, I want to see him. Don't I have that right?"

"Why haven't you ever tried before?"

"I did. Once."

"When?"

"If you'll let me see him, I'll try to explain everything. It's complicated."

Now Kirsten's own curiosity was piqued. Grady had tried to see David? "David doesn't need my permission anymore. He's old enough to make his own decisions. If he really does want to see you, perhaps he could check into a hotel in the city, and the two of you could meet there."

"I've got a better idea," Grady said. "Let him come down here. Then we'll have a real visit. Do you mind if I ask him?"

Kirsten thought about it. If David was determined to meet his father, that might be the best arrangement. "No, I don't mind. That probably would please him very much."

"I'd love it if you'd come along. I'd like to see you, too."

"Me? Oh, I don't think so."

"Why not?"

"Well, I—"

"Look, Kirsten, I'm not trying to turn this into a traumatic experience for anyone, but there are a lot of things I'd like to tell you, things that are almost impossible to explain over the telephone. I suppose I could write, but I really would like to see you. Aren't you just a tiny bit curious about me?"

Kirsten smiled. "I guess I am."

"If you're worried about your in-laws, tell them you have some family business to take care of and David's going along for the ride. Hell, you're from Jackson. Surely you can think of a reason for going back."

"It's not that, Grady. I don't have to explain my every move to the Patricks."

"I wonder. They must be pretty powerful people, judging from the house you live in." *There,* he thought. *If that doesn't whip her curiosity into a frenzy, nothing will.*

Kirsten gasped. "How do you know what kind of house I live in?"

"That's part of what I want to talk to you about. Please, both of you come."

They talked back and forth for another ten minutes or so. Every argument Kirsten came up with against making the trip was met with a more forceful one from Grady. She was aware that David was pacing the floor outside the room, ready to jump out of his skin. Finally, when it became obvious that either she and David would have to go see Grady or he would come to see them, she said, "All right, all right. For a couple of days."

Kirsten gave it some thought. It was imperative that she be here for a party Denise was throwing since she had agreed to cohost it, but that wasn't until a week from Saturday. That left plenty of time for a quick trip to Mississippi. Maybe David would get it out of his system once and for all. "This is Thursday. We'll come...Monday."

"That gives you a long time to change your mind."

"I doubt David would let me change my mind. We'll be there Monday and stay until...oh, Thursday."

"Good. David has my phone number. Give me a call when your reservations are firmed up. I don't care what time of day or night you get here. I'll be in Jackson to meet you."

"Fine."

"Thanks, Kirsten. Now, tell me something. Have you changed much?"

She laughed lightly. "Probably. But I haven't gotten fat, and I'm not silver haired yet."

"You're only forty-one."

"Forty-two pretty soon."

"That's right. November 30."

Kirsten was stunned. "Grady! You remember!"

"But I'll bet you don't remember when mine is."

Her mind went blank. "I'm . . . sorry."

"Why? There was no reason for you to remember. May I speak to David again?"

"Of course. I'll get him."

"By the way, it's April 22."

"What?"

"My birthday is April 22."

"Oh, well...I'll try to remember to send you a card next year. Goodbye, Grady."

Kirsten placed the receiver on the desk and went out into the hall to get David. "He wants us to come to see him. If you don't want to go, just tell him so."

David went into the study, and as Kirsten reached the foot of the stairs, she heard him say, "I think I'd really like that."

She found it hard to believe she'd actually agreed to this, and she hoped she didn't regret it. She hadn't exactly been honest when she'd told Grady she didn't have to account to the Patricks for her actions. The first hint that she and David were leaving town for a few days would have the phone ringing off the wall. Every Patrick she knew—and the North Shore was saturated with them—would call. That was the way the family operated; no one made a move without informing all the others. She'd do her best to keep the trip a secret, but in case word got around and the Patricks started asking questions, she had to have something to tell them....

She started thinking, but then she recalled the earlier confrontation with T.G. She owed him no explanations. Too much of her life was ordered and measured by what the Patricks thought as it was. She wouldn't tell them a damned thing.

But that thought had no sooner formed than another took its place, and a sardonic smile touched Kirsten's lips. Maybe she'd tell everyone she was thinking about moving back to Mississippi. They'd probably arrive en masse to help her pack.

CHAPTER THREE

FOR THE NEXT THREE DAYS Grady existed in a state of excitement and anticipation. David's upcoming visit took precedence over everything else. It had been a long time since he'd been excited about something, and he was enjoying every minute of this.

When David had called to tell him when they would arrive, Grady planned to make reservations for them at Culver's lone luxury hostelry, a bed-and-breakfast inn that reeked with history and quaint charm. However, due to a recent article about the inn in *Southern Living*, the place was booked solid right up until Christmas. There wasn't another motel or hotel for miles that was remotely suitable for people who lived the way the Patricks did, so that meant they would have to stay with him.

Which suited him fine. Grady didn't want to miss a second of David's visit. But it also meant giving some serious thought to the kind of accommodations he had to offer. Up in the loft that served as his study, there was a sleeper sofa; David could have that. The spare bedroom was small but very nice, thanks to his secretary's good taste. Phyllis had picked out most of the house's furnishings when he had pleaded ignorance about such things. Of course, Kirsten was accustomed to much more elegant surroundings, but she would only be in Culver a short time. A couple of

days, she had said. Maybe he could talk her into adding a day or two on to that. Two days wasn't much
time for a man to get acquainted with his son.

Grady walked through his house with the air of a
sergeant making a barracks inspection. Nothing escaped his critical eye. Considering that he'd always
thought his house to be the last word in comfort, he
was amazed at how many flaws he found in it. The
towels in the bathrooms didn't match. The glasses in
the kitchen cabinet were the oddest assortment of sizes
and shapes imaginable. He wondered why he'd never
noticed that. And since he ate alone at the breakfast
bar most of the time, he didn't own even one table-
cloth. He began making a list, and by the time he'd
finished his inspection, the list was a lengthy one.
When he went into town the following morning, he
didn't make his usual rounds but went shopping, instead. Afterward, he bought more groceries than he
alone could consume in a month, but wouldn't a
nineteen-year-old be hungry all the time?

Once he'd pronounced the house as guest-ready as
he could make it, Grady was hit by an unexpected
thought. What if he and David didn't get along? What
if he was a disappointment to his son? The kid was an
Ivy Leaguer, while he himself was...well, pretty ordinary. He suspected that he and Kirsten would feel
awkward with each other, at least at first, but somehow he'd imagined that he and his son would hit it off
from the start. Now he supposed he had been naive to
think they would take one look at each other and the
years would simply melt away. What would they talk
about? Two days could seem like an eternity when two
people had nothing to say to each other.

Asking Kirsten to come along had been a spontaneous move on his part, not rooted in thought, but now it seemed a pure stroke of genius. David could always talk to his mother.

AFTER ACCOMPLISHING the mission he had set out on four years ago, David suddenly was overcome by uncertainty. One minute he wanted the trip to Mississippi more than he'd ever wanted anything; the next he was seized with panic at the thought of facing a father he remembered nothing about. Then he would remind himself that Grady had contacted him immediately upon receiving the letter and that he had insisted on a meeting between the two of them. If his father hadn't genuinely wanted to see him, he would have ignored the whole thing.

That thought would make David feel better for a while; then the doubts would resurface. However, he mentioned none of his fluctuating moods to his mother, sensing that Kirsten harbored plenty of doubts herself. Not until the plane's wheels were in the well on Monday did he relax and begin to look upon the trip as an adventure.

On the other hand, that was the exact moment when Kirsten grappled with her first bout of real nervousness. For the past three days she had tried to recall happy incidents from her marriage to Grady, some pleasant memories they could reminisce about, and she'd come up with almost nothing. Unfortunately, it was the difficult time after his return from prison camp that she recalled most vividly. That was sad. They once had been lovers and, she supposed, happy. Now she was wondering if either of them could put together enough sentences to make conversation.

Except for a maddening delay in Atlanta, the flight went smoothly, and the last leg from Atlanta to Jackson passed in a flash. "Do you think he'll recognize you, Mom?" David asked anxiously as they inched toward the plane's exit.

"I have no idea, but—" she patted his arm. "—I'll bet he recognizes you."

Actually, it was Kirsten whom Grady noticed first, and the sight of her knocked the breath out of him. He remembered that she had been an unusually pretty young woman—it was her beauty that had first captured his interest at that dance in 1969—but he could see that his memory hadn't done her justice. Her hair was still the color of midnight, and though he wasn't close enough to see her eyes, he remembered them well—so blue they were almost violet. She wore a simple rose-colored dress that clung to her body's bountiful curves. Standing there all poised and graceful, she epitomized understated elegance. Grady thought that anyone seeing her would peg her as the product of wealth and privilege. With some difficulty, he forced himself to tear his gaze from Kirsten and look at the young man whose arm she clung to so possessively.

His son! He almost choked on a dozen different emotions, and for a minute, he was too overcome to move. Then, as the crowd began to thin out, he stepped forward, hand extended.

"David?"

The young man's head spun around. For what seemed an eternity but could only have been a few seconds, father and son simply stood staring at each other. Then David's young face broke into a wide

smile, and he took Grady's hand, pumping it vigorously. "Sir," he acknowledged.

"Sir?" Grady pretended to be horrified. "We're
going to have to come up with something else. If you
don't feel comfortable with Dad, call me Grady."

"Well, sure...er, Dad." David's face colored
slightly. The word sounded strange coming from his
mouth. He'd never had anyone to call by that name.

"Welcome back to Mississippi."

"Thanks. It's good to be here. I...I mean, we're
glad you invited us."

Kirsten watched the exchange between Grady and
David, and her heart knocked against her ribs. She
wouldn't have had a bit of trouble recognizing Grady,
no matter where on earth they had met. He was an
older version of David. He looked wonderful—ma-
turely handsome, composed, self-assured and extremely virile. How had he managed to stay single all
these years? It had to have been his choice. Then her
heart stopped altogether as he turned to her.

"Hello, Kirsten."

"Hello, Grady."

Impulsively, he bent and placed a light kiss on her
cheek. "You look wonderful."

"Thanks. So do you."

"I trust you had a pleasant flight."

"Yes, it was...fine."

An awkward minute of silence passed. Then Grady
stepped forward and sandwiched himself between
Kirsten and David, placing an arm around each.
"Let's get your luggage and be on our way. We have
about an hour's drive ahead of us, just enough time to
start getting acquainted."

Kirsten hadn't realized she was holding her breath until it oozed out of her. Thanks to Grady's easy charm, there were no more awkward moments. It was as easy as that.

KIRSTEN RODE in the back seat during the drive, idly scanning the lush Mississippi countryside, experiencing some unexpected feelings of nostalgia and listening to the animated chatter from the front seat. Grady and David kept up a running conversation; they had clicked from the beginning. One of them occasionally would make a stab at including her in the conversation, but for the most part, father and son were completely absorbed in each other. One would have thought they both had been waiting a lifetime for this encounter. The guilt that brought on was difficult for Kirsten to deal with. She never should have kept them from each other, never should have gone along with Travis's lie.

Then she quickly reminded herself that an entire year had passed between the time of the divorce and her marriage to Travis, a year in which Grady did not contact her or try to see David. That assuaged the guilt somewhat and served to remind her of the main reason she had made this trip. At some point Grady had decided to see David but had apparently changed his mind. Obviously he had come to Long Island since he knew about the house. She wanted to know when that was and why he had waited so long. She wanted to know a lot of things, and she found herself studying the man she once had been married to.

The Grady O'Connor she was seeing now seemed so open and cheerful, a man at peace with himself—not the gaunt, troubled stranger who had returned from

Vietnam. This Grady was more like the man she had met at that long-ago dance and married five months later.

Even then, however, she had quickly learned that the sunny facade was only one side of his personality, that there was a more complex man lurking beneath the surface. During his formative years in the orphanage, he had erected emotional fences that no one could scale, not even an adoring wife. Kirsten had respected the barriers, even though it had meant many lonely moments for a young bride who was away from home for the first time and learning to cope with military life. Then, with the ink on their marriage license barely dry—or so it now seemed—and in the midst of troops withdrawing from battles, his squadron had been deployed to Vietnam, and she had gone home to Jackson to wait out a year that turned into more than three. Perhaps if he'd only been gone a year, perhaps if they'd had more time to grow close, then everything would have turned out differently.

As it was, when Grady at last had come home, the fences were higher and more impossible to scale than ever. Kirsten had tried to understand, but it all had been too much for a young working mother who often had been tired herself at the end of the day. Now all traces of that brooding stranger seemed to have vanished, but she couldn't help wondering if the fences were still intact.

It was nearing five o'clock when Grady braked and pulled off the main road. A steady stream of vehicles passed them going in the opposite direction, and most of the drivers waved to Grady. Kirsten forced her thoughts back to the moment and looked around at the impressive compound they had entered. She heard

Grady tell David that this was his "shop," the place where he lived and worked. David, whose knowledge of agriculture and the great outdoors was severely limited, was goggle-eyed, and his questions came in rapid-fire succession. Finally, with a promise to give them the grand tour tomorrow and explain the entire operation, Grady drove straight to his house. It was time to get them settled in and start giving serious thought to dinner.

Kirsten was immediately charmed by the house. It had everything the Long Island mansion lacked— openness, pale walls and plenty of glass. It was, she thought, exactly the kind of house she would want if she had spent her childhood in an orphanage and too much of her young adulthood in a prison camp.

After Grady showed David to the loft, he led Kirsten down a short hall to the room across from his own. "It's small," he apologized, "but I think you'll be comfortable."

"It's lovely," she said, meaning it. "You have good taste."

"It's my secretary who has the good taste."

"Ah, I thought I detected a woman's touch."

Grady set her suitcase at the foot of the bed, then made a move toward the door. A step or two before reaching it, he stopped and turned. "Kirsten, thanks for coming. It means a lot to me."

"You're welcome, but I don't think any thanks are necessary. David started this, and I think he was determined to see it through. As for me . . . there are certain things I want to explain to you. I'm going to feel a lot better when I do."

A bare suggestion of a smile touched his lips. "I've got some things I want to tell you, too, and believe me, it's going to be good to get them off my chest. I'll leave it to you to decide how much of it David should know."

"Agreed," Kirsten said.

"Surely we'll find time to talk before you leave."

"I hope so." But Kirsten knew it would be difficult. David would begrudge every second he had to be away from his father.

"You did a real good job with him," Grady said. "He's a fine young man, very self-confident for his age."

"The kind of life he's led builds self-confidence."

"Obviously. Is there any...resentment toward either one of us because of...what happened?"

Kirsten pursed her lips. She wasn't sure. As close as she and David were, there was a large part of her son she couldn't touch. David could be a very private person. "I don't think so. Certainly he's never expressed any. I have to guess that if he does feel an occasional flash of resentment, it would be directed at me...because of the lie."

Grady nodded solemnly. "Well, I'll go start dinner. Come on in the kitchen when you're settled."

"I'll only be a minute or two."

David was already there, sitting on one of the stools at the breakfast bar, when Kirsten joined them a few minutes later. She took a seat beside him and accepted the glass of wine Grady offered her. Normally, she was a master of the art of cordial conversation, a skilled technician when it came to drawing others out and making them comfortable. Now, however, in the company of her son and her ex-husband, she felt inexplicably shy and tongue-tied. Technically, they were three people who once had been a family. Actually, they never had been, not really. They couldn't indulge in "remember when," because there was almost nothing to remember.

Fortunately, Grady took the initiative, and soon they were asking the sort of questions that strangers ask each other. He wanted to know what David's favorite school subjects were and whether or not he followed or participated in sports. He asked Kirsten about her mother's death and how she liked living up north. She, in turn, wanted to know how he had come to be doing the kind of work he was.

"Pure blind luck," Grady told her. "I had some vague idea that I wanted to work outdoors and was thinking about the forestry service when I saw an ad in a Jackson paper that sounded interesting. It stated that the applicant should like outdoor work, which I did, and should know something about professional horticulture, which I didn't, but I figured what the heck. It couldn't hurt to apply. Vanessa Hamilton herself was in Jackson doing the interviewing, and we hit it off right away. It was that simple. There were about half as many Hamilton House restaurants then as there are now, and this operation was a fourth as big as what you saw earlier. I got on with the company at a good time. It grew, and I grew along with it."

"Obviously you like your work," Kirsten commented.

"I love it."

"How fortunate you are."

And the conversation did not lag when they sat down to dinner. They talked and talked and laughed a lot. Kirsten thought it was amazing that they got along so well, considering everything. But she noticed that Grady never mentioned his childhood, the war or their brief time together. It was as though his life had begun in 1976. If he still had the old hang-ups, she knew she might never find out the things she wanted to know. One thing was for sure: she wouldn't be the one to bring them up for fear the fences would be erected again. She worried that David might innocently mention one of the unmentionables, but he was too concerned with the immediate to be interested in Grady's past. The reunion was going far more smoothly than she would have dared hope.

Kirsten didn't think she and Grady would find time to talk alone that night, but by ten-thirty David looked ready to drop. He hadn't been able to sleep the night before, and they had been on the go since dawn. Kirsten would have welcomed bed, too, but when it looked as though David was going to call it a night and Kirsten's eyes met Grady's, his unspoken message was clear. *Let's talk now.*

When David finally said good-night and climbed the stairs to the loft, Grady got to his feet, turned off all but one small lamp, then wordlessly went out onto the front porch. Kirsten waited behind for a minute before joining him. The evening air, thick with humidity and the smell of growing things, assaulted her senses. The first aroma she identified precisely was honeysuckle. Grady was seated in a wicker chair, and as she approached, he half rose and smiled.

"Please, don't get up," Kirsten said, pulling another chair over and placing it next to his. When she sat down she took a deep breath. "Mississippi air. It smells good. I'd forgotten."

"It smells good, all right," Grady agreed, "but it has the consistency of something you pour over pancakes. Had you forgotten that, too?"

"Maybe, but the humidity here isn't nearly as oppressive as New York's can be."

"Is this your first trip back?"

"Yes."

"Any particular reason?"

Kirsten shrugged. "I didn't think there was anything for me here."

They lapsed into silence, but it wasn't uncomfortable or awkward. It was, in fact, almost companionable. Finally Kirsten spoke. "Grady, I want to talk to you about the lie I told David."

"Forget it. I'm sure you had your reasons for telling him I was dead."

"Not very noble ones, I'm afraid. Actually, it was my husband who told the lie first."

"Why?"

Kirsten smiled ruefully. "Travis was more his father's son than he wanted to be or knew he was. You see, I married into a wealthy, powerful family that disapproved of divorce. That sounds pretty thin, but since they disapproved of almost everything about me to begin with, Travis thought it might be easier for me if they thought I was a widow. It was the wrong thing to do—I can see that now—and to be honest, it didn't do much good. They still disapprove of me." She paused and cast a sidelong glance at Grady, but his face registered no emotion. She sighed and continued.

"I hadn't seen you in a year, had no idea where you were, and I had to guess you had no interest in being a father. We were leaving Mississippi anyway, so... I've regretted it many times, and I'd like to apologize."

Grady didn't say anything immediately. Then Kirsten heard him shift in his chair. "Accepted. How did David find out I hadn't died in the war?"

"He was rummaging around in some old boxes of mine and found the divorce papers."

"That must have been a shock, for him and for you."

"It was."

"When was this?"

"Four years ago."

That got a rise out of Grady. "Four years? Then why—"

"He was only fifteen. He wanted to find you then, but—"

"Your husband's family?"

"Oh, that and other things. I just assumed you would be married and have a family. I was afraid he would open a can of worms. And I couldn't forget the year when you'd made no attempt to get in touch with us. Suppose he'd located you, written to you and you hadn't responded. I worried about David's reaction to that kind of rejection. There were a lot of reasons, but I'd be lying again if I told you the Patricks weren't a big factor."

Grady stared out into the black night, tugging on his chin. "Then why now?"

"David never forgot about finding you, and this time he was determined. He also was older and smarter and knew how to go about it. Travis was gone, so none of this could affect him. And from the way things have been going lately, I'm sure my fragile ties to the Patricks will, for the most part, soon be severed. Again, a lot of reasons."

Grady twisted in his chair so he could get a good look at her. Her profile was a study in perfection—long lashes, pert nose, lush mouth. Throughout dinner he had found his gaze wandering to her time and time again. She was a stunning woman with exquisite manners and a regal bearing. What kind of family wouldn't be proud to claim her as one of their own? "What the devil kind of people are these Patricks anyway?"

Kirsten chuckled lightly and tried to think of a good way to describe the majority of Travis's family. "Very old money. Steeped in traditions and family. They all live in Tudor mansions clustered on the same hill, and the first thing Travis's mother does every morning is to phone all her children and grandchildren to find out what they're going to do that day and to tell them what she's going to do. Like the president's press secretary. Maybe the best way to explain the Patricks is to tell you that twenty-five years ago they decided to buy a house in Vail. My father-in-law refers to it as 'the new place.'"

Grady smiled. "I figured they would be something like that when I saw the house."

Kirsten's head snapped around, and their eyes met. "Now it's your turn."

A muscle twitched in Grady's cheek. "It's hard to know where to begin."

"You told me to get a divorce, and you left to return to duty," she prompted. "I thought you were going to make the Air Force a career, yet you didn't. Why?"

"I stayed a year because I needed what the Air Force could give me—medical attention. As you know, I was an emotional mess, but it was worse than

I thought. I was flirting with mental illness. I would forget the simplest things. I was jumpy as hell and couldn't concentrate on anything for more than a few minutes, so I didn't dare get into a cockpit again. They gave me an office job, and I damned near climbed the walls. My commanding officer was the one who suggested I get help. Fortunately, the Air Force babied us POWs in those days, so I got great medical care. But it took a while." He laughed mirthlessly. "I'll say! I was in and out of the hospital for a year, mostly in."

"Oh, Grady," Kirsten breathed, shocked. If she had known he was actually on the verge of mental illness, what might have happened? "You . . . seem to have recovered."

He nodded. "Mentally, I'm probably in the best shape of my life. The therapy finally did the trick. My shrink had this theory that everything wrong with me started in the orphanage and was compounded by prison. He probably was right. That home I grew up in had long, dark corridors and tiny, high windows. When I lived there it reminded me of prison, and when I was in prison it reminded me of that home."

It occurred to Kirsten that this was the first thing he'd told her about the orphanage, except to say it had been a "crummy place." Furthermore, he seemed to welcome talking about it, about everything. She kept silent while he continued.

"But, who knows, maybe my experience there helped me get through my many stays in solitary confinement. When I first got thrown in the prison camp, I had a smart, quick mouth . . . but the guards knew how to take that out of me. Anyway, when the doctor pronounced me fit to return to polite society, he suggested I buy a farm and always live in houses with a lot of big windows. I think he was joking, but it sounded great to me. And that's when I thought—holy hell, I've got an ex-wife and kid out there somewhere! I decided to get out of the service, try to find the two of you, and if you thought you could stand it, we'd try it again. Maybe I would buy a farm.

"So...I went back to Jackson. When I couldn't find you, I tried to find your mother, but she had moved. Then I went to your old office and found out the name of the resort where you'd gone to work. I got there two weeks after your wedding." Grady made some sort of imperceptible sound deep in his throat. "But I decided I needed to find you anyway, to make some kind of arrangements about seeing David. First, though, I had to find out where you were, and that proved to be easier said than done. The hotel employees were a closemouthed bunch, but I finally hooked up with a golf pro who knew your husband pretty well. While I pretended to be serious about taking lessons, I got enough information out of him to get to the North Shore, and after that it was easy. Everybody knows the Patricks."

"What happened to make you change your mind about seeing David?" Kirsten asked.

"Oh, it was a combination of things. I was in a rented car, parked across the street from that monstrous house, and my feet were getting colder by the minute. I thought about how I'd just up and left the two of you, and I wondered if I had any right to charge back into your lives, even briefly. You were lost to me for good, and I doubted David even remembered me. About that time a limousine pulled up to the gate, and there was a young boy in the back seat. I thought it was David, but I couldn't be sure since I'd paid so little attention to him when he was around. But there had been a light snow earlier, and a man was clearing off the driveway. When he saw the limo, he waved and called David's name. Then the gates swung open, and the car drove through. I remember thinking—he doesn't even know me. What am I doing here? Look at the life he has now. What do I think I can offer him?'' Grady's voice suddenly sounded weary. ''I sat there for a long time, but I finally drove off and caught the next plane back home.''

Kirsten rubbed her eyes, and a feeling of incredible sadness overcame her. If Grady had contacted them, Travis's lie might have come to light, and all hell would have broken loose, but that would have passed. Or if Grady even once had called to let her know he was in the hospital, she would have gone to see him, she just knew it. Maybe she wouldn't have changed jobs, wouldn't ever have met Travis. If, if, if. How different life might have been.

''I...don't know what to say, Grady. That can't have been an easy decision for you to make.''

''I thought about it a lot for a long time afterward. I've always felt sorry for kids of divorce—forced to spend every other weekend and two weeks in the summer with a parent they don't know very well. Maybe it was best that David didn't know the truth about me until he was older. Or...maybe I'm rationalizing the decision.''

''You, at least, had David's best interests at heart, and that makes me feel absolutely rotten. When I went along with Travis's lie, I had my best interests at heart.''

''I was the one who left in the first place.''

"You were ill and couldn't be responsible for your actions. I wish I had been mature enough to understand that."

Kirsten felt Grady's eyes settle on her. "Why?" he asked. "Haven't you been satisfied with your life?"

"It's not that. Travis was a wonderful husband, and he couldn't have been better with David. It's just that . . . it was a terrible time for you, and you didn't have anyone."

"That was mostly my fault, I guess. I'm the one who threw in the towel. If there's one thing I've learned, Kirsten, it's not to waste a minute on regrets and what ifs. Life's so short. Besides, it's all worked out great. I'm hoping David and I will see each other many times in the coming years. You wouldn't object, would you?"

"It's not my place to object. David's growing up, and he'll do as he pleases."

Kirsten hoped she meant that, but she experienced a pang or two as she said it. Except for the past year, during which he was away at school, David had been all hers for nineteen years. All the years Grady had been a POW, it had often seemed that she had stayed sane only by focusing on her small boy. Later, while she struggled for acceptance by the Patricks, her release from tension had been to laugh and talk and play with her son. Now all that would change. He would return to school, develop new interests, and she would have to share him with his newly expanded world. Not only that world but with his father. Surely she could do that and do it graciously.

Kirsten chanced a glance at Grady, but he was staring ahead, lost in his own thoughts. It was odd to see him again after so many years, to know he was part of her past even though he seemed like someone new and interesting. She had trouble thinking of him as David's father, and she couldn't think of him as her ex-husband at all. She admitted to herself that if she were meeting him for the first time ever, she would think of him as attractive, someone she would like to know better.

Stirrings began inside her, and she recognized them for what they were. Hardly surprising. She had been widowed almost a year, and she and Travis had remained lovers to the end. She supposed she felt deprived. When a deprived woman came face-to-face with an attractive, very masculine man, it didn't take a genius to predict the response.

Good Lord, she thought with a start. *I can't believe I'm thinking like this!* She gave herself a shake and almost bolted out of the chair. "Thanks so much for telling me all this, Grady. I don't know why it makes a difference after all this time, but it does. Now, if you'll excuse me, it's been a long day. I'm going to say good night."

Grady got to his feet. "Good night, Kirsten. Again, thanks for giving me a chance to meet my son. I hope you sleep well."

She nodded distractedly, turned and went into the house. Grady stared after her for a minute, long after the door had closed. Well, he thought, that hadn't been so bad. Pretty damned easy, in fact. She was such a beautiful woman, and he was anything but immune to beautiful women. He had expected Kirsten to be pure class, and she hadn't disappointed him.

What he hadn't expected or wanted was to be attracted to her all over again, exactly the way he'd been at that dance in 1969. The attraction had been instantaneous then, and it had been again today. That was the biggest surprise of the visit, and it was something he was going to have to come to terms with.

CHAPTER FOUR

THE FOLLOWING MORNING Kirsten woke with a start, totally disoriented for a minute. When she finally remembered where she was, she glanced at the bedside clock and did a double take. Nine o'clock! She hadn't slept so late in years, but the room was dark, cool and completely quiet. She wondered if David was up. Cocking her head, she listened for sounds but heard nothing. She flung back the covers, dressed hurriedly, then ventured out to see what David and Grady were up to.

There was no one in the house, but the coffee maker was on in the kitchen, and nearby was a plate of breakfast rolls. Kirsten could smell the lingering aroma of bacon, but it was faint, so she assumed Grady and David had eaten quite a while ago. She would have felt like a complete sluggard if the laziness hadn't seemed such a luxury. After pouring a cup of coffee, she picked up a roll and carried her breakfast out on the front porch to have a look around.

Already the day was very warm. Fall took its sweet time about arriving in Mississippi. The chairs she and Grady had used the night before still stood in the center of the porch. Taking one, she sat, sipping her coffee, munching on the roll and simply enjoying the solitude. In the distance she could see workers in the fields; otherwise, all was still. Grady's Cherokee was nowhere in sight, so she guessed he and David were together, probably touring the place. In a way she wished she was with them, but in another she was grateful for the peace and quiet. Besides, they needed time alone in order to get acquainted.

And this was the perfect opportunity for her to do some serious thinking about the situation with Travis's family. Here in Mississippi she could, for the first time in years, relax and be herself, whoever that self was. Trying her damnedest to be a Patrick had taken a lot out of her. There wasn't much left of the woman who had captivated Travis in the first place. She hated admitting that she had allowed her husband's powerful family to destroy a lot of the spontaneous enthusiasm she once had possessed in abundance, but it was true. She had to be "on" so much of the time. Her own identity had been submerged and had surfaced only on those blissful occasions when she had been alone with Travis and/or her son.

Whenever Kirsten thought of T.G.'s "request"—and she had thought of it many times since last Thursday—she bristled with indignation. The Patricks had more than their fair share of nerve. They always had. How she wished she had been more assertive right from the beginning of her marriage, less malleable and less eager to please. Instead, for Travis's sake, she had tried so hard to win their approval. To no avail. She doubted if their collective opinion of her had changed one iota, while she had changed far too much.

But wishing she had behaved differently years ago was a waste of time. What mattered was what she did now, and her options were limited. She wasn't emotionally attached to the house; more often than not it was a huge nuisance. Old houses, she often thought, were like old bodies—in need of constant attention if they were to look their best. The easiest, and probably smartest, thing to do was quit the premises and break her ties with the Patricks—all but Denise, of course. An apartment in the city would be more convenient for her, and think of the fun she would have decorating it.

Still, a perverse but very human part of her balked. She was all but being ordered out, and that went directly against the intent of Travis's will. Kirsten suspected she would have a pretty good case if she wanted to fight it. Then she was reminded of how powerful the Patricks were, of that battery of high-dollar lawyers they kept on retainer, of the unpleasantness of a court fight, of a lot of things.

It was a dilemma, and not one that would be solved by a few days of pondering. As with most vexing problems, there probably would be a catalyst, something out of the blue that would help her make a decision. Draining her coffee, Kirsten went inside for a refill. Later, as she was putting on her makeup, stroke by practiced stroke, she wondered how Grady and David were getting along. Now that she'd had time to think things through, she'd decided it would be nice if they saw each other periodically in the future. And she hoped their meetings would stem from a real desire to see each other, not from any sense of obligation.

A tiny frown creased her forehead as she leaned closer to the mirror while putting on her lipstick. Realistically, though, she didn't expect them to get close, certainly not like father and son. What did they have in common except the blood coursing through their veins? Grady was so down-to-earth, a self-made man; David was fairly sophisticated for a nineteen-year-old. Her son was well traveled and had been around great wealth long enough to treat it casually. Grady, she imagined, knew exactly what a dollar was worth. Frankly, Kirsten couldn't think of a thing they would find to talk about.

GRADY AND DAVID had not stopped talking since they had left the house. David was clearly fascinated by the Hamilton House farm, with its vast fields of vegetables and the enormous greenhouses in which new varieties were being tested constantly. Before today, he had thought a carrot was a carrot, a tomato a tomato. He was astonished to learn that the farm grew more than twenty varieties of lettuce, twelve kinds of squash, as many of green beans, and the list went on and on. There were bush tomatoes, vining tomatoes, cascading tomatoes. The habits of each variety were recorded in thick logbooks every day by Ramon Cuellar, the man in charge of the fields, and Grady himself was a walking encyclopedia when it came to gardening.

David found himself listening raptly. He had spent most of his life surrounded by businessmen and business talk. But to him, business meant men in three-piece suits carrying briefcases and hurrying to board meetings. Yet his father was a businessman, successful by any yardstick, and he was able to conduct his affairs dressed in khakis, strolling through open fields with the breeze and the sun in his face. David thought it would be very easy to get used to such an unstructured way of life.

But as interesting as the huge gardens were, it was the aquaculture operation that fascinated him most.

He asked dozens of questions. Grady wondered if he really was that interested or just making conversation. His son, he'd already discovered, was extremely poised and knew how to make others comfortable. However, he proceeded on the premise that David genuinely was curious and eager to learn anything he knew nothing about. "Basically," he told him, "fish farming is like managing a giant aquarium. Have you ever had an aquarium, David?"

"Once, when I was a little kid. I was supposed to take care of it, but the fish kept dying. When I asked the lady at the pet shop what was wrong, she started talking about oxygen content and pH balances and purifiers. I figured all that was a bit much just in order to raise a few goldfish and black mollies, so I gave up."

Grady smiled. "And those are exactly the things we worry about here, too, only on a grander scale. In order to raise fish in commercial quantities, you have to make the conditions as ideal as humanly possible. Fish have to have oxygen to survive, so our ponds are constantly aerated. That doubles the harvest. The pH balance is kept at 6.5, and the water is recirculated and kept at a perfect temperature. Catfish thrive in much warmer water than trout do, so here we raise cat in warm weather and trout during the cooler months. And they're fed commercial feed that has the right proportions of protein, vitamins and minerals. They're also fed at the same time every day. There's a great deal more to it than throwing some fingerlings into the water in the spring and harvesting them when they reach a pound."

"No wonder my black mollies didn't do so well," David said with a grin.

Grady glanced at his watch. "Do you suppose we ought to check in with your mom? We've been gone longer than I realized. She might be climbing the walls."

"Mom's not much of a wall climber, but yeah, you're probably right. It's not fair for us to have all the fun."

David had no way of knowing how much that off-hand remark pleased his father. Grady was proud of what he had built here in the lush Mississippi countryside and could become quite rhapsodic when talking about it, but he hadn't expected a city person to be more than mildly interested. "Somehow I don't think your mom will be too enthusiastic about taking the tour we just did," Grady said as they walked to where the Cherokee was parked. "I thought I'd take both of you into Culver and introduce you around. We'll have lunch there."

David swung himself up into the passenger seat. "You don't mind?"

"Mind?" Grady asked, puzzled.

"Having your friends see us together," David explained. "I noticed the way the man who runs your fields . . . er, Ramon, looked when he saw us together. It's pretty hard to recognize yourself in someone else, but . . . I guess you and I do look an awful lot alike. Won't people you know start asking questions?"

"Let 'em."

"What are you going to tell them?"

"That you're my son, of course."

"Just like that?"

"Just like that. Look, David, your mother and I were married when you were conceived. There's no juicy gossip involved, no dirty linen to air. Who knows, if it hadn't been for the war and all those years in prison, we might still be married."

"Would you have liked that?"

Oh, boy! He was one straightforward young man. "Yes, I think I would have liked that very much."

David looked down at his hands a minute, then back at Grady. "Why didn't you ever try to contact us?"

"I did once. At least, I came close."

David's eyes widened slightly. "Mom didn't tell me that."

"She didn't know the whole story until last night."

"So... what happened?" David asked. "Why did you only come close?"

Grady hesitated. He had told Kirsten he would let her decide what David should and shouldn't know, and he intended on sticking to that—up to a point. This was the point. This he wanted to explain himself. He and David were getting along great, better than he would have dared hope, and he knew the young man had to be wondering about all those years without communication. "When I got out of the Air Force, I found out where you were. I went to see you, and I got as far as those gates."

"Gates? You mean, the gates at our house?"

Grady nodded.

David swallowed hard. "When was this?"

"Not long after your mom and Travis Patrick were married."

"But why... why didn't you come on up to the house?" David ignored the fact that Grady's doing so would have caused an unholy stink.

"Think about it, David. Your mother had just married a man who could give her—both of you—everything. I was only recently out of the service and didn't even have a job. You didn't know me, and I had nothing to offer you at that time—nothing. It wasn't a snap decision. I sat there for a long time before deciding to turn around and come home. Actually, I botched everything from the beginning. I probably shouldn't have asked Kirsten to marry me, not when I knew my outfit had Vietnam breathing down our necks. When I finally got home, I should have worked harder at the marriage and at getting to know you."

"Yeah, but I understood from what Mom said you were all messed up in your head when you got home." David rushed to Grady's defense; why, he wasn't sure. "Maybe she was the one who should have worked harder."

"She did all she knew how to do, son," Grady said. "You can't waste time on what ifs. Besides, if your mom and I had stayed together, you never would have been a Harvard man."

It was meant to be a lighthearted remark, but Grady alertly noticed the way David's eyes clouded over. "Maybe," the young man said, "maybe that wouldn't have been all that bad."

"You don't like school?"

"Let's just say I don't like it as much as I thought I would."

"I see." Grady tugged on his chin and looked at his son thoughtfully. "Well, David, the longer you live the more you'll realize that it's often the things we look forward to the most that disappoint the greatest. What made you decide on Harvard in the first place?"

David uttered a sound, part laugh, part grunt. "I don't ever remember making a conscious decision. It's where Travis wanted me to go, and he talked about it all the time I was growing up. Somewhere along the line it became what I was going to do after high school."

"Were you and your stepfather close?"

"Pretty much so. Travis was the nicest guy you could ever meet, but he never understood Mom's and my position with his family. I think Travis honestly believed that if I graduated from Harvard, the Patricks would accept me with open arms, maybe even take me into one of the family businesses. But there was no way that was going to happen, ever."

Grady was beginning to work up an active dislike for the whole Patrick clan. Who in hell were they to say that Kirsten and his son weren't good enough for them? "They sound like a bunch of snobs."

"Not all of them. Aunt Denise is first-class, but the rest..." David shrugged.

Grady burned with questions. He wanted to know all about David's background. He thought it would help him get to know his son better. And he wanted to know everything that had happened to Kirsten, too. Which reminded him...

He hoped he and David would find time for a long discussion before this visit was over, but right now the hours were fleeing, and he had another guest. He wanted to spend time with Kirsten, too. He slapped David on the knee and turned the key in the ignition. "Come on, let's rescue your mom and see if she wants to go into town for lunch. You and I can talk later."

WHAT PASSED for the noon rush in Culver was in full swing when the Cherokee turned into Lee Avenue. The streets were as traffic-choked as they ever got. "This is a cute little town," was Kirsten's comment after they'd traveled a few blocks. "I guess *quaint* is the word."

"Yeah," Grady agreed, "it's not a bad place to live. Pretty hassle free."

"But what do people do in a place like this?" David asked from the back seat.

"You mean people your age, right? Well, most of them are off at Mississippi State or Ole' Miss right now. And when they're home, I imagine they do what young folks in small towns all over the world do— make their own fun. Or occasionally go into Jackson."

Once they got to Slick's Café, they had to wait a few minutes for a table, which gave the other customers ample time to stare openly at Kirsten and David, especially Kirsten. Grady had told her to dress very casually, and he supposed the simple navy-and-white dress passed for casual with her. But in the crowded café she stood out as though a spotlight had been trained on her. She could have been dressed in sackcloth and the effect would have been the same. She was an incredibly beautiful woman.

No one in the café gaped at her with more astonishment than Loretta. The waitress came very close to spilling a tall glass of iced tea on one of the customers while she craned her neck to get a better look. When a table was cleared at last, Loretta motioned to Grady, and though she addressed him, she couldn't take her eyes off his companions.

"Hi ya, Grady. How's it goin'?"

"Not too bad, Loretta." He held Kirsten's chair while she sat down, then took the chair on her left. "As you can see, I have company this week. All the way from New York."

"City?" Loretta asked incredulously.

"Long Island, actually. This is Kirsten Patrick."

"Pleased to meet you."

"Thank you, Loretta. It's nice to meet you, too," Kirsten's smile was friendly and warm, and Long Island gentility dripped from her voice.

"And this—" Grady patted David's shoulder "—is my son, David."

"Your..." Loretta's eyes widened, and she looked as though she'd swallowed her tongue for a minute, but she recovered nicely. "Hi, David."

"Hello, Loretta."

"What's the special today?" Grady asked.

"Huh?" Loretta reluctantly tore her gaze away from David. "Oh, the special. It's fried chicken."

Kirsten made an appreciative sound. "It's been a number of years since I've had real southern fried chicken."

"That's what you want, then?" Grady asked.

"I think so. It sounds wonderful."

"David?"

The young man shrugged. "Guess I've never had any but the fast-food kind. Sure, I'll have that, too."

Grady addressed Loretta. "Three specials."

"You may have to wait a bit," the waitress said, scribbling on her pad. "We've really had a run on it. Slick's cookin' up a fresh batch right now."

The consensus around the table was that time was not of the essence. Loretta scurried away, and Grady's eyes followed her. The waitress placed their order at the serving window, took a quick, expert look around the café, then hurried through the kitchen door. Grady would have bet his last dollar she had gone in search of Rosemary.

Sure enough, seconds later the door swung open and Loretta reappeared, this time with Slick's wife quick on her heels. While the waitress resumed her duties, Rosemary's gaze made a full sweep of the café, then landed squarely on Grady. Feigning surprise, she marched straight for him. He hid his smile. By tonight, half of Culver's citizens would know about Kirsten and David; the other half would know by noon tomorrow.

"Hi, Grady," Rosemary greeted him.

"Hello, Rosie. How's it goin'?"

"Not too bad. You didn't tell us you were having out-of-town company." Her tone was accusing, intimating that it wasn't right of him not to have informed the gang at Slick's beforehand.

"This was sort of a spur-of-the-minute thing, Rosie." Grady made the necessary introductions. Rosemary, he noticed, did not react in the slightest when he introduced David as his son. But, of course, that startling news would already have been relayed to her via Loretta. He could well imagine the third degree that was in store for him the next time he came into the café alone. This would give the two women a week's worth of gossip.

Rosemary didn't appear to be in any hurry to leave, so he had no choice but to ask, "Won't you join us?"

"Well, I..." She grabbed the fourth chair and sat down. "Are you going to be staying long?" she asked Kirsten in an overly polite voice.

Kirsten shook her head. "No, we'll be leaving the day after tomorrow."

"That's too bad," Rosemary said obscurely, then turned to Grady. "Your guests explain why you weren't at the spaghetti supper last night. We had a real good turnout."

"Did we raise much money?"

"Oh, we never raise a lot of money at anything, but I guess every little bit helps."

Grady explained to Kirsten and David. "The town's trying to raise money to build a birthing center at the hospital. It's slow going, though. I don't think we ever dreamed it would be so hard to get people to part with their money."

"Heck, you ought to hire Mom," David said jokingly. "She's raised more money for more causes than you can shake a stick at."

All eyes focused on Kirsten. "That's . . . just something the women in my husband's family are expected to do," she said lamely.

"She's a great organizer," David added.

"That's what we need, an organizer," Rosemary said. "None of us really know how to go about this. Maybe you could give us some pointers."

Kirsten hesitated to say anything because her experience with fund-raising wouldn't do these people any good. There was a big difference between a small town trying to raise money for a hospital addition and her inviting three hundred of the Patricks' dearest friends to a five-hundred-dollar-a-plate dinner in order to keep a ballet company alive. "It's something you get better at the longer you do it," she finally said. "But I have learned one thing—if you need to raise money and can't count on friends to cough it up, bring in some big-name entertainment. People who won't donate five dollars will gladly pay four times that much to see a good show."

"But what big name is going to come to Culver?" Rosemary asked reasonably.

"The best bet is to find someone famous who's from here. You'd be surprised at some of the really big stars who'll do a benefit for their old hometown. It makes great press."

"Shoot!" Rosemary scoffed. "If anybody famous had ever come from Culver, it'd be in the paper every other day."

"Are we sure, Rosie?" Grady pursed his lips. "Maybe we ought to start asking around. Somebody might know of someone. At least it's something to look into, something we hadn't thought of before."

At that moment Loretta appeared with their food, which effectively put an end to the conversation. Rosemary realized she wasn't going to have her curiosity satisfied, not today, so she excused herself and went back to her office and her ledgers.

But she was about to pop! The young man, David, was Grady's son—that much they knew. Not that anyone would have to be told. Talk about two peas out of the same pod.

That, however, wasn't the most intriguing part of the surprising turn of events. David had referred to Kirsten Patrick as Mom, so that meant Grady and the stunning woman from New York had, at one time, been...close. Rosemary's mind raced, and her fertile imagination shifted into high gear. The possibilities for the story behind all this were limitless.

Learning such delicious news about anyone in town would have tongues wagging, but since it concerned Grady, the gossips would have a field day. He had always been Culver's mystery man. Handsome and eligible, he naturally was the focus of feminine attention wherever he went, but no one knew a thing about his past. Now his past had shown up, and he wasn't doing a thing to hide it.

Oh, wait until Loretta heard! It had been a long time since anything this interesting had happened in Culver. This made the alleged affair between Alice Howard and Claude Brown seem like stale stuff, indeed.

"THAT WAS WONDERFUL, Grady," Kirsten said as they drove back to the farm.

"I'm glad you liked it. Slick is one heckuva cook."

"Oh, I don't mean just the food, although it was great. I mean the café and the people we met and...everything. A real slice of Americana. It's so easy to forget that kind of down-to-earth folksiness when—"

She checked herself, remembering David's presence. Naturally David was aware of her situation with Travis's family, but they never discussed it—or almost never. From the beginning, David instinctively had given all the Patricks but Denise a wide berth, which wasn't difficult for him to do. Kirsten, on the other hand, had been surrounded, inundated, smothered by the family. Small wonder that today had seemed so liberating, and she would have another day just like it before going back to face the problems at home.

As Grady drove through the brick archway, David leaned forward. "Dad, do you suppose Ramon was serious when he said I could hang around with him while I'm here?"

"I'm sure he was completely serious. Why? Would you like to do that?"

"Yeah, I really would."

"Who's Ramon?" Kirsten wanted to know.

"The man in charge of the fields," Grady explained. "Sort of my foreman, I guess. David asked him a hundred questions this morning, thus endearing himself to Ramon forever. Come on, we'll go find him."

Once they'd located Ramon and deposited David with him, Grady and Kirsten drove to his house. "I feel certain we're keeping you from your work," she said as Grady parked the vehicle. "I want you to know we don't expect you to spend every minute with us."

"My secretary knows how to reach me if something comes up that no one else can handle. You'll be here such a short time as it is. I'd hate to waste a minute of it."

"All right," she said with a soft smile. "I just don't want to keep you from more meaningful pursuits."

"What could be more meaningful than this?"

Kirsten had noticed that he never locked the front door when he came and went. Now he pushed it open for her, and she preceded him into the house. "You know, of course," he said, "that at this very minute you and David are the chief topics of conversation in Culver."

"We are?"

"Sure. It's a gossipy little town in the first place, and now that I've announced to one and all that I have a son, now that Rosemary distinctly heard David call you Mom . . . well, you get the picture."

"Does that bother you?"

"Not at all."

"Then it doesn't bother me. I doubt I'll ever see any of those people again."

Hearing her say that did something peculiar to Grady's stomach. He guessed he'd harbored the hope that she would come back, many times. Now that the three of them had opened the lines of communication, he had allowed himself the luxury of thinking they might spend holidays together, take trips together, that sort of thing. Apparently nothing of the kind had entered Kirsten's mind.

He watched her as she sat down on the sofa and crossed her legs. They were as fine a pair of legs as he'd ever seen, trim and shapely. Then her eyes surveyed the room. "This is a nice house," she said. "Very livable."

"Thanks. I like it."

"But I want to ask you about something I noticed this morning when I was here alone. I hope I don't touch a nerve."

Grady hitched his trousers at both knees and sat down beside her. "Ask anything you like. My nerves are pretty touchproof."

With her hand, Kirsten made a sweeping gesture to include the house as a whole. "No mementos of your Air Force days. Not one. I don't think I've ever known anyone who'd been in the service who didn't have something around to proclaim it to the world. Especially a pilot."

Grady shrugged. "Oh, I guess I've got a bunch of stuff stashed away in boxes. I don't know why I don't have anything displayed. I just never thought about it."

"Perhaps your memories of the military aren't particularly happy ones. Understandable."

"No. When I think of the service, mostly I remember the good times. Pilot training, all the gung ho nonsense before the war. And I think of those funny base quarters we lived in right after we got married."

"You think of that?" Kirsten asked in surprise.

"Sure. Remember the couple who lived below us? Sam Collins, and I think her name was . . . Janice."

Kirsten closed her eyes, trying desperately to recall them. "Yes!" she finally exclaimed. "I don't remember much about him, but Janice was a little blonde who had grown up on a farm. She taught me how to cut up a chicken." A slow smile spread across her face.

"Those cookouts we had every weekend," Grady prompted. "Everyone in the building would chip in. There were always about fourteen little kids underfoot. God, we were all so young."

He began to reminisce about days Kirsten thought she had forgotten entirely. He remembered far more about their short time as husband and wife than she did, but little by little, prodded by his memories, she began to recall some of the good times.

Yes, they had been young, she especially so. Grady had been a handsome, dashing captain, and since they'd had no children, they had been financially better off than the other couples they had chummed around with. Free to come and go as they pleased, they had been greatly envied by their friends. Kirsten went from remembering almost nothing to remembering almost everything, particularly how much in love they had been. Their lovemaking had been spectacular. Did Grady remember that, too?

Kirsten looked at him. Their eyes met, and she knew that he did, that he was thinking about it as he spoke. Her cheeks suddenly felt flushed, and she had to glance away. The memories were a revelation for her. They actually had had some wonderful times together. Sadly, there just hadn't been enough of them to keep the marriage from falling apart after a long separation.

Why sadly? she wondered. Why was all the reminiscing leaving her with such a sense of loss? To regret, even vaguely, the breakup of her first marriage was to do an injustice to the years she had shared with Travis.

She had no idea how long they sat there talking—a long time. And then David was bounding through the front door, full of enthusiasm about the things he had learned under Ramon's expert tutelage. "And I met his daughter, Mona," he informed them. "She's a real looker."

"A fine young lady," Grady agreed. "Ramon's pride and joy. He has six kids, but Mona's the only girl. She must be about your age, maybe a year younger. She's working in the processing plant, making money for college."

"She invited me to a cookout this Thursday night, but—" David looked at his mother "—I had to tell her maybe next time."

Grady alertly caught the "next time," but it seemed to have gone right by Kirsten, as did David's beseeching look. In fact, she'd heard almost nothing of what David had said, and for the remainder of the day and all through the evening meal, she tried very hard not to look at Grady. It wasn't until much later, when they were getting ready to retire for the night, that they spoke directly to each other again. She was on her way to the guest room, and Grady caught up with her just as she reached the door. Touching her lightly on the shoulder, he forced her to turn and face him.

"Kirsten, I can't tell you how much I enjoyed today," he said huskily.

"Thank you, Grady. So did I."

"Would you like to go to Jackson tomorrow to look around, visit some of your old haunts?"

Oh, Lord, more memories. "I ... guess so. Maybe David would enjoy seeing the place where he was born."

Grady wondered if it was completely unconscionable for him to wish he and Kirsten could go to Jackson alone. Probably. Even so, for one brief moment that was exactly what he wished. During that moment he went so far as to envision the two of them strolling hand in hand along the street where she had lived when he courted her. Ridiculous! "Then that's what we'll do."

Grady stood awkwardly for a minute, hands at his side. Then, unable to help himself, he touched her arm, lightly stroking it. "Must you go home Thursday? I could tell that David really would like to go to that cookout Thursday night."

"What cookout?"

"Weren't you listening? Mona Cuellar invited him to a cookout."

"I ... who's Mona Cuellar?"

Grady smiled. "You weren't listening. Mona is Ramon's daughter. She's about David's age. He wants to go. Does one more day mean so much, one way or another?"

"I need to be back before Saturday night. Denise and I are cohosting a party."

"So, change your reservations to Friday."

What good would one more day do? Kirsten wondered. She'd been with Grady only two nights, with one more to go, and she could feel some kind of magnetic force urging her toward him. Nothing positive could come of that. It was best to keep this duty visit as short as possible, then let Grady and David decide when they would see each other again. "I . . . don't know. . . ."

"Please. For David's sake?"

"I . . . well, let me sleep on it."

"I guess I can't ask for more than that."

Impulsively, he bent his head and placed his lips on hers. It was nothing more than a simple, light caress, the sort of kiss one might give an old and dear friend. It occurred to him that even that light brush of lips might seem bold to Kirsten, but all afternoon he had been aware of a burning need for some physical contact with her.

Kirsten stood as still as a statue, afraid to move for fear she would lean into the kiss and deepen it. When Grady lifted his head, his eyes seemed to have turned to liquid.

"Good night," he said.

"G-good night." Quickly she slipped into the room and closed the door. A second later she heard his door close. She placed her hand to her heart, as if that would somehow still its racing. She felt ridiculous, gauche, like a silly schoolgirl. The hours she had spent alone with Grady today had had the most curious effect on her. Try as she might, she couldn't stop thinking of him in man-woman terms.

Which wasn't particularly surprising. He'd always appealed to her in a very masculine way, even during those difficult months after he returned from prison. But now she found herself wishing for . . . what? Did she actually think something might develop between herself and Grady again? It was impossible. Too many years had passed. Now he had his life and she had hers, and they were light-years removed from each other.

She shook her head clear and quickly undressed for bed. Still, her last conscious thought before sleep claimed her was of a dashing young man in uniform who'd told her she was wonderful and had made her believe it. If it hadn't been for the war and prison, their life together might have been quite beautiful.

CHAPTER FIVE

SLEEP WAS COMPLETELY ELUSIVE for Grady that night. First he congratulated himself. All that reminiscing had had exactly the effect on Kirsten he had hoped for. It had caused her to begin thinking about their marriage and how much they once had meant to each other. And he blessed whatever fates had sent David to rummage around in those boxes four years ago. It eventually had led to today. He found it difficult to believe that Kirsten had sailed into his life after all these years and captivated him all over again, but that was precisely what had happened.

Often in the past, he had wondered why he, normal heterosexual male, had steered clear of serious romantic entanglements for so long. Now, at last, he understood why he had been content to settle for sporadic affairs that only involved his body, never his heart. Now he knew why there had been no room in his life for another woman. He had never gotten over the raven-haired beauty he had married years ago. It was foolish to think he ever could.

So what next? Even if he did nothing, they would see each other from time to time because of David, but Grady wanted more than that. He didn't bother asking himself if Kirsten could learn to care for him again or if she would want to leave New York. He'd make her care, and once she did, she would want to be wherever he was. He would focus every ounce of energy his job didn't use up on making Kirsten and David a part of his life.

But right now he was a long way from having them, particularly Kirsten, be a part of anything. Just how he intended to accomplish all the grand things he had in mind wasn't yet clear to him. He only knew he had to do it. He felt joyous for the first time in too long, so he couldn't lose them again.

So went Grady's thoughts throughout much of a restless night. Yet, though he slept little, his inner alarm clock went off at precisely six-thirty, just as it did every morning. Rousing, he shaved and dressed and went into the kitchen to make coffee. To his surprise, David soon joined him.

"You're up and about awfully early this morning," Grady commented.

"I couldn't sleep," David said. "You mentioned needing to do some work first thing. I wondered if I could come along."

"Love to have you. We'll have a quick bite to eat first."

After a hasty breakfast they left the house, and Grady made his customary early morning inspection of the fields and tanks, then stopped at his office for a few minutes, just to see if there were calls needing to be returned or mail requiring his personal attention. He and David entered through the side door.

"Neat," was David's assessment of the stylish office.

"Thanks," Grady replied.

"You must be the luckiest man alive. Your house, your office, your work—all right here. No rat race."

"Don't think I don't realize that." Grady punched the intercom.

"Yes?" Phyllis responded.

"I'm checking in before leaving for Jackson for the day. Any messages?"

"Vanessa Hamilton wants you to call the minute you can."

"Get her for me." He glanced at David and motioned him toward a chair. "It's the big boss herself. Have a seat. This shouldn't take long."

Grady thumbed idly through the mail until the call to Dallas went through. After he'd exchanged the customary pleasantries with Vanessa's secretary, he heard a very familiar voice come over the line.

"Good morning, Grady."

"Good morning, Vanessa. How are you?"

"As fine as one can be at seventy-nine, I suppose. I want you to do something for me."

"Of course."

"I'd like to see you here in my office Monday morning. Can that be arranged?"

Grady almost laughed out loud. Anything Vanessa wanted could be arranged. "Sure. I'll be in Dallas Sunday night."

"Prepare to spend a few days here," Vanessa said. "At least three. Possibly four."

That got Grady's attention. Three or four days? Vanessa's time was so valuable that he rarely got to spend more than a day with her. "Great! I'm looking forward to it."

Vanessa's voice softened. "So am I. I don't get to see nearly enough of you."

"Call me more often, and I'll be on your doorstep."

Vanessa chuckled delightedly. "There'll be reservations at the Anatole for Sunday night, and my driver will pick you up at the hotel at eight-thirty Monday morning."

"I'll be there in my best bib and tucker."

They spent a minute or two on small talk, but Vanessa gave him no inkling of the reason for this unexpected summons. When Grady hung up, he was alive with curiosity. He normally made two trips a year to the home office to brief Vanessa on the agricultural operation, but his next one wasn't scheduled until just before Thanksgiving. That was almost two months away. He couldn't begin to imagine what Vanessa would want to see him about that would require three or four days at the home office.

But his was not to reason why, his was but to do or die for Hamilton House. And a trip to Dallas might help get his mind off Kirsten and David. Already he knew he was going to miss them far more than he was sure he could handle. He had been alone a long time and had thought he liked it that way. Now he knew with certainty that he was damned tired of it.

Grady glanced at David, seated across the room. He thought his son seemed preoccupied, but it wasn't until they were back in the Cherokee, heading for the house, that the young man voiced what was on his mind.

"I wish we didn't have to leave tomorrow."

"So do I, David," Grady said, "and maybe you won't have to. You might be able to tell Mona you can go to that cookout, after all. I asked your mom to stay another day, and she said she'd sleep on it."

David brightened for a minute, then shook his head. "I doubt it. She wants to be back for Aunt Denise's bash. She's promised to cohost the thing."

"But that's not until Saturday night, right?"

"Yeah, but you don't know the kind of parties the Patricks give. They're really swanky affairs, with tons of champagne, food, flowers, an orchestra . . . I don't know what all. Of course, Mom and Denise don't have to do much but send out invitations, since between them they have enough servants to staff a motel. Saturday night, all they'll have to do is throw on their latest twenty-thousand-dollar designer original and try to outdazzle every other woman there."

Grady's spirits plummeted. What made him think for a minute that a woman who was accustomed to that sort of life would be interested in anything he could offer her? He was dreaming.

"You don't sound as though you approve," he commented.

David shrugged. "It's not my place to approve or disapprove. It goes with the territory, and Mom does it very well. If you ask me, she does it better than a lot of those women who have 'position' out the kazoo." He lapsed into silence for a minute, then asked, "Can I come back soon?"

"I'm counting on it."

"I mean . . . right away. Maybe in a few weeks. And next time I'd like to stay awhile."

"How is your mom going to feel about that?"

David expelled his breath. "I don't imagine she'll be thrilled, but I don't think she'll try to stop me if she knows it's what I really want to do. I guess what I really wish is that we all lived closer together. Then seeing you wouldn't have to be a major hassle."

"That . . . would be nice," Grady managed to say with deceptive calmness. That was exactly what he wished, too.

"I like it here," David went on, "and that's pretty funny. If someone had asked me before I came here if I would be interested in farming, I'd have said no way, but this is different from just farming. I think Ramon called it agribusiness."

Grady smiled. "There are those who call it agribigness, and they don't mean it as a compliment."

"Whatever it is, it's appealing. I think I might like to study something like it, and I don't think I need to go to Harvard for that. I could go almost anywhere I wanted, right?"

This was getting interesting. Grady pulled to the side of the road, turned off the engine and studied his son solemnly. "Where, for instance?"

"Oh . . . for instance, a school near here. Then I could come to see you on the weekends."

"That would be great for me, but would you really like being so far from home? It would be a drastic change for you. Don't you have a girl you'd hate to leave?"

David shook his head. "No girl. Most of the ones I know I've known since I was a kid. Dating them is like dating your sister."

"Okay, so there's no girl, but there are other things—friends, places, a way of life that's vastly different from what you'd have here."

"It's hard for me to explain, and probably harder for you to understand, but . . . I think I've been wanting something different for a long time now."

A part of Grady was thrilled beyond words that David wanted to be close to him, but another part knew with certainty that going to school so far from home was not going to sit well with Kirsten. From a word dropped here and there, he had come to realize that mother and son were closer than most. Grady doubted Kirsten would let David go without a fight, and if they started fighting over their son, all would be lost before it could begin.

"Well, David, no one would be more pleased than I to have you close by. We could have us some good times together. But I don't think you ought to hit your mom with this just yet. You go back home and think about it a few days. Then if you still feel the same way, give me a call. We'll put our heads together and see if we can't come up with something she won't find too hard to accept."

"You mean it?"

"Of course."

"My being around wouldn't screw up your life-style?"

Grady chuckled. "Hardly."

"I know you think I'll change my mind when I get home, but I won't. You'll find that out about me. Once I make up my mind to do something, I don't change it. Four years ago I decided I was going to find you someday, and I finally did."

"I'm glad you did, son. Yes, I'm certainly glad you did." Grady felt choked with emotion. There was a lot he would have liked to say to David; he just didn't know how. Fearing he might turn embarrassingly maudlin, he decided to say nothing. He switched on the engine and eased the vehicle back onto the road. "Now, let's go see what your mom's up to. We have the day ahead of us, and we don't want to waste a minute of it."

THEIR SOJOURN TO JACKSON took up the remainder of the day. Kirsten enjoyed every minute of it, even though wandering through the city where both she and David had been born dredged up more poignant memories than she felt equipped to deal with. Grady drove her to the house she had grown up in, and while sitting parked in front of it, reminiscing, they had been approached by a frail, white-haired woman who introduced herself as Eve Bishop. Eve had been Kirsten's mother's neighbor and best friend for at least two dozen years. That encounter prompted more reminiscing. Kirsten was certain that David didn't find the trip down memory lane as fascinating as she did, so she reluctantly cut it as short as possible. But it was wonderful to see the house, the elementary school she had attended and to see Eve again. Everyone needed roots, and it was nice to touch base with hers. It served to remind her that there had been life before the Patricks and there would be life after them.

Before starting for home that evening, they had a superb dinner at the city's Hamilton House, where Grady was well-known and well liked. Consequently, Kirsten suspected, they received some special attention. The food and service were impeccable. The elegant restaurant impressed even two New Yorkers who had dined in some of the world's finest places.

During dessert and coffee, Grady—aided by David—again gently pressured Kirsten to stay one more day. Feeling wonderfully mellow, she agreed. One more day couldn't matter, she reasoned. She would still be home in plenty of time for the party, and David was having such a good time. If he was that keen on attending tomorrow night's cookout, why not let him? Except for Denise's party, there wasn't a thing waiting for her back home.

It was after nine when they returned to Grady's house. David got the Cuellar's phone number from his dad and immediately phoned Mona, who seemed genuinely pleased to hear he would be available.

"Hey, that's great," she enthused. "It's my uncle's birthday, and there'll be everything from babies in strollers to grandparents. I've been trying to get out of the thing for weeks, but Dad wouldn't hear of it. Family, you know. But now I'll have someone my own age to talk to."

"Trouble is, I'm here minus wheels," David said.

"No problem. I'll pick you up at five-thirty."

"I'm looking forward to it," he told her just before they hung up. "And tell your dad I'd like to follow him around tomorrow, if it's okay."

"Will do. Goodbye, David."

"Goodbye, Mona."

David really was looking forward to tomorrow night; why, he wasn't quite sure. A family cookout, for Pete's sake! But it would be the first time in a long time he'd had a date with someone he didn't know well. More importantly, it would be the first time he'd had a date with someone who didn't know of the Patricks. He was grinning when he turned away from the phone and back to his parents. "Well, it's all set."

"You'll have a good time," Grady predicted. "Like I said, Mona's a wonderful girl."

"Yeah, she seemed to be. Well…I guess I'll hit the sack. I want to be up bright and early to pester Ramon tomorrow." David kissed his mother's cheek and patted his dad's shoulder before climbing the steps to the loft.

Kirsten stared after him, shaking her head in wonder. "How could I not have granted him another day? It's been a long time since I've seen him so up. I can't imagine what magic this place has."

"It's something different," Grady said. "I think all young people long for a change of pace occasionally."

Kirsten nodded. "I guess so. Now...I think I'll say good night, too. It's been a busy day. And a lovely one. Thanks, Grady."

"You're welcome. I enjoyed it, too."

"Good night."

"Good night, Kirsten. Sleep well." The only thing that kept him from following her down the hall was the knowledge that tomorrow they would have virtually the entire day to themselves. It would be his chance to begin worming his way inside her head and heart. The thought was so delicious he had to smile. He didn't bother speculating on what would happen after that. He was taking this one step at a time.

IN THE PRIVACY of her room, as she undressed, Kirsten reflected back on the day. She and Grady had not spent one minute alone the entire time, which was probably for the best. Several times that afternoon she had caught him looking at her—wistfully, longingly, enigmatically, with just a trace of sadness. Always the looks were more like caresses, and they caused odd flutterings in her stomach. He was such an attractive man and so real. If their worlds were not so far apart, if there was a reasonable hope of seeing him often...

However, there wasn't. One more day, then she would be leaving, and only heaven knew when she would see him again. True, he had stirred something inside her, but being the sensible woman she thought she was, she was confident that would settle down once she returned to her familiar world.

But David? David was another matter altogether. It was so easy to see that her son had become enchanted with his father. Watching them together, one easily could imagine they had seen each other every day of David's life. Kirsten couldn't help wondering if that would become a problem. She knew David so well, knew how his interests often became obsessions. A tiny tingle of trepidation swept through her. What she was vaguely afraid of, she didn't know. She didn't think she was jealous; she hoped she wasn't. She liked to think that the sensible side of her nature extended to motherhood. For years she frequently had reminded herself that her son was growing into a man, that she would have to loosen her hold on him.

Still, she'd had David to herself for a long time. Except for a grandmother who hadn't been around often, he'd had no other family. Now he did. The instant rapport that had sprung up between father and son was touching to see. As wonderful as Travis had been with his stepson, Kirsten had always been aware that something was missing. That something was definitely there where Grady and David were concerned.

She was only human. Maybe she was jealous... just a little.

WHEN KIRSTEN VENTURED out of her room the following morning, it was to an empty house again, but by the time she had showered and dressed for the day, Grady was back. "David has his day all planned. He and Ramon are meeting Mona in the employees' dining room for lunch. So all that's left is for you to tell me what you want to do."

She shrugged. "I . . . really don't know."

"Then, if it's all right, I'd like to give you an idea of what I do for a living."

"Lead on."

The tour Grady gave her wasn't nearly as extensive as the one he'd given David. He didn't imagine Kirsten would be that interested in the nuts-and-bolts operation. Rather, he wanted to give her an insight into the scope of his job. In plainer words, he wanted her to know how successful he was, that he was an important executive who was in charge of a vital part of a dynamic corporation. She had to realize that, while he was far from being on the same plane as the Patricks and their ilk, he wasn't exactly a nobody, either. And somehow he managed to do just that without coming across as a pompous braggart. Kirsten was impressed.

When lunchtime rolled around, Grady suggested the employees' dining hall. Again there was a purpose. He was treated with cordial deference by all the people who worked for him, and he wanted Kirsten to see that. He'd never in his life done any showing off, but never before had someone's admiration mattered to him. Kirsten's did.

They sought out and joined David and his new-found friends, Ramon and Mona. One look at the Cuellar daughter and Kirsten understood why David had referred to her as a looker. Mona was a beautiful girl, with lustrous dark hair and big eyes the color of pitchblende. She also was an amiable, witty chatterbox, the kind of person who never met a stranger. Her gaiety was spontaneous and contagious. It rather

startled Kirsten to see the expression on David's face
when he looked at Mona. Never, at least not to her
knowledge, had he shown so much overt interest in a
girl. She had often wondered how she would feel when
he came home with one special young woman in tow.
Now she got a taste of her reaction. It was a peculiar
sensation.

All in all, the day turned out to be another memorable one, surprisingly so, considering that she and
Grady did nothing unusual. She sat in his office while
he went through the mail. He had some errands to run,
and she tagged along. Much later, after David had
driven off with Mona, Grady fired up his barbecue
grill and cooked her one of the best steaks she had ever
eaten. And they talked…and talked and talked. Even
when they didn't talk, the silences were comfortable.
It was after eleven when Kirsten decided to call it a
day.

"Another lovely day, Grady," she said as she got to
her feet.

"I thought so, too." He stood and turned off the
one lamp that remained burning; moonlight streamed
through the windows. As Kirsten turned to go down
the hall to her room, he fell into step beside her and
paused with her at the door. Placing his hands on her
shoulders, he detained her a moment.

"As much talking as we've done today," he said,
"the one thing we haven't done is established some
ground rules."

Kirsten frowned. "Ground rules?"

"I'm going to want to see David as often as can be
arranged. Is there going to be a problem with that?"

"None."

"He's already told me he wants to come back here sometime soon."

"I rather imagined he would."

"Would you find it awkward if I came to New York occasionally?"

"No, David will be delighted."

"And you? I won't be coming only to see David."

She offered him a small smile. "Yes, I'll be delighted, too."

The pressure of his hands on her shoulders increased. "Kirsten, I . . ." Grady's chest heaved. There was so much he wanted to say to her and so little time. "This visit . . . has been a major event in my life. I don't expect anything to be the same for me again. I'm sure tomorrow is going to be one of the most difficult days I've ever spent. In some ways it seems you've been here only minutes. In other ways, it seems we've never been apart."

Kirsten's heart seemed to swell to twice its normal size. The expression on his face was so intense that she experienced a great surge of tenderness for him. Raising her hands, she placed them on top of the ones gripping her shoulders. "Grady, it's been marvelous for us, too. Perhaps when I decide what I'm going to do and life settles down a little, we can have you come for a nice long visit. Really show you the city. Strangely enough, I . . . I think I'm going to miss you."

That was all she needed to say. With one deft motion, his arms went around her, and he pulled her to him, holding her so tightly she could scarcely breathe. Twisting his head, he groped for her mouth. Finding it, he kissed her with a hunger that staggered her.

It seemed to Kirsten she should remember what his kiss felt like, but she didn't. This was the kiss of someone new and exciting and desirable. Too desirable, she thought as she mindlessly leaned into the kiss and returned it ardently. He felt so good, and she was so starved for affection. It was glorious to melt against him, to feel her breasts crushed against his chest and the hardness of his erection pressed against her stomach. Her legs turned to absolute liquid, and when one of his hands dropped to cup her buttocks and pull her even more tightly to him, she aided the action with a thrust of her hips.

The drugging kiss ended finally, and Grady looked down at her with eyes glazed by desire. "I know this is going to sound crazy, but I wanted to do that the minute I saw you Monday. Don't tell me things like that can't happen, because I know they can."

Kirsten uttered a nervous little laugh. "It is crazy, Grady, and you know it. Three days together and we're wound around each other like coiled snakes."

"Remember how fast it happened before?"

"At least then it took five months."

"It barely took five hours for me."

"No, no, we shouldn't even be thinking this way. We're letting this entire thing turn too emotional."

"Dammit, you kissed me back. I felt that much."

Kirsten gave a shake of her head, not to deny that she had kissed him, which she had; rather, the gesture was prompted by her own confusion. This was so irrational. For years she had been a proper society matron, filling her days with orderly preciseness, doing the same things her acquaintances did. When one lived as a Patrick, one did not act impulsively, and this attraction to her ex-husband was impulsiveness personified.

Grady watched her. He felt he could read her thoughts and, surprisingly, he understood. He would accomplish nothing by moving too fast at this point. Their worlds might seem a million miles apart now, but planes flew back and forth every day. Direct dialing still existed, and he might even remember how to write an irresistible love letter. If there was one thing he had learned during his stay on the planet it was patience. One day Kirsten would be his again; he vowed it on the spot.

"I won't press now," he said softly. "I'll just tell you that I once thought you were very special, and I still think you are. You got to me then, and you're getting to me now."

"Oh, Grady, I . . . You're adorable . . . and impossible." Feeling completely graceless, Kirsten backed into her room and closed the door. Her heart was pounding like a hundred drums. He was getting to her, too, and that couldn't happen. These insane, unruly feelings he aroused had no place in her life. What could possibly come of them? Snatched intervals here and there? She didn't know.

She only knew one thing; if that kiss had lasted two seconds longer, she feared she might have invited him in so she could rediscover the joyous ritual of making love to him. . . .

SOME THIRTY MINUTES after Kirsten and Grady had retired, Mona's car pulled to a stop in front of the house. She switched off the engine and turned to David with a smile. "Thanks for coming. I hope you weren't too bored."

"Not at all. I enjoyed it—I really did. Thanks for asking me. That's quite a family you have there."

Mona rolled her eyes. "Tell me about it. I've been hemmed in by family all my life."

"That's nice. There was always just Mom and me until now. Oh, there was my stepfather's family, but that's different."

"That's the neatest story about you finding Mr. O'Connor. Will you be coming back from now on?"

"I sure hope so. I'm planning on it."

"Give me a call, will you?"

"Sure...if your dad won't mind. Seemed to me he—" David paused to chuckle softly "—he looked at me kind of suspiciously."

The lines of Mona's pretty mouth set grimly. "Don't take it personally. He's that way with any guy who's anywhere near my age. I'll tell you, David, the worst thing in the world is being the only girl in a family of six kids. My folks were in their late thirties before I came along, and Dad's always treated me like I was made of porcelain or something. He'd keep me in a convent if he could."

"Yeah, that must be rough."

"I can hardly wait to go away to school even though Dad almost has a cow when he thinks about it."

"Where are you going?"

"Mississippi State. Not exactly Harvard, but I'm sure looking forward to it." Her bright smile returned. "To think I actually knew a Harvard man."

David looked uncomfortable. "It's not that big a deal. In fact...can you keep a secret, Mona?"

"I'm the best. You say don't tell anybody, I don't tell anybody."

"I'm...sort of thinking about going to school down here."

"Really? To State?"

"I haven't gotten that far yet. You have your dad to deal with, and I'll have Mom. She's not going to do a dance over it, I promise you."

"Parents! Gosh, it'd really be neat if you did come down here. We could drive back and forth together on the weekends."

Strange how appealing that sounded, David mused. He didn't really know this girl, but already he liked her enormously. "Yeah, well, keep the good thought." He reached for the door handle. "I'd better go in. You have to work tomorrow, and Mom and I have to be at the airport by ten. Thanks again. I had a great time."

"So did I, David. Get in touch next time you're here. Maybe I can find something for us to do other than hang around with my family."

"Count on it. Good night, Mona."

"'Night, David. Have a safe trip."

He stood and watched until the taillights of her car disappeared, then hopped up the steps, opened the front door and went inside. He was whistling softly under his breath. Suddenly he had one more reason for wanting to return to Mississippi.

WHY IS IT, Grady wondered the next morning as he watched the plane to Atlanta lift off, that the planes carrying loved ones away were always on time? Because of David's presence, he and Kirsten had, with some difficulty, kept the goodbye from becoming too emotional, but a feeling of the most abject loneliness overtook him when she turned and walked away from him. He had to get out of the airport, out of Jackson and back to work fast.

Once he was driving out on the open highway he felt a little better—not much, but a little. He patted his shirt pocket. The check for five thousand dollars Kirsten had handed him just before boarding had been a surprise, and he had felt peculiar taking money from her.

"For the birthing center," she explained. "It's not a lot, but as Rosemary said, every little bit helps."

Not a lot? It was the largest individual donation they'd had. Hamilton House's check had been larger, but that was a corporate thing, donated by many people.

Grady sighed. He wondered how long he should wait before contacting her again. David wanted to come back right away, which was great, but he had to see Kirsten, too. Maybe it wasn't rational to want her, to want the three of them to be a family, but there it was. There wasn't a thing he could do about it.

He had to accept that he was one of those men who truly love only once. Kirsten! He liked rolling her name over on his tongue. They had had such a short time together—five months of dating and six months as husband and wife before he'd left for the war. But what they had compressed into those short months had been the stuff of dreams. Now, with single-minded purpose, he had to find a way of recapturing the magic.

CHAPTER SIX

ON SATURDAY MORNING, Denise stopped by, supposedly to go over last minute details of that evening's gala, but actually it was her burning curiosity about the trip to Mississippi that prompted the call. "How was it?" she asked.

"Not at all what I expected," Kirsten told her candidly. "I honestly thought it would be awkward as hell, but Grady and David hit it off immediately. It was amazing to watch. It really must be true that blood is thicker than water. Here was this kid who Grady hadn't seen in years, and David didn't remember Grady at all, yet there was an instant rapport. Actually, we had a very good time."

"How did seeing him affect you?"

Not even to Denise would Kirsten admit the unvarnished truth—that she had thought about Grady incessantly throughout the previous day, and he had been her first conscious thought upon awakening that morning. "It was...strange at first. I couldn't seem to think of him as my ex-husband, and I felt terrible that I remembered almost nothing about the time we spent together. Grady remembers, though, and the more he talked, the easier it got."

Denise loved the soap opera aspect of such a reunion, and she tried to break down Kirsten's obvious reluctance to reveal all the details. "What's he like?" she probed.

"Very nice," Kirsten said with as much nonchalance as she could manage. "Easy to be with. Sort of laid-back. That was a surprise, since he was so mixed-up the last time I saw him. It was good to see him looking so fit. He's changed a lot, and, of course, he's become quite successful."

"Is he good-looking?"

"Yes, I think any woman would say that Grady is handsome. He's an older version of David. Does that tell you anything?"

"Ooh, would I love to get a good look at him. Did you invite him to come here?"

"Well . . . no, not in so many words. He said he would want to see David often and asked if I would object to his coming to New York. I said it would be fine. And I know David is going to want to go back to Mississippi one of these days. He's so enchanted with Grady." Kirsten grew pensive. "It's difficult for me to get used to the idea of sharing him with someone else, but now that the first step has been taken, I have to encourage him to be with his father whenever it can be arranged. And I wonder if that might become a problem."

"Problem?" Denise asked. "I don't understand."

"It's something that occurred to me during the flight home, when David was chattering away about Dad this and Dad that. Grady's a very busy man, and David will be returning to school for the spring term. As much as they might want to see each other, there'll be many times when it just won't happen. I wonder how that will affect David."

"Good grief, Kirsten, you find the damnedest things to worry about. Busy fathers and grown kids always have a hard time lighting in the same place at the same time. If they want to see each other, they will. What about you?"

"Me?"

"Do you want to see Grady again?"

"Well . . . I'm sure we will . . . occasionally."

Denise waited, hoping to hear more, but when nothing else was forthcoming, she gave Kirsten some news of her own. "Guess what happened to me while you were away."

"You met a man?"

Denise shrieked. "How did you know?"

"I didn't, but what else puts that look in a woman's eyes?"

"Well, you're right. I met him at Mom and Dad's Monday night. His name is Raymond Billingsley, and he's British. Very British. Old family, with ancestors stretching back forever. He's taking over the Patrick interests in Europe, so he'll be sitting on the board. You'll meet him tonight. We've had dinner together every night this week."

Kirsten found this intriguing. It was the first time in eight years she had heard Denise speak with enthusiasm about one particular man. Dinner every night this week? It came to Kirsten with somewhat of a jolt that she was feeling exactly the way she felt about David finding his father. There was that same sense of loss, that same flash of jealousy. She and Denise had been good friends from day one, but since Travis's death, they had become as thick as thieves, always there for each other. If the attraction to Raymond Billingsley grew and proved to be mutual, the days of picking up the phone and having Denise come right over would be a thing of the past.

Kirsten was appalled at herself. She couldn't believe that her own life was so sterile that the thought of sharing her son with his father and Denise with a man could shake her so. "I can hardly wait to meet him," she said feebly.

"You'll like him, I just know it," Denise said. "Now, how about coming to the florist with me? I want to be standing right there when she starts putting those bouquets together. Then we'll have lunch."

"Good. I need to stop at the jeweler's, anyway. Let me tell David I'm leaving."

WHILE KIRSTEN AND DENISE were driving away from the house, Grady was walking through the door of Slick's. He'd thought he might as well get it over with. As expected, the minute Loretta spotted him, she went in search of Rosemary. He had come prepared to be bombarded with questions, and the two women didn't fail him.

"Grady, you devil!" Rosemary exclaimed. "How dare you not tell us you have a son."

"I don't recall that the question ever came up, Rosie."

"You know what I mean. And that gorgeous woman! If David is your son and she's his mother, then we ... well, obviously at one time the two of you were ..."

"Married," Grady finished for her. "It was a long time ago."

"Oh."

Grady grinned. Rosie and Loretta obviously had been hoping for something a little juicier.

"But where have they been?" Loretta asked.

"All right, ladies. I'll satisfy your curiosity." And he did, telling them the basic facts about the breakup of the marriage, Kirsten's subsequent remarriage and David's recent discovery of his father's whereabouts. He told them just enough to keep them from manufacturing some preposterous scenario of their own.

"Oh, Grady," Loretta said with a sigh. "That's positively the most romantic thing I ever heard! After all these years! You could make a movie out of that story."

"And there's not an ending to it yet," Rosemary said. "What next?"

"Next?"

"Sure. Are you going to New York to see her? Is she coming back here? What?"

Grady wished he had the answer to that one himself. Kirsten had been gone a scant twenty-four hours, and he already ached to see her. He wanted to see David again, too, of course, but it was a foregone conclusion that would happen. The doubtful part came when he thought about Kirsten. Would he throw her life completely out of kilter if he simply showed up on her doorstep some Friday night? And was that what he wanted—to see her for a couple of days whenever he could get away?

No, he wanted her here all the time, but it wasn't realistic to think that would actually happen. He could indulge in wishful thinking, but it was unlikely she would want to give up her high society life. Who would? He imagined that whatever filled up her days and nights—charity affairs and dazzling parties and opening nights—would grow on a person. They'd never grow on him, not in a million years, but in many ways he was a strange case.

"Grady?"

He looked up to see Rosemary's eyes quizzing him. "Oh, well . . . I'm not sure. I'll see David, of course. That's already been established."

"But what about Kirsten? You're not just going to let it lie, are you?"

"No, Rosie, I'm not about to do that. I can promise you that much."

IT WAS AFTER FOUR O'CLOCK that afternoon when Kirsten returned home. Once she and Denise started shopping, the hours flew by. As soon as she stepped through the front door, she went in search of David. She found him stretched out on his bed with his nose in a book. He looked up when she entered his room. "Hi. You were gone a long time."

"You know Denise and shopping. David, let me ask you something. How would you feel about leaving this house, moving somewhere else?"

David looked surprised. "Like where, for instance?"

"I don't know. I haven't given this too much thought. I just wanted to know how you would feel about moving."

He didn't have to think about it. "It suits me fine."

"Just like that?"

"Just like that."

Kirsten had expected a little bit of uncertainty. "It's the only home you've ever known."

David glanced around the room and pursed his lips. "I guess that should make a difference, but it doesn't."

Kirsten studied her son intently. He was in such a strange mood, and whatever else David was, he wasn't a moody person; only quieter and more thoughtful than a lot of young men his age. Still, he was rather blunt when it came to speaking his mind, but something was bothering him now that he wasn't interested in sharing with her. She'd noticed the preoccupation at dinner last night.

However, she wouldn't pry. David would tell her what it was if he wanted her to know. At least she'd found out one thing: leaving this place wouldn't make any difference one way or another. That made her own decision much easier. "You know, it just occurred to me that the yacht club singles' party is tonight. Do you have a date for it?"

He shook his head. "Nope."

"For goodness' sake, why not?"

"Aw, Mom, who would I ask?"

"What about Katherine Withers? What's wrong with Katie?"

"There's nothing 'wrong' with Katie, but I've known her since I was seven. I think if anything was going to develop between us it would have by now."

"Well . . . there's Marcia Spencer."

David groaned. "You don't know Marcia, Mom. She's a self-centered bore. If I go tonight, I'll just go alone and come home early."

"That doesn't sound like much fun."

"The yacht club party stopped being fun years ago."

Kirsten frowned. *It's Grady,* she thought. *Three days with his father and he's bored with everything else.* But that would change, wouldn't it? The visit was too fresh in his mind; the memories were too sharp and distinct. And she couldn't really blame David. She herself seemed to be having a damnably hard time keeping Grady out of her thoughts. But again, time would take care of that ... wouldn't it?

When his mother had left the room, David gave up all pretense of reading. He gazed first out the window, then at the ceiling. He'd spent all day forcibly restraining himself from calling his dad. It was too soon, and he really didn't have anything to say. He'd even entertained the notion of calling Mona tonight, but again, what would he say? And she'd probably be busy on Saturday night, another dispiriting thought.

It promised to be a long weekend. He would have dinner alone tonight, then go to the party, more to pass time than because he wanted to. And tomorrow he would set himself to the mindless task of watching twenty-two hulks fight over a football.

David rubbed his eyes. He'd always loved football. He didn't know what was wrong with him.

No, that wasn't true. He knew. After visiting his father, he had returned to the myopic society in which he'd been raised, and he felt more out of place than ever. The Patricks and their kind were fond of saying they didn't mind outsiders as long as they "knew their place." Well, he'd never found his place. He'd never even told his mother how much of an outsider he felt he was. Why lay that on her? His friends, most of them third or fourth-generation money, were so self-assured, so comfortable in the world they'd been born into. Here they would stay, North Shore society through and through, as would their children and grandchildren and on and on. David had always been aware that it wasn't his world, that his future lay somewhere else, in a place where he wouldn't have to try to be a Patrick while knowing he could never be one.

Maybe it was crazy to say he had discovered where that somewhere else was, but it was true. And having found it, he was impatient to return. But he wasn't naive enough to think leaving would entail nothing more than throwing some things into a suitcase and buying an airline ticket. What if his mother cried when he told her? Come to think of it, what if his dad didn't even want a son on a full-time basis?

David sighed. Pushing himself up, he decided to get on his bike and ride as far and as fast as he could before dinner.

DENISE'S LOVELY HOME was resplendent with all the trappings of Patrick wealth and social position. She and Kirsten couldn't stop congratulating themselves. Hardly a month went by that one Patrick or another didn't throw a gala affair of some kind, but none of them had ever outdone this one. Spotlights flooded the wood-and-stucco facade of the grand Tudor mansion and its surrounding grounds. Gowned, jeweled ladies and their tuxedoed escorts stepped from chauffeured limousines, which were then turned over to hired parking attendants. At the door more servants took wraps and hats and invited the guests to join their hostesses for drinks in the ballroom.

Though this was only the second time that Kirsten and Denise had cohosted a large affair, they were accomplished party givers who had instinctively developed a routine for circulating among their guests. The number one rule was that T.G. and Evelyn Patrick were personally greeted by every family member present. Kirsten found Travis's parents situated slightly apart from the mainstream—purposely, she was sure, so they could hold court. Evelyn was seated in a brocade chair, wearing a gown of the inevitable powder blue, which was her favorite color. Beside the chair stood the distinguished T.G. One hand rested lightly on his wife's shoulder. They looked for all the world like the aging monarchs they were.

Kirsten bent to kiss the air beside Evelyn's cheek. "Good evening, Evelyn. You look wonderful." She'd never had any real difficulty in dealing with her mother-in-law, although Evelyn's manner toward her was more aloofly cordial than genuinely warm. The older woman's total deference to her husband precluded her ever completely embracing a daughter-in-law whom T.G. did not approve of.

"Kirsten, dear, how sweet you look," Evelyn said, fingering the lipstick-red silk Kirsten wore.

"Thank you." Kirsten then straightened and gave T.G. her best party smile. "Good evening, Mr. Patrick."

"Kirsten." T.G. executed a slight bow. "I understand you and your son were in Mississippi this week."

How did the man find out everything? "Yes. It was sort of a nostalgia trip."

"And did it prove to be nostalgic?"

"Very."

"That's good. So often a trip back to a place where one once lived can be such a disappointment."

"This wasn't. We had a very nice time. Now, if you will please excuse me, I must speak to the other guests. I hope you have a nice time tonight."

As Kirsten sailed off, she wondered if T.G. and Evelyn ever had a really good time anywhere. In fact, she wondered if any of these people were having as good a time as they appeared to be. For the most part, it was the same group who attended all the parties. The guest lists rarely varied. These same faces clustered together two or three times a week in various places. The men discussed golf courses, banking and mergers. The women talked clothes, jewelry and antique auctions. These ladies possessed unlimited reserves of energy and cash, yet not one aspired to any title higher than best dressed.

Kirsten saw so much of these people that it taxed her brain to find something new to talk about. There was one unfamiliar face that night, however. After Kirsten had spoken to everyone present, Denise signaled to her. Threading her way through the crowd, she approached her sister-in-law and found herself being introduced to Raymond Billingsley.

Without seeming to, Kirsten made a rapid survey of Denise's new interest and approved of what she saw. Attractive, distinguished, in his late fifties, Billingsley cut a dashing figure. Kirsten noticed the new light in Denise's eyes and sent up a silent prayer that Raymond wouldn't turn out to have a wife living in a luxury London flat. She hoped he was respectably widowed or properly divorced, although a man his age rarely came completely unencumbered.

"I am delighted to meet you, Kirsten," the man said in his clipped accent. "Denise speaks so highly of you."

"Thank you. I'm delighted to meet you, too."

"You ladies did a marvelous job with tonight's party."

"Mostly Denise's doing, I'm afraid."

"Nonsense," Denise said. "Kirsten's parties are legendary. It's just so much easier for us to pool our resources. That way we're both off the hook for another couple of months."

They spent another minute or two on that sort of inane "party talk," then Kirsten moved on, smiling until her face hurt. Later, when everyone was seated and starting a magnificent dinner that began with an ethereal lobster bisque, she glanced around as if seeing Denise's home for the first time. Tonight it was beautiful. Creamy table linen, fine china, gleaming crystal and silver, lavish flower arrangements. A chamber music trio played in the background, and all around her was the cacophony of the voices and laughter of sixty-eight guests.

Suddenly a heaviness settled over her. It seemed to squeeze at her chest. There were, she thought, legions of women who would regard her as the most enviable of women. They would gladly give their all to even once be invited to such a dinner. They would be deliriously happy with a fraction of the wealth and glitter displayed in that room that night. They would single her out as a woman who truly had it all.

So what was wrong with her? Why then was she so incredibly bored with it all? Dear God, was this the way she wanted to spend the rest of her life?

CHAPTER SEVEN

DAVID SOMEHOW MANAGED to wait until Monday, but finally the urge to talk to Grady became irresistible. He placed a call to his office and was connected with his secretary. He seemed to remember that her name was Phyllis.

"Phyllis, could I speak to my...to Mr. O'Connor, please?"

"I'm sorry. He'll be in Dallas until later in the week."

David's spirits sank. "Oh, yeah, I forgot."

"May I take a message?"

"You might tell him David called."

"Is that all?"

"Yes, that's all. Just David."

"Does he have your number?"

"Yes, ma'am, he has it."

"All right. He'll get the message the minute he returns."

"Thanks. Thanks a lot." Days more. An eternity. David couldn't remember ever feeling so down.

THAT EVENING, a servant in a starched white apron ushered Grady into Vanessa Hamilton's lavish estate north of Dallas, then led the way down a hallway to the paneled study at the rear of the house. He had been in the grand mansion perhaps half a dozen times in his life, and always he was overcome by the heady richness of the place. Vanessa and her husband, Stuart, had traveled extensively when Stuart had been alive, and the house reflected that. Their art collection alone was worth a tidy fortune, to say nothing of the formidable array of Georgian and Victorian antiques they had amassed through the years. The Hamiltons had had no children, and Grady imagined several museum curators would swoon with ecstasy when Vanessa's last will and testament was read.

The servant gestured him through the door and hurried away. As he stepped into the den, the regal matriarch of Hamilton House turned to him, as beautifully dressed as always, tonight in a jade silk gown. Vanessa's hair was a blaze of silver that shone as brightly as the diamonds on her earlobes and at her throat. As she flashed him her incomparable smile, Grady was struck anew by the sheer radiance of the woman. She alone, of all the people he had ever known, possessed that indefinable quality called presence. He had always thought her strikingly handsome, but it seemed that in the past ten years or so her beauty had changed; she had become even more aristocratic looking. Her eyes, though heavily lidded with age, still could mesmerize with their clarity and directness. Part of that was attributable to her enthusiasm, her absolute zest for living. She was a business wizard and a motivational expert who inspired almost missionary zeal in her employees. Even those who thought her intimidating, demanding and imperious admitted that her like had seldom been equaled. Whenever Grady entered her presence, he felt as though he were being presented at court. It was impossible to believe she was nearing eighty, just as it was impossible to believe she would ever really age, or die.

"Good evening, Grady," Vanessa said, offering her cheek for his kiss. "My, you look handsome tonight."

"I do?" he asked in mock astonishment. "I feel like a pallbearer. I'd sure like to run into the guy who invented the necktie. I ask you, is there anything more absurd than winding a strip of fabric around your neck and tying a knot in it?"

Vanessa laughed lustily. She had a soft spot in her heart for Grady and had from the first day they had met in Jackson. He was earthy, unpretentious and thoroughly charming. Of course, he also was capable, innovative and loyal, and those were the qualities—not her fondness for him—that had prompted her to make him a vice president, to the complete astonishment of almost everyone in the organization. "The farmer?" they'd said among themselves. But "the farmer" had made Hamilton House untold millions in a relatively short time; the vice presidency had been her way of showing her appreciation.

"Let me fix you a drink," she offered. "Dinner should be ready before long."

"No, let me fix you one. What'll it be?"

"Sherry."

"Coming right up," Grady said, and headed for the sideboard that housed the liquor. Minutes later, he handed her the sherry and sat down to enjoy his Scotch and water. Vanessa, sitting on the couch across from him, was sending out some puzzling vibrations. In fact, from the minute he'd stepped into her elegant office suite that morning he'd felt that this trip was no ordinary summons from on high. All day he had been led in and out of offices, had met key people at every level of the company's vast operation and had been bombarded with facts and figures until his head spun. Tomorrow he was scheduled to spend the morning with the director of acquisitions, who was to brief him on the company's plans for the coming decade.

Why? He ran the agricultural operation. It might have a grander title, but it was a giant farm, nevertheless. Except for marketing and distribution, he had little contact with the various departments. Yet, he had the oddest feeling he was here to receive a crash course in the way the entire organization was run. Again, why?

"How was your day?" Vanessa asked as she sipped daintily at her sherry.

"Very informative. I met a lot of interesting people."

"You'll meet more tomorrow. We employ a lot of bright people. Being able to get and keep them has been one of the reasons for the company's success. Remember that."

Again the puzzlement. He was eaten up with curiosity, and Grady never hedged, hemmed or hawed around Vanessa. "Do you mind if I ask you something, Vanessa?"

"Of course not."

"What in the hell is this all about?"

Vanessa chortled delightedly. "I take it you've guessed that I asked you here this time for a specific reason."

"Obviously."

She turned serious. "To be blunt about it, I'm going to be eighty in January, and I'm finally getting around to putting my affairs in order. My attorneys and I have been rewriting my will for months. Disposing of my estate is no easy task."

Her eyes strayed across the room to a console that stood against the wall. Grady knew what she was looking at—an old framed photograph of a tiny café on a side street in south Dallas, the place she and Stuart Hamilton had turned into Hamilton House, Incorporated. It was a homey sight among all the expensive art and fine antiques. "Stuart and I spent a lifetime acquiring art and antiques and fine furniture, and now I find myself trying to decide to whom to give them. But they are only things, after all. Hamilton House is something else altogether."

Now she faced Grady squarely. "I'm in the process of choosing my successor. It's past time."

Grady's eyes widened. "But I thought—"

"Dolph?" Vanessa's lips compressed tightly. "You thought Dolph Wade would take over when I'm gone—is that what you were going to say?"

"Yes, everyone did." Dolph Wade was the company's executive vice president, a man who had been with Stuart and Vanessa from the beginning. Since Stuart's death, Vanessa had relied on him heavily. Dolph had been a shoo-in...or so Grady had thought.

"Well, he won't be," Vanessa said tersely.

Grady sat back, taken completely by surprise. What a startling development this was, one that would shake the organization from top to bottom. What could have precipitated Dolph's fall from grace? Grady waited for the explanation he felt sure was coming.

"I suppose you heard about the buy-out offer from Barrington International," Vanessa said.

Grady nodded. "Uh-huh."

"What did you think of it?"

"Nothing. I knew you'd never sell Hamilton House. I didn't imagine you'd give the offer a second's consideration."

"I didn't. Dolph, however, did."

"Oh?" That didn't make much sense. The conglomerate had admitted to wanting to bring in its own people, do things their way. That might have put Dolph out of a very high-paying job. "You mean, he thought you ought to sell?"

"Yes. In fact, he was so in favor of it that I smelled a rat from the beginning. Oh, Dolph and I have had our differences in the past, but when it came to the Hamilton House image—keeping the restaurants exclusive, never putting more than one in any city, stressing regional tastes in food and the like—we agreed right down the line. Yet, here were these international banking types admitting they intended implementing certain 'standardizations,' and Dolph was urging me to sell out to them. The entire thing positively reeked. So I investigated. Snooped, if you will. It seems the Barrington reps offered Dolph a great deal of money if he could persuade me to sell."

Oh, boy, Grady thought. That would really rip it with Vanessa. One could get away with bad advice or an occasional inept move, but never disloyalty. "Are you sure?"

"Of course I'm sure. Dolph did something incredibly stupid. He taped a conversation between himself and the Barrington people. His insurance, I'm certain, in case they tried to renege later. Unfortunately for my once trusted associate, I found the tape."

Grady had wondered why there had been no sign of Dolph all day. Always before, Dolph, as second in command, had been in the center of things. Often when Grady visited the home office, he spent more time with Dolph than with Vanessa.

"Does Dolph know all this?" he asked.

"No, and he won't until I announce my successor. Call it malice if you like, but I want to see the look on the schemer's face. Oh, he knows I'm miffed at him, but he thinks I'll get over it. He's wrong." Suddenly Vanessa's manner changed completely, and she gave Grady a soft smile. "I'm considering several people as the next C.E.O. You're one of them."

Grady almost choked on his drink. "Me?" he cried.

"Of course, you. Why not you? I like your style, Grady. I always have. You're bright and innovative. There are a lot of people who can run an organization, manage personnel, take care of administrative tasks. But coming up with new and profitable ideas is a rare talent. I have no trouble envisioning you as president of the company."

Grady was stunned. "Maybe you don't, but I certainly do. Ask anybody in the company—I'm a farmer."

"You've always been more than that, and you know it. You wouldn't be a vice president if you didn't have the skills. I've talked to both Matt Logan and Paula Steele about this, and I've narrowed my choices down to the three of you."

"Either Matt or Paula would be perfect. They both have C.E.O. written all over them."

"But not you?"

"Not me. Vanessa, I don't even like to wear a tie!"

She chuckled. "I rather imagine you'd get used to it. It sort of goes with the position. However, if you chose not to wear one, who do you suppose would complain? Oh, Grady, I know that any of you three would have to make adjustments. Sacrifices would be involved. Matt adores San Francisco, and he has a new wife, a local woman who doubtless wouldn't want to leave. Paula's new husband is in the music business, and I'm sure they would prefer staying in Nashville. I don't know how attached you are to Mississippi, but—"

"It isn't that," Grady said quietly. "It's ... being confined to an office, being confined anywhere. It's something I've fought ever since being released from that damned prison, but it's still with me. Walls start closing in on me after a few hours."

Vanessa nodded in sympathy. "You know the size of the home office, dear, and there are so many outside obligations, plus the travel. I don't think you'd ever feel confined."

She didn't understand; nobody ever really did. "And I like being outdoors," he went on, more to remind himself of these things than to inform Vanessa. "I love it in the spring when the fields are being tilled and replanted. I like the smell of dirt. Hell, I even like the smell of manure."

Vanessa grinned impishly. "Oh, there's quite a bit of that at the home office, too. It's just called by a different name." She leaned forward and spoke earnestly. "Grady, are you telling me that if the top spot is offered you, you won't accept it?"

There was his out. Just say no, thanks, and Vanessa would remove him from consideration with no hard feelings. And he was tempted, sorely tempted, to do just that. He meant every word he'd said. It just didn't seem as though his name and the term C.E.O. should have been mentioned in the same sentence. He wasn't the type.

Then he looked at Vanessa, and something held his tongue in check. He'd always thought her an uncanny judge of character, and she never allowed emotion to intrude upon her decision-making process. Why was he questioning her now? She wasn't considering him for this plum because she liked him; she honestly thought he could do the job. Obviously, she saw something in him that he couldn't see.

Grady sighed. "I...don't see how I could do that," he said. "And I'm flattered as hell to be on any kind of list with Matt and Paula."

Vanessa smiled broadly. "Good. I think I came up with three superb choices. Now, I'll tell you my plans. I'm giving myself a birthday bash in January. I'll have made my decision by then and will announce it that night." She sobered. "Grady, whoever occupies my office will automatically become the single largest stockholder in Hamilton House. That means wealth, of course, but it also means power, enormous power. No one will be able to ignore you. That's one reason I've had to be so careful about choosing my successor. Naturally, I wanted someone intelligent and capable, but all of my vice presidents are that. What I was looking for above all was an individual who had proved his or her loyalty many times over, and you, Matt and Paula have all done that. And I'm going to ask you now to promise me something. I might add that I've extracted the same promise from both of the others."

"Of course, Vanessa. Anything."

"If you sit in my chair, promise me you'll keep the company intact, no matter what. It frightens me to death to think of what a cartel like Barrington could do to it. Stuart and I gave our lives to Hamilton House."

The passion in her voice touched Grady. "I know. And I promise nobody will buy us out or take us over. Even if I'm not sitting in your chair, I'll fight to keep control as long as I draw breath."

"Thank you, dear. I would have bet you would say just that." Vanessa settled back comfortably and toyed with the stem of her glass. "Now, let's simply visit. Tell me what's going on in your world."

Grady was not ready to tell anyone, not even Vanessa, that he had been reunited with his son or that he'd discovered that his ex-wife still was the woman of his dreams, so for the next twenty minutes or so he and Vanessa only chatted amicably about nothing of consequence. Then dinner was announced, they dined on a superb meal, and Grady left at nine, returning to the hotel before ten. Then and only then was he able to sit down and reflect on the incredible evening. That he actually was being seriously considered to head Hamilton House staggered him.

A very large part of him was flattered, elated and humbled. President of Hamilton House! The mere thought electrified him. He derived immense satisfaction from knowing his work had been so appreciated by the woman he held in such high esteem.

Yet an equally large part of him wrestled with all the negative aspects of the promotion. Proud of what he had built in Mississippi, he was loath to leave it. And a job change would require other changes in his life that he simply hadn't counted on and wasn't prepared for, which made him reflect on his capabilities and limitations.

Grady had never considered himself a business-man, not in the accepted sense of the word. The world of staff meetings, briefcases and three-piece suits held no appeal for him, but that world fit Matt Logan and Paula Steele like a glove. Matt's Western Division and Paula's Southeastern Division were small-scale repli-cas of the overall organization. Neither of them would have a bit of trouble expanding their horizons, whereas he knew how to raise food and distribute it in record time, period. And he was damned good at it. Essentially, he guessed he feared falling victim to the Peter Principle—rising to the level of his own incom-petence.

Dwelling on these inner thoughts, Grady chastised himself. Why was he questioning his intelligence, re-sisting change? It was easy to prefer his simple, insu-lar world to the challenge of running a corporation, and that made him a coward. Given a little time and some studious application, was there anything he couldn't learn to do and do well?

Hell, no! As for adapting to a new life-style, he had spent most of his life adapting to situations he hadn't been prepared for. Vanessa Hamilton was no fool. If she wanted him to be president of Hamilton House, she had her reasons. When the time came, if it did, he'd prove to her that she had chosen well.

Grady felt better. At least he thought he could sleep. And he fervently hoped this was the end of his con-fusion.

IT WASN'T. Doubts resurfaced many times in the next two days, during which Grady felt as though he were a study in perpetual motion. Only by carrying a note-book and taking down page after page of notes was he able to remember half the information fed him. One of the reasons he had been successful was his ability to clear his mind and focus on one thing at a time. And so for those two days he concentrated solely on the inner workings of Hamilton House. He saw for the first time what a truly vast organization it had become. Its restaurants tentacled the nation, and plans for expansion into Canada were well underway.

Vanessa had put together a thorough indoctrination, and at some point during it, Grady's mind suddenly seemed to turn a corner. Everything slipped into place. The pieces of the immense jigsaw began to fit. On Wednesday afternoon, he stood at the window in Vanessa's plush office, gazing down at the incredible hustle and bustle of Dallas at rush hour, and decided he could do it. By the time he boarded a plane Thursday for the return trip home, Grady's self-confidence was at an all-time high.

It was five-thirty when he drove through the brick archway south of Culver. All of the work force would have gone home, but he decided to stop by his office and check the mail that had accumulated during his absence. When he opened the side door and stepped into his office, he was hit with a feeling of homecoming. He'd never tried to explain the feeling of peace and belonging that the agricultural compound gave him. Who would understand? But this place was his, and the thought of leaving it tore at him.

He shook off the feeling. There was a very good chance he wouldn't be going anywhere else.

Nothing in the mail seemed to require immediate attention, but a note Phyllis had prominently propped against his telephone did. David had called Monday afternoon. Smiling, Grady tucked the note in his shirt pocket and left the building. As soon as he got home, he left his luggage in his room for later unpacking, changed into comfortable clothes, then picked up the telephone and dialed the Patricks. A servant answered and summoned David.

"David?"

"Dad!"

"I just got back and saw the message that you'd called. How are you?"

"Oh, pretty good, I guess."

"How's your mom?"

"Ticked off at the Patricks, but that's nothing new. How was your trip?"

"It was...interesting. Did you have anything particular you wanted to talk to me about?"

There was a long pause before David said, "Oh...not really."

To Grady he sounded like someone who had something on his mind. "Are you sure?"

"Well...I know this sounds dumb, but I was hoping I could see you pretty soon."

"That suits me," Grady said. "How does your mom feel about it?"

This time the pause lasted longer. "She doesn't know about it yet. And when I tell her what it is I want to do...well, I'm not sure how she'll take it."

"Then maybe you'd better tell me what it is you want to do."

"I'm...not exactly talking about a visit. I'd like to come down there for good. I want to live with you."

Grady sat in dumbfounded silence for a minute. Then his breath escaped in a whistle. "You're really going to knock the props out from under your mom with this one."

"Yeah, I know, but if I can talk her into it, is it all right with you?"

Grady cleared his throat. "You know it is, son. But, David, you don't just walk out on someone who's devoted nineteen years to you. Unless you handle this with the tact of a diplomat, you're going to hurt her terribly."

"I'm not walking out on her. She's my mom, for Pete's sake! I'll come back to see her all the time. Or she can come to see us. I...just want to be down there, to learn to do what you do." David's voice sounded shaky. "I hate it here. I've always known I'd be leaving someday. I never had anywhere to go before, but now I do. I guess you think I'm being impulsive, but I'm not. I wouldn't have said a word about this unless I was absolutely sure it was what I want to do."

At first Grady was at a loss to know how he should handle this startling development. He had known David would want to come back soon, which had pleased him no end, and even Kirsten was prepared for that. But to hear his son say he wanted to live with him, no ifs, ands or buts...

Then the first faint glimmering of an idea formed in the back of Grady's mind. "Tell me something—is your mother at home right now?"

"Yes."

"Let me speak to her."

"What are you going to do?" David cried in alarm.

"Trust me. Just let me speak to her."

"Well...all right."

While he waited for Kirsten to come on the line, Grady thought of the best way to approach this. It wasn't something that could easily be discussed over the phone. In fact, that would be impossible. So in an instant he knew what he had to do. His heart raced. David had surprised him. Stunned him might be more accurate, but it was exactly the opening Grady needed.

"Grady?"

The soft, sweet voice made his insides melt. "Kirsten, how are you?"

"I'm fine. And you?"

"Fine. Listen, Kirsten, I want you to know I'm not in the habit of inviting myself places, but I'd like to come to see you for a couple of days. There's something very important I have to discuss with you."

"You want to come here?"

"Yes, it's... I don't mean to your house, exactly. I could stay somewhere nearby."

"Well, I..." She faltered, then her tone turned brisk and defiant. "Oh, that's ridiculous. Of course you'll stay here with us. There's so much room, and... Grady, can you give me some idea what this important something is?"

"I'd rather do it face-to-face."

"I see." She sounded concerned, puzzled, and Grady could understand that. He knew he was being damned mysterious, but he didn't want to give her so much as a clue as to what he had on his mind—not yet. He was counting on his powers of persuasion and the chemistry between them to do the rest. "All right," she said softly. "When do you want to come?"

"I need to be in the office tomorrow after being gone all week, at least for part of the day, and I'll have to check with the airlines. If I can get out tomorrow, I will. Otherwise, I'll leave as early Saturday as I can. Don't bother with meeting me. I'll take a cab, but I'll let you know ahead of time what time I'll arrive."

"Fine. Goodness, you certainly have me curious. This has to be in regard to David."

"Not . . . entirely."

"Oh?"

"I'll explain when I see you."

"Of course. And that will be soon. Do you want to speak to David again?"

"I don't think so. Just tell him I'll see him tomorrow night or Saturday morning. Goodbye, Kirsten."

"Goodbye, Grady. Take care."

When Grady hung up, he stared across the room for the longest time, cautioning himself against getting his hopes up. Sure, Kirsten's life was in a state of flux, and she didn't get along well with her in-laws, but that didn't mean she was ready to pack up and leave her glittering life-style. It was a pretty farfetched scheme.

But if he succeeded . . . Simply contemplating such success was so delicious he had to smile. The three of them here together. A real family again. And this time nothing would interfere—not a war, not a prison camp.

Then something occurred to him with such force that he slapped the heel of his hand against his forehead. Oh, God, there was Vanessa! What if she, in her wisdom, decided to turn over the reins of the company to him? What would a change like that do to these grand—and perhaps fanciful—plans of his? Should he tell David and Kirsten right off that he was being considered for the promotion? Or should he wait until what he wanted had become reality?

But he was getting ahead of himself. He didn't have the promotion, and he certainly didn't have a green light from Kirsten. She might nip all these grand plans in the bud. The immediate task was getting reservations to New York. First talk to Kirsten. If her answer was in the affirmative, he could work out anything else. If it was negative . . . what in hell would anything else matter, anyway?

CHAPTER EIGHT

"Do I HAVE NEWS!" Denise exclaimed as she sailed through the door to the solarium the following morning.

Kirsten glanced up from the newspaper she was reading. "I don't have to ask if it's good or bad. You look as bubbly as champagne. Coffee?"

"No, thanks. I've had my caffeine jolt for the day." Denise sank into one of the chintz-covered chairs. "My news is of the divine variety. Raymond has to go back to England next week. Something to do with his family's property."

"That's good news?"

"He wants me to go with him."

"Denise!" Kirsten exclaimed. *At least there's no wife,* was her immediate thought. Not in England, at any rate. "Are you going to do it?"

"You better believe I am!"

"Well, I'll be. For how long?"

Denise shrugged. "Who knows? We'll definitely be back in time for next month's board meeting. Raymond is taking his new position with the institute very seriously. For the past ten years or so, his only job has been to look after his family's property and investments, and it seems to embarrass him that he doesn't have to work. Dad's offer was a godsend for him."

Kirsten looked at Denise, seeing the new radiance in her eyes. "You really like the guy, don't you?"

"I'm nuts about him," Denise said without hesitation. "Maybe that can't actually happen in just two weeks, but I'm not about to ask myself a lot of damned fool pertinent questions. I'm simply having the time of my life. Raymond's good-looking and fun, and he knows how to treat a woman. Beyond that, he's interesting. When I'm with him I don't have to listen to the same old gossip about the same old people. And he's unimpressed with my last name. In England, his family is at least as big a deal as mine is here." She paused and smiled. "You know, I didn't think this would happen to me again, and it might not last, but while it does, I'm taking advantage of every minute I have."

"But if it does last?" Kirsten prodded.

Denise laughed gaily. "I rather imagine I'll become a globe-trotter, jetting here and there—London, Paris, Rome, wherever the Patrick interests are."

"Tough life."

Kirsten was thrilled for Denise, of course, but a selfish part of her still hated that it was happening. Some of her happiest times were spent in her sister-in-law's company. Who would she talk to now? The sad fact was, although she knew many people, she had few real friends in their exclusive social circle. Her very nature prohibited it, for she simply couldn't live the life to the hilt. She liked lovely clothes, but she didn't take the Concorde to Paris twice a year to view the designer collections, as so many of her acquaintances did. She didn't make grand entrances, wooing society columnists and photographers, nor did she suffer angst about being seated at a less than perfect table.

She avoided people she didn't like, no matter how much they could "do" for her. All of which made her something of an oddity. Denise, being cut of the same cloth, was her best friend and confidante, to say nothing of her nearest neighbor. Life would be so much lonelier without her.

One more reason in favor of moving to the city. Denise would be away much of the time, and David didn't care if they left. Why stay in this mausoleum?

"Well, not to be outdone," she informed Denise, "I have a bit of news of my own. You're about to get your wish. Grady phoned last night and again this morning. He'll be here tonight."

Denise's mouth formed a little O of surprise. "What's up?"

"I don't have the slightest idea. He was very mysterious."

"What time will he get here?"

"He's leaving work early this afternoon and expects to be standing on our doorstep around eight-thirty. We'll have a late dinner, and then I guess he'll tell me what's on his mind. David is very excited."

"Are you?" Denise asked expectantly.

"Excited? Well . . . I'm certainly curious."

"Oh, Kirsten, you've only been home a week, and already he has to see you. I'm receiving some very interesting vibes from this."

"Are you?" Kirsten frowned slightly. "I'm receiving something, too. I just don't know what it is. Anyway, you drop by sometime tomorrow and get your good look at him."

"Oh, you can count on that."

IT WAS A LONG DAY for Kirsten. She didn't know why she was so nervous. She had asked Maddie to prepare something "very special" for an important guest who would be staying overnight, so that meant the cook would pull out all the stops and the meal would be flawless. Still, Kirsten fussed over the table setting as though she were preparing to entertain a head of state. In the late afternoon she went upstairs to make her umpteenth inspection of the guest room Grady would be using. There were many guest rooms in the mansion, but the one she had chosen for him was the most masculine—a beautifully appointed retreat with cherry-wood furniture and a thick paisley spread on the bed. Not a ruffle or posy in sight. Knowing Grady would be staying in it made her inspect it with an extracritical eye. But the room was perfect. The meal would be perfect. She wondered if he would even notice. Of one thing she was certain: Grady was not flying in from Mississippi to have a delicious meal or to admire her home furnishings.

So that prompted her to seriously consider what his "important" something could be. It was more, she was sure, than making arrangements for David's next trip to Mississippi. That could be done with a five-minute phone call. But the holiday season was fast approaching. Perhaps Grady wanted to feel her out about having David spend Thanksgiving or Christmas with him. If so, she would suggest Thanksgiving. Christmas was out. Kirsten knew she now had to share David, but she wasn't yet ready to spend Christmas without him.

But again, such arrangements could be made over the phone. It was useless for her to speculate; Grady would tell her before the evening was out. She moved around the room, flicking at imaginary dust, unnecessarily straightening and rearranging accessories. Finally, when she had killed as much time as she could, she went into her bedroom suite, drew her bath and began the ritual of getting dressed for the occasion.

THE DOORBELL RANG at eight-forty-seven that night. David knew because he had been pacing the study and keeping an eye on the grandfather clock for a full twenty minutes. Bounding from the room, he hurried down the hall and across the foyer, leaving Kirsten behind in the study. He threw open the heavy door with a flourish. Hoping his grin didn't look as foolish as it felt, he reached for Grady's hand. "Hi."

"Hi." Grady grinned back.

"Come on in."

As Grady stepped inside, he and David embraced. It was a very masculine embrace that included much hearty backslapping. "I'll take your bag upstairs. Mom's waiting down there, the room at the end of the hall." He gestured toward the study.

"Have you said anything to her?" Grady asked.

David shook his head. "No. I thought we could do it together. After dinner. Rule number one in this house is that we don't discuss troublesome subjects at the dinner table."

"Do you think this is going to be that troublesome?"

"I...don't know." David bent and grabbed the handle of Grady's luggage. "Go on in. I'll be down in a jiffy."

Grady squared his shoulders and walked toward the room David had indicated. When he crossed the threshold, Kirsten got to her feet. The sight of her took his breath away. She was wearing black pants in a drapey fabric and a shimmering white top that criss-crossed in front, emphasizing the shape of her breasts. Long silver earrings hung from her lobes. What was draped over her curvaceous body probably had cost thousands of dollars, but the clothes took a back seat to Kirsten herself. She was without a doubt the most beautiful sight he had ever seen.

In long strides he crossed the room. "Hello, Kirsten. How lovely you look."

"Thank you, Grady." She lifted her face to receive what she expected to be a light brush of his lips on hers, but the kiss was solid, heartfelt, and he held her tightly for a few seconds after it. Kirsten's equilibrium teetered precariously. She steadied herself by pressing the back of her legs against the sofa. "This must have been a terribly hectic week for you."

"I'll admit it's been pretty rushed."

"Maybe you can rest tomorrow." Sitting back down, she patted the sofa cushion beside her. "Please sit down. Would you care for a drink?"

He spotted the tulip-shaped glass in front of her on the coffee table. "Whatever you're having is fine."

Kirsten poured from the bottle in the wine cooler. She had expected to be glad to see him. She hadn't expected to be absolutely thrilled to see him. He was dressed in a dark business suit and wearing a tie, and he looked every inch the successful executive. Yet, as handsome a picture as he presented, she thought she liked him better in his starched khakis.

"Dinner should be ready soon," she said. "Are you starved?"

He was starved, all right, but not for food. He'd been starved for the sight of her, and now that that craving had been satisfied, he was starved to hold her. But that wouldn't be enough, either. "No, not at all," he lied.

Grady sipped the wine and surveyed the room. It was a study or den, that much was obvious, and in many ways it reminded him of a more masculine version of Vanessa's den. This room, however, overpowered him. A certain aura permeated the walls, the furnishings, the very air—one of immense wealth and power. There was nothing of Kirsten in the room, so he had to assume it had been her husband's retreat. He didn't know why that made him feel uncomfortable, but it did.

In fact, now that he was actually here, he was overcome with apprehension. What had seemed a fairly plausible idea back home now seemed ridiculous. He'd known Kirsten led a life of extreme affluence, but he hadn't been prepared for the opulence of her house. Now he understood that the wealth she was accustomed to was on a par with Vanessa's. Did he honestly think she would give it up for what he had to offer? Grady could feel his steely resolve melting like ice on an August afternoon. He wasn't sure he could summon up the nerve to actually say all those brilliant words he had rehearsed so carefully during the plane ride. An involuntary sigh escaped his lips.

Kirsten's head turned with a jerk. "Is something wrong, Grady?"

"I . . . no, nothing's wrong."

At that moment, David joined them, and the atmosphere became tense. Kirsten knew she wasn't imagining it. It was as though a switch had been activated that immediately altered the mood. In spite of all the friendly repartee between them, Grady and

David seemed nervous. She had expected unabashed delight over another reunion, but both of them were as skittish as frightened rabbits.

She studied them. There wasn't much she could tell about Grady, except he didn't seem as relaxed as he had in Mississippi, but back there he had been on his home turf, where he felt completely comfortable. Maybe the house intimidated him. She could understand that; sometimes it intimidated her.

But David? She knew her son like the back of her hand, and that too bright chatter was a dead giveaway. It was a defense mechanism he used to disguise a rising tide of panic. What was it all about? Kirsten was at a loss to understand any of it.

She was relieved when dinner was announced. Nothing relaxed people more than a good meal, and that night's dinner was excellent. From the asparagus vinaigrette to the lemon soufflé, everything was a study in perfection, and the food and the general ambience had the desired effect. Smiles became warmer, the conversation less strained. When coffee was served, Kirsten suggested they have it in the solarium, and she led the way into the cheerful room.

They had no more than taken their seats, however, when a servant appeared to inform Kirsten she had a phone call from a Mr. Harding. She got to her feet. "I'll take it in the study, thanks," she said, then turned to Grady, who also had stood. "One of the family's attorneys," she explained. "This shouldn't take but a minute."

The call turned out to be personal rather than business, an invitation to a small, intimate dinner at the Hardings' house. Kirsten accepted warmly and spent a few minutes on small talk before hanging up. She wasn't gone from the solarium more than five minutes, but when she returned, Grady and David were deep in conversation. Seeing her, they exchanged quick glances and fell silent.

The suspicious silence that greeted her annoyed Kirsten beyond measure. Again the air was heavy with tension; it was like a tangible object she could hold in her hand. The expressions on their faces spoke of private caucusing and scheming. She'd had about all of it she could stand.

As she stepped across the threshold, Grady again got to his feet. "Will you please stop jumping up and down like a jack-in-the-box?" she snapped, more harshly than she had meant to. Crossing the room, she sat in the chair she had vacated earlier and regarded both men stonily. "I don't know what's going on here, but something definitely is. Both of you are behaving strangely and making me nervous. Now, Grady, suppose you tell me what 'important' thing has brought you here."

Grady clasped his hands in front of him and glanced at the young man seated next to him. "Fair enough. David, how about it?"

Kirsten saw her son's Adam's apple bobble up and down, as though he were swallowing with difficulty. She sat back and waited for whatever was coming, which she now suspected was far more complicated than she had even imagined.

"Mom, I..." David cleared his throat. "I want you to know this isn't a rash decision. I've thought and thought about it, and it's definitely what I want to do. You remember how restless I was all summer, not knowing what I wanted to do, at loose ends, but then this thing came along, and I knew right from the start.''

Kirsten stared at him blankly. "Darling, I don't have the slightest idea what you're talking about. Could I have it in plain English, please?''

David hesitated and cast a sidelong look at Grady, who encouraged him with a slight nod of his head. David turned back to his mother. "I want to go to Mississippi to live with Dad.'' His chest heaved with relief at having gotten it out.

A heavy silence that seemed to last forever followed his announcement. He'd said it so fast that Kirsten was sure she hadn't heard correctly. "You what?'' she cried.

"I mean it, Mom. I want to go live with Dad and go to school down there. Mississippi State... or someplace.''

Kirsten was too stunned to move, too stunned to think clearly. The blow had been unexpected and devastating. Her chest suddenly felt constricted. She put a hand to it and closed her eyes, trying to bring herself under control so she could think. Her breath came out in labored puffs, and her eyes stung. Again Grady and David exchanged glances: Grady's, worried; David's, fearful.

When Kirsten finally opened her eyes, she stared coldly at her son, ignoring Grady altogether. "I see. And just where does that leave me?''

"I... don't know what you mean,'' David said, his voice rising. He was sure he had never seen such an expression on his mother's face, not even when he was young and had misbehaved badly. He would have much preferred an avalanche of tears. "It wouldn't change you and me. It would be like it was last year.

I'll just be away at school. I'll come home whenever I can."

"Are you sure? And just where will home be, David?" she asked icily. "Here or with dear old Dad?"

"You're leaving this house. You'll be busy with your new place, and you have all your friends. I guess now I'll . . . have two houses, two places to go."

"But you want to live in Mississippi?"

"Well, I . . . Yes."

Kirsten's head snapped in Grady's direction. "What incredible power do you have over him? Three days with you, and he's ready to pack up and follow you anywhere. Of course, I've only given him nineteen years of my life, but what does that count for now that he has Daddy?"

"Kirsten, please," Grady pleaded, "there's something else I have to tell you. I—"

"I don't want to hear it, not another word!" She shot to her feet. "This is the most absurd thing I've ever heard." As she stared at Grady, her chin lifted defiantly. "I can't imagine what you hoped to accomplish by putting such an idea into his head. Now I know how Caesar felt. I promised that you could see David whenever it could be arranged, but that wasn't enough for you. Now you want him full-time. Well, the answer is no! Not only no, but hell, no!"

"Kirsten, it wasn't like—" Grady stopped; she had already swished out of the room.

Father and son sat silently for several minutes, staring at the floor. Finally David stirred. "Wow, I really didn't think she would freak out over it."

"Well, son," Grady said ruefully, "we probably didn't handle that so well. It was quite a shock for her."

"For Pete's sake, you'd think I want to run away and join the French navy or something."

"She probably could take that better than this. I'm afraid you've inadvertently made your mom think you're choosing me over her."

"That's dumb. Mom's smarter than that."

"But right now she's hurt, and that can play the devil with a person's intelligence." Grady sighed heavily and raked a forefinger across his mouth. He should have done the talking. David had been so nervous he'd just blurted it out. Something this delicate required a softening-up process, a certain finesse.

Fine time to be thinking that. So now, with only one day to accomplish it, how did he undo the harm that had been done? Sadly, he conceded that he might not be able to.

"So now what do we do?" David asked.

"I don't know, son. I wish I did.... Now, David, there's something else I have to tell you that may put all this in a new light. There's a chance—a small one, I happen to think, but a chance, nevertheless—that I'll be receiving a promotion after the first of the year."

David couldn't imagine what that had to do with anything. "Well, that's great. What kind of promotion?"

"President of the company."

"Are you serious? That's really something!"

"Two other people are in the running, and I think either of them is more qualified than I, but still the possibility exists. If it comes about, I'll be transferred to Dallas."

"Dallas?"

"Yes. Would you still want to go to Mississippi State?"

Fleetingly, David's spirits sagged. Nothing about this was easy, and nothing was working out the way he'd hoped. Still, he thought it over carefully, as he did everything. Finally he said, "Yes. I want to study the kind of work you do, and Dallas is a lot closer to Mississippi than this place is. Sure, I still want to move. Like you said, there's a chance it won't happen."

Grady placed his hand on his son's shoulder. "All right. If you're sure, I'll do what I can with your mom."

"Why couldn't she just cry like any other mother would?" David asked morosely. "I've never seen her like she was tonight. It won't be easy."

"I'll just have to give it my best shot." Grady had a feeling it was going to be a long night.

UPSTAIRS IN HER ROOM, Kirsten paced agitatedly. *I want to go to Mississippi to live with Dad.* The words rolled over and over in her mind. Just like that, David wanted to live with his father. Grady had never bought the boy so much as a toothbrush. He had no idea whether or not David had ever had measles or chicken pox, while she had worked hard to be a good mother, to deserve her son's love and approval. Yet Grady had simply strolled in from left field and voilà—instant approval. She'd never been so hurt in her life.

Well, it wasn't going to happen. He was going to stay here where he belonged. He was going back to Harvard in the spring. If he wanted to visit his father occasionally, that was fine, but there was no way he was going to live with him. The whole idea was absurd. How had she ever let things go so far? She should have squelched David's attempts to find Grady the minute he mentioned it.

That thought had no sooner formed than Kirsten's shoulders sagged. Who was she kidding? She stopped pacing and sank onto a chaise longue, miserably admitting that it had all been out of her hands from the beginning. She wasn't dealing with a little boy any longer. If David didn't want to stay here, if he didn't want to go to Harvard, he wouldn't, period. She might delay his leaving a year or so, but if she did, he would leave full of resentment instead of with her blessings. If he wanted to be with his father, he would be...someday.

He wants to be with Grady, her inner voice taunted. *Wants to. That's what's stuck in your craw, right?*

Of course. It was like a knife in her stomach.

And you're jealous, right?

Yes, dammit, she was jealous.

Grady's a novelty right now.

And she was old hat, was that it? Just someone who had been around all his life to tell him to hang up his clothes, not to slouch, not to talk with his mouth full of food.

Think about it Kirsten. David's never had a father figure in his life. As wonderful as Travis was, the age difference was just too great. Grady's a new face, a different type of person from anyone David's ever known.

Kirsten rested her head on the chaise and stared across the room. Maybe it *was* just the novelty of it all, having a father when there had never been one before. And novelties could become stale stuff pretty quickly. If she let him go without a fuss, he might come back before long...and when he did, he'd stay.

Getting to her feet, she crossed the room to her closet, peeling off her lovely clothes as she went. Once they'd been carefully hung up, she slipped on her nightie and robe and went into her bathroom. The sleekly modern room looked like something one could find at a beauty salon. It had taken a team of workmen weeks to turn the old bathroom into this private spa, and T.G. had all but gone into cardiac arrest when Travis had shown it to him. It was the one room that Kirsten herself had designed, right down to the last of the dozens of pale pink light bulbs encircling the huge mirror over her vanity. She wondered what Roger and Constance would do with it.

The kind of sadness that produces overwhelming lethargy engulfed her. Her life was unraveling. Travis's death had been hard on her, but she had gotten through it because everything else had remained constant. Now she accepted that she would be giving up the house soon. No great loss there. Denise wouldn't be around on a full-time basis anymore, not if the relationship with Raymond Billingsley continued. That was a wrench. Now David. A new house, but no husband, no best friend, no son. What on earth would she do with her time?

Impatient with her melancholy, Kirsten washed her face and brushed her teeth. She was feeling sorry for herself, and that was a feeling she despised above all others. Flipping off the lights, she returned to the bedroom and pulled down the bed covers. Minutes later, as she was lying with her hands propped behind her head, staring at the ceiling, she heard a door close down the hall. Grady and David were probably through commiserating with each other and were calling it a day.

She'd behaved badly, she decided. She'd been a bitch to accuse Grady of purposely scheming behind her back. She didn't know how any of this had really come about, so she should have asked some questions instead of flying off the handle. David hadn't been the same since their return from Mississippi. If Grady could have that profound an effect on him in so little time, it was meant to be. Fate, Kismet—whatever— had to have had a hand in this.

Yet, she wondered if she had it in her to look them both in the eye and say, "Okay, you two go do your thing. Come to see me when you can."

Kirsten tossed and turned for more than an hour, and as the minutes ticked by, she grew more and more wide-awake. Finally, giving up, she got out of bed, put on her robe and stepped out into the hall. Several small lamps were always left burning in the cavernous house. There was one on a console in the hall, under the portrait of Travis Patrick I, the horse thief. Another sat on a small Victorian table on the landing and another in the foyer at the foot of the stairs. Kirsten silently padded down and crossed through the formal dining room into the kitchen.

The room was a stainless steel marvel, Maddie's personal domain, and the cook was fiercely possessive of it. Kirsten was careful to make no noise as she took a glass out of the cupboard, opened the refrigerator and poured some milk. She carried it into the solarium, where light from a full moon streamed through the uncovered windows. She hadn't taken more than a few steps when a tall figure uncurled from the sofa. The glass almost slipped from her grip.

"Oh!" she exclaimed.

"I'm sorry if I frightened you," Grady apologized. The coat and tie were gone, and his shirtsleeves had been rolled to the elbow. His hair was tousled from being raked by his fingers.

Once she recovered from her fright, Kirsten's first thought was of her unlovely, unadorned face. Thank heavens moonlight camouflaged a multitude of flaws. "Couldn't you sleep?" she asked.

"I don't know. I haven't tried." His eyes took in the robe and slippers. "Apparently you couldn't."

"I rarely can after behaving like a witch." She set the glass on a nearby table, folded her arms across her chest and looked at him contritely. "I'm sorry about earlier."

"I'm sorry, too. You should have had more warning than that. And, Kirsten, I want you to know I didn't conspire behind your back. It was David who first brought up the idea of going to Mississippi State. At least he said he'd like to go to school somewhere down there. I have no idea when he settled on State."

"When was this?"

"Believe it or not, it was the second morning of your visit, before we went to Jackson."

Her chin quivered. "It certainly didn't take you long to make a great impression on him."

Grady stepped closer to her. "I don't think it's me as much as it is being young and uncertain and wanting something new and different. At least, he thinks he does. He might discover he doesn't like it as much as he thinks he will."

"I doubt that. David thinks before he acts. I'm sure that being with you in Mississippi is what he wants more than anything." Her voice broke, so she paused a minute to steady herself. "And I know the smart thing for me to do is let him give it a try. He'll just re-sent it terribly if I don't. He's nineteen. My influence with him isn't what it once was."

"Oh, don't think that for a minute. He was very unhappy over upsetting you tonight. You did such a good job with him. You should be proud of yourself."

"Thanks." She flicked away a tear with a finger. "Grady, promise me something."

"Anything."

She shoved her hands into the pockets of her robe and looked down. "Promise me you'll make him stay in close touch with me. He's terrible when it comes to writing letters, so he'll have to call me frequently. He has his own money, so make him pay for the calls, but don't let him get so busy he forgets. And if you ever have reason to believe he doesn't like it down there, send him back."

Grady smiled down at her bent head. She looked so sad and terribly vulnerable. A great wave of tenderness washed over him. Taking her by the shoulders, he pulled her closer. "You were so upset earlier that I didn't get a chance to tell you everything I came here to say."

She looked up. "Don't tell me there's more. I don't think I can stand it."

"Kirsten, I love the idea of having David come to stay with me. It's brought a whole new purpose to my life. But that's not the end of it. I want you to come, too."

Her eyes widened. "Me?"

"Of course you."

"You mean, you want me to move to Mississippi?"

"That was the general idea."

"But...that's impossible. What would I do? Where would I live?"

Grady hesitated, then taking a deep breath, he continued. "I was hoping the three of us could live together."

"Oh..." She uttered a nervous little laugh. "Oh, good grief, I—"

"Look, our relationship, yours and mine, can be anything you want it to be. But I'm going to tell you straight away that I'm hoping you'll like it, that you'll want to make it permanent."

If Kirsten had been stunned over David's announcement, she was flabbergasted over this. "Grady, there is no way you can know at this point that you want...what you're suggesting. No way. So many years have passed. You and I are different people now."

"I know that any sensible person would say exactly what you're saying, so I guess that means I'm not the sensible sort. I do know it, Kirsten. You hadn't been in Mississippi twenty-four hours before I knew it. I want us to be a real family."

"Whew. I'm going to have to sit down on that one." Backing away, she slumped into a chair.

Grady took a seat on the sofa and looked at her intently. "David tells me you're leaving this house, anyway."

"Yes, that's true...but I thought an apartment in the city...or something like that."

"You wouldn't be sold into bondage, Kirsten. Naturally, you could leave anytime you wanted. I'm only asking that you give it a try. And you'll be the one who decides exactly how...things will be between us."

She looked at him skeptically. "If we're living under the same roof, could you really do that?"

He grinned charmingly. "I'd have to if that's what you wanted. I'm not in the habit of ravishing women who don't want to be ravished."

Kirsten closed her eyes for a minute. "This is insanity."

"Unusual perhaps, but not insane. And not impossible. Don't you remember how well we got along when we were married?"

"Grady, we weren't much more than kids then."

"But there's still something special between us. Don't you feel it? Look, I know what I'm offering is nothing like what you already have, but—"

"This, you mean?" She gestured to indicate the house as a whole. "It means nothing to me. Things aren't the reason for my hesitation. I...this entire thing is so preposterous."

She couldn't understand why she just didn't say no. Why wasn't she laughing uproariously? Of course it was preposterous, ludicrous. True, there wasn't much for her here, but she did have a few friends and a few obligations. What was there for her in Mississippi?

Nothing but her son...and his father. Now she looked at Grady and recalled her immediate attraction to him that first night at his house. She had put that down to missing the love of a man but she had to admit there was something about him she liked, and there always had been. "I'm going to have to think long and hard about it" were the surprising words that came out of her mouth.

"Of course. I expected you to."

"You think about it, too."

"I already have...constantly."

Kirsten didn't know what else to say. What could she say? It was time to go back to bed and reflect on the evening's startling events. Everything would be clearer to her in the morning. Getting to her feet, she shoved her hands back into the pockets of her robe. "Good night, Grady. We'll talk tomorrow."

"Yes, tomorrow." He, too, got to his feet. "Kirsten, there's one more thing...." In a swift motion he closed the space between them, slid his arms around her waist and captured her mouth with his before she knew what was happening. He held the kiss until he heard a tiny gurgle of pleasure rise up in her throat. Then he broke away and cupped her face in his hands. "Sweet dreams," he murmured huskily.

Kirsten opened her mouth to say something, but nothing came out. Finally she managed a whispered "Good night," slipped away from him and left the room.

Grady watched her leave, a smile touching the lips that still tasted of her. Perhaps he shouldn't have felt so encouraged, but he did. At least she hadn't said no.

CHAPTER NINE

"DENISE," KIRSTEN SNAPPED into the phone, "I want you to get over here and talk some sense into my head before I do something utterly rash and foolish."

It was nine-thirty, and she was trying to shake off the vestiges of sleep after a restless night. At some point after returning to her room last night, she had decided that to even consider doing what Grady wanted was idiotic, and she had fully intended on telling him just that this morning. Yet, when she woke, her first thought had been of Mississippi and the three of them there, a family again. Thus, this frantic call to Denise.

"I don't know, Kirsten," Denise said. "I might not be the one you should talk to. I seem to be leaning heavily toward the rash and foolish myself these days."

"Give me some time to get dressed and have a bite to eat. Then get over here. I've got to talk to you."

"I'll be there in about forty-five minutes."

Kirsten hurried with showering and dressing and was downstairs in less than half an hour, looking for Grady or David or both. She found neither of them, and there was only one place setting left on the dining table. Instead of sitting down and ringing for Maddie, she went straight into the kitchen. The cook, unaccustomed to seeing the mistress of the manor in this part of the house, looked startled. "Is something wrong, ma'am?"

"No, no, everything's fine."

"Are you ready for breakfast?"

"Just coffee and a roll, something simple. Maddie, has David had breakfast yet?"

"Oh, yes, ma'am. He and your guest were down quite early. They had breakfast together."

"Do you happen to know where they are now?"

"I believe they said something about going for a walk."

Kirsten nodded distractedly and accepted the coffee and roll Maddie offered her. "I'll be out on the terrace if anyone is looking for me."

"Yes, ma'am."

It was a beautiful morning. From the terrace, Kirsten could look across the sweeping lawns of the various Patrick estates with their commanding views of the sound. But the vista, as breathtaking as it was, did not make its usual impression on her. Grady would have by now informed David of her dramatic change of heart, so the die was cast. There would be no turning back from that decision. About all that was left to be decided was when David would leave.

Well, there was one more thing: would she be going with him? She found it hard to believe there was an "if" associated with the decision. Such a move would be so drastic, so bold, so unlike anything she would have thought herself capable of. Yet, the pull was unmistakable, the temptations easy to pinpoint: her reluctance to completely release her hold on David, plus the force of Grady's personality. Being with both of them was so much more appealing than anything she would have here.

Grady had approached her at a good time—or a bad time, depending on the way one wished to look at it. Even if she stayed put, her life would be undergoing change. Why not make the changes extreme?

Still, it was pretty pie-in-the-sky to think that, after all these years, she and Grady and David could settle down cozily in that house in the woods and live happily ever after. Fairy-tale nonsense.

At that moment she caught a glimpse of Denise topping a rise and striding across the great expanse of lawn that separated their houses. Kirsten waved, then sipped her coffee and watched her sister-in-law approach. Reaching the terrace, Denise plopped into a chair, her face flushed with exertion. "Here I am," she said, slightly out of breath, "reporting in as ordered."

"Want something to eat or drink?" Kirsten asked.

"No, thanks. I just met David and his dad."

"Oh?"

"David's showing him the territory. Oh, Kirsten, Grady is one good-looking man! Whatever this rash and foolish thing is you're thinking of doing, if it includes him, I'm voting for it."

Kirsten paused, then said, "David wants to go live with Grady."

Denise's smile faded, and she looked at Kirsten, her expression conveying her sympathy. "Oh, Kirsten, I can imagine how you must be feeling right now. What a blow!"

"I must say, it took me by surprise."

"Listen, you know this is nothing but a temporary whim." Denise reached across the table and laid a comforting hand on Kirsten's arm. "Grady's new and exciting to David right now, but that's bound to pass.

I know this is easy for me to say, but I think you should let him go, let him get it out of his system. He'll be back before you know it. Don't do anything impulsive, like try to spirit David out of the country or anything like that. That would only make Grady more attractive to him. Just let him go. I give the whole thing a month, tops."

"It's not like that, Denise. I've already told Grady that David can go with my blessings, and I'm sure he's told David by now."

Denise sat back, frowning. "Then I don't understand. What's the rash and foolish part?"

Kirsten took a deep breath. "Grady wants me to come, too."

Denise's eyes brightened. "Really?"

"Really. He's painted the rosiest little picture of the three of us living together, just like a family."

"Are you going to do it?"

"I was hoping you would come over here and talk me out of it."

"Why in heck would I do that?"

"Because even thinking of moving to Mississippi is irrational. Everything is here."

Denise uttered a sound of disdain. "They're not going to chain you up down there, are they? If you don't like it, you can always come back here."

Kirsten sighed. "That's what Grady said. But he also said he hopes I'll want to make it permanent."

"That is incredibly romantic."

"Only because you're an incurable romantic. What it actually is is foolish."

Denise smiled softly. "But you want to go, don't you?"

Kirsten glanced down, then back up. "Yes . . . and that's even more foolish."

Denise smiled softly. "But you want to go, don't you?"

Kirsten glanced down, then back up. "Yes . . . and that's even more foolish."

"I disagree. I think it's wonderful, and it's come along at exactly the right time for you. Just like Raymond did for me. No mid-life crises for us, kiddo."

"And to think I asked you over here hoping you would talk me out of it."

Denise smiled knowingly. "No, you didn't. You asked me over here hoping I would tell you to do what you want to do. And that's exactly what I'm doing. Go, for heaven's sake! Bed the man. Wallow in pleasure. Discover if whatever you saw in him years ago is still there. If it doesn't work out, at least you tried it. Go find something that will work. Above all, don't sit and analyze every tiny step, every detail. Take things as they come and don't worry too much about tomorrow."

Kirsten looked at her thoughtfully. "You've never been afraid of making waves, but this seize-the-moment philosophy is a side of you I've never seen before."

"Oh, it's always been here," Denise said, "but so much of what composes my life—the family, my 'position' in society—tends to keep my baser instincts well hidden. But no more. I'm going to really live out my remaining years, and I suggest you do the same. End of advice."

"You're a big help," Kirsten said with a smile.

"I just told you what you wanted to hear. Isn't that always the best advice we can receive?"

Kirsten stared over Denise's left shoulder. She supposed that at some point going to Mississippi with David had become more attractive to her than staying put. She didn't even remember making the decision. It wasn't quite real to her, but she knew that was what she was going to do. At least she was going to give it a try, to see if this time she and Grady could pass the test. In essence, it would be a trial run to determine if they could build something permanent. If they did, it would be wonderful for David. If they didn't, she could say she'd made the attempt. She wouldn't forever regret having not done it.

The really sad part would be saying goodbye to Denise. "When you're a jet-setter, you'll drop me a postcard now and then, won't you?"

"Absolutely," Denise said. "Buckets of them. You, too?"

"Yes, sure. But who will I pour out my woes to?"

Denise's eyes seemed misty. "Maybe your woes will all be over. Honestly, Kirsten, I'll let you know where I am every second. If you need to talk, pick up the phone."

Kirsten's breath escaped in a soft sigh. So many changes.

"THERE ARE SOME BENCHES over there, Dad," David said. "In front of that hedge. Why don't we rest a minute?"

Grady grinned. "Believe it or not, I'm still good for another mile or two, but if you want to rest, we'll rest."

A tall, manicured hedge separated the estate of Roger and Constance Patrick from the one Kirsten and David occupied. It was the only barrier among the four estates that comprised the Patrick compound, the result, if family lore was to be believed, of a long-ago feud between two brothers. Along it, at exact intervals, stood four stone benches. Grady sat down on one, hating to admit how good it felt to get off his feet. David had given him quite a workout.

"Why the benches?" he asked as David sat down beside him.

"Years ago, when I was a little kid, we used to have huge Sunday afternoon croquet matches out here. The benches were for the spectators."

"Did you enjoy croquet?" Grady asked.

David grinned. Unconsciously, he had adopted many of his father's mannerisms, to the point that now their grins were almost identical. "Do I look like the kind of guy who would enjoy croquet?"

Grady laughed. "No, I guess not."

"I played for the same reason I did almost everything else—to pretend I belonged. Thank God, that's over. I can't believe Mom changed her mind, not after that fit she pitched last night."

"Ah, David, that was a very normal reaction to what had to have been startling news for her. Then she thought it over and changed her mind. It was her decision, hers alone."

"When I went to bed last night, I thought I was going to have to openly defy her. I didn't know if I could do it."

"No need for that now. Everything is working out exactly as I hoped. Or almost."

"Almost?" David asked, puzzled.

"I guess I should tell you.... I asked your mom to come, too."

David sucked in his breath. "To Mississippi?"

"Yes."

"What did she say?"

The corners of Grady's mouth twitched. "She didn't say no. That's all I can tell you."

David sat back in disbelief. "Wow! Wouldn't that be great? Would you . . . I mean, would you and Mom get married again?"

"It's too early to even think about that, son. We've been apart a lot of years, and the divorce, after all, was my idea. I thought I was doing the right thing at the time, and it did give you and your mom a chance at this kind of life. A lot has happened to both of us since we were last together. We're not the same people we were back then. But who knows? We had it once—maybe we can find it again. The first hurdle is convincing your mom to give it a try."

The two men lapsed into silence, each with his own thoughts. Finally, Grady stood up. "Maybe we should get back to the house. I can't very well convince Kirsten of anything if I'm not with her."

"Yeah," David agreed. "Tell you what, Dad—I'll make myself scarce after lunch. Then maybe you can talk to her."

Father and son walked off in the direction of the house, each clasping the other's shoulder. On the other side of the hedge, a woman sat in stunned shock. Constance Patrick had been sunning in her favorite spot, reading and enjoying the solitude. When she'd first heard masculine voices, she'd felt a flash of irritation at having her reverie interrupted, if only momentarily. She had recognized David's voice immediately. The other, a masculine southern drawl, had captured her attention only because of its unfamiliarity. But once she'd caught the gist of the conversation, her book had been forgotten, and she'd sharpened her hearing. Slowly it had dawned on her that what she was hearing was of monumental import.

David's natural father was alive! Not only alive but here. That meant her ladyship had lied to the family all these years. Doubtless had lied to poor Travis, too. A widow, indeed!

All of Constance's breeding and poise had never prevented her from overtly resenting Travis's wife. Though none of the Patricks, with the exception of strange Denise, had sanctioned or accepted Kirsten's marriage to one of their own, some of their less particular and more forgiving peers had. It annoyed Constance no end that the urchin was considered the prettiest, best-dressed, most charming hostess in their closed social circle. Before Travis had returned from the hinterlands with a bride in tow, it was Constance who had enjoyed that distinction. There were many members of the *Social Register* who actually professed to admire the pluck of the young widowed mother.

Kirsten was a fraud! How absolutely wonderful! Constance's heart began to beat rapidly in anticipation of the commotion this would cause within the family. What a time for Roger to be out of town. She'd have to wait till she saw him to tell him her news. She'd burst! But Constance, like every other woman in the family, wouldn't have dreamed of going to T.G. without talking to her husband first. And she wanted to do it in person.

She slipped off her lounge and went to a spot where the hedge parted slightly. Squinting, she made out the two figures walking away from her. Same height, same coloring, that was for sure. Then they stopped and faced each other; both were laughing. The profiles were so much alike it was unbelievable. Constance went back to the lounge, laughter trying to bubble up from her throat. That she had been the one to stumble onto this incredible information was poetic justice, she thought. She'd been forced to live in the elegant hillbilly's shadow much too long.

IMMEDIATELY AFTER LUNCH, David mumbled something about needing to do some shopping and made a hasty exit, leaving Kirsten and Grady alone. The big house always seemed eerily quiet on Saturday afternoons. Normally it was the time Kirsten saved for personal correspondence or reading. This afternoon, however, she had a guest to entertain.

"Can you think of anything you'd like to do, Grady?" she asked. "Sight-seeing, a ball game on TV? I want you to do whatever you like."

They were sitting in the solarium, a room, Grady realized, that was one of her favorites. He could understand that. It was the only room he'd seen that suited her personality. "The only thing I really want to do is find out if you've thought any more about last night."

"I've hardly thought about anything else," she admitted.

"And?"

Kirsten was holding the glass of iced tea she hadn't finished at lunch. Now she stared at it. "You know, this is the one southern habit I've never been able to break myself of—drinking iced tea all year long. Travis thought I was absolutely crazy to drink iced tea on Christmas day."

"Kirsten," Grady groaned, "you're digressing."

She took a deep breath, and a funny sort of smile touched her lips. "I . . . guess I'll be coming with David."

Grady hadn't realized he was holding his breath. Now he released it. "Thanks" was all he could think to say at the moment.

"It will take some time for us to be ready. At least a week."

"I think I can wait just about a week."

"Please don't ask me why I'm doing this," Kirsten said with a somewhat sheepish smile. "I don't have a logical answer for it."

"If either one of us were being logical, this wouldn't be happening." There was nothing sheepish about his smile. It was one of absolute delight. "Was there a bolt of lightning, a stroke of insight? What made up your mind for you?"

"Oh, several things. Being at a crossroads in my life, for one. Wanting to leave this house. Not wanting to completely release my hold on David just yet. Hating it that Denise is following her heart to England, even though I'm happy for her." She looked at him. "Maybe I'm curious to see if two people can rebuild a relationship after years of being apart. I don't know—a lot of things."

Grady would have felt better if she'd sounded more certain about her action. "Well, I'm not about to inspect and examine this too closely. I'm just glad you're going to do it."

"I'm not making any promises, Grady."

"I'm not asking you to."

"I've more or less accepted that the move will probably be permanent for David. But for me...I don't know."

Impulsively, Grady stood and walked to where she was sitting. He cupped her face in his hands and, bending from the waist, kissed her tenderly. When he raised his head, he smiled at her in a way that made her heart actually flutter. "Then I guess it'll be my task to convince you that it's the smartest thing you've ever done."

"I don't know how you can be so positive you really want me with you on a permanent basis."

"It's not supposed to make sense."

"Guess I'll have to learn to say 'y'all' again."

Grady smiled. "There won't be any learning to it. It's contagious."

"I remember how hard it was to stop saying it when I first moved here." His hands still cupped her face; she rested hers lightly on both sides of his waist and looked up at him. "You know, I wouldn't do this insane thing if I didn't feel so comfortable with you."

"That's not a bad way to start a relationship."

Kirsten heard a throat being cleared. Peering around Grady, she saw one of the maids standing in the doorway. "Pardon me, ma'am, but Mrs. Patrick is here to see you."

"Which Mrs. Patrick?" Kirsten asked.

"Mr. Roger's wife, ma'am."

Constance? What the devil was she doing here on Saturday afternoon? Of all the Patrick women, Roger's wife was the one who mystified Kirsten the most. She had her ways of dealing with the others, but she'd never learned to deal with Constance's animosity toward her.

Grady felt Kirsten stiffen. "Shall I get lost?"

"I'm sorry, Grady. It might be best. Wait next door in the study."

He nodded, turned on his heel and left the room. Kirsten sat back, composed herself and said to the servant, "Please show her in."

A minute later, Constance swept grandly into the room. Two years older and as many inches taller than Kirsten, she was a handsome woman with blond hair, pale gray eyes and an angular body that wore clothes beautifully. From a *Social Register* family that took traditions as seriously as the Patricks did, she was T.G.'s darling. Her only "fault," in the patriarch's eyes, lay in her production of only female offspring—three, to be exact.

Kirsten got to her feet. "Well, Constance, what a nice surprise," she said. "Please, have a seat. May I get you something to drink?"

"No, thanks." Constance's eyes darted around the room; Kirsten couldn't imagine what she was looking for. Then she took a seat and folded her manicured hands in her lap. "I was on my way to see Mom and Dad and thought I'd stop by and see how you're doing."

Liar, Kirsten thought as she smiled politely. It always annoyed her when Constance referred to Travis's parents as Mom and Dad. That was petty of her, but she couldn't help it. "That was nice of you. I'm doing fine."

"The folks will be asking about you. Is there any...news?"

"News?"

"I suppose I should have asked, is anything new?"

This was too damned much of a coincidence to suit Kirsten. Who knew she was leaving? She and Grady, that was who. No, there was Denise, but Denise and Constance were barely civil to each other. *Ah, I'm being overly suspicious.* "New? Well, let's see... You might tell Mr. Patrick that David and I will be vacating the house very soon. Possibly within a week, if everything goes well."

"Isn't this awfully sudden?" Once again Constance's eyes darted around the room.

What in the hell is she looking for? Kirsten wondered irritably. Or maybe those were covetous eyes she was casting around, making a mental inventory of all she soon would "own." "Actually, I've been thinking about it ever since our father-in-law asked me to get out."

"Really, Kirsten, that's a bit harsh. It's family tradition, you know. The oldest male heir lives in this house."

"How could I not know that, Constance? It's mentioned six times a week."

Constance was accustomed to a much more docile Kirsten—a little mouse striving for acceptance. This uncharacteristic harpishness flustered the older woman, but she recovered quickly. "You and David must have plans. Where are you going... or is that a deep, dark secret?"

"Why on earth would it be a secret? For the time being, at least, we're going back to Mississippi."

"Good heavens, how provincial!"

"We've talked about it quite a lot since returning from our trip there."

"Oh, yes, family business, didn't you say? Since your mother was your only family, and since she's been gone several years, we did wonder what kind of business would need taking care of at this late date.'' Constance smiled.

Kirsten's matched hers for lack of warmth. ''Did you? Goodness, I wouldn't have thought the Patricks would give a minute's thought to my family business. We—David and I—thought Mississippi might be a refreshing change of pace.''

''Well, they do say that one never completely rids oneself of one's roots.''

''Yes, they do say that, don't they?''

Constance, apparently realizing that the conversation had reached an impasse, sought to divert it into another channel. Her eyes fell on a framed photograph of David on one of the end tables. ''David is very handsome,'' she said. ''It's strange that he's never become seriously involved with a girl.''

''Do you think so? At nineteen?'' was Kirsten's vague reply.

Constance again looked at the photograph. ''He doesn't favor you much. He must resemble his father.''

Kirsten made a show of studying the picture. ''I really hadn't thought about it. Yes, I guess he does...in a way.''

''Your late husband—what did you say his first name was?''

''I don't believe I ever said. I never discussed him with Travis's family.''

''Perhaps not. Well—'' Constance got to her feet ''—I guess I'd better be running along. The folks are expecting me.''

Kirsten stood, too. ''Have a nice time.''

"I always do. Mom and Dad are such delightful hosts."

"Are they now?"

Kirsten walked with Constance to the door, made sure she was safely gone, then went back into the solarium just as Grady emerged from the adjacent room. "Who's that charmer?" he asked with a hint of sarcasm.

"Travis's sister-in-law."

"I don't think I would like knowing her."

"You're very perceptive. I spent years trying to like Constance and wondered why I couldn't. Then it came to me. She's self-centered, vindictive and snobbish. She brings out the absolute worst in me." Kirsten frowned and chewed on her lip. "Beyond that, I smell a rat."

"What do you mean?" Grady asked.

"Coming over here at this particular time, asking the sort of questions she's never asked before. Grady...did you and David see or meet anyone while you were out on your walk this morning?"

"Just the woman David introduced as Aunt Denise."

"Hmm. Well, I'm probably conjuring up monsters where none exist. I'm an alarmist where Travis's family is concerned. I'll just chalk it up to coincidence." She slipped her hand into the crook of Grady's elbow, a casual gesture on her part, but one that seemed delightfully intimate to him. "Let's go sit on the terrace. It's such a beautiful day, and the cold weather will be here before we know it."

"Not where you're going."

Kirsten stopped, a bemused expression on her face. "That's right. It's going to take some getting used to. I've spent so many winters here."

For the next half hour or so, they sat on the sunny terrace, making plans. Grady told her about the possible promotion, but that made little impact on Kirsten. He kept emphasizing his doubt that he would be the one chosen, but even if he was, that was next year. How did she know she would still be with him? She was having enough trouble coming to terms with a move to Mississippi; she certainly wasn't going to worry about Dallas. Her decision seemed like one that had been made for another person. She supposed she would do as Denise had suggested—take each thing, each day, one at a time.

When David returned home, he wandered through the house, looking for them. Finally he spotted them on the terrace, but before joining them, he stood at the door, watching them before they saw him. His mother and father were seated close to each other at the round, glass-topped table, deep in conversation. At one point, Grady reached for Kirsten's hand and held it. David was at a loss to understand why that touched him so. He stood there another minute, simply staring at their interlocked fingers; then he opened the door.

At the sound, Kirsten and Grady both turned. Their hands separated, and Grady got to his feet. "Come here, son. Your mom has some wonderful news for you."

IT WAS SETTLED. Monday morning Kirsten and David would decide what they absolutely, positively had to have with them in Mississippi. No excess baggage. Into storage would go her timeless designer suits and dinner dresses. David saw no need for his yachting or polo attire in Culver. They were embarking on a brand-new way of life. How long it lasted remained to be seen.

Once everything was done, they would leave, driving Kirsten's car. If everything went smoothly, they would be at Grady's within ten days. While merely discussing it, it seemed simple enough, but Kirsten wondered when she would start believing it was actually going to happen.

CHAPTER TEN

THE FOLLOWING WEEK passed in a blur of activity. Once Grady left for home Sunday afternoon, Kirsten and David threw themselves into the task at hand. Virtually everything in the house belonged to the house. It was strange, she reflected, to have lived with so many lovely things for so long, only to realize how few of them were really hers. The items of furniture that actually belonged to Kirsten went into storage, along with her designer originals and her personal memorabilia. As drawers and closets emptied, the servants were instructed to clean the place from top to bottom. Kirsten wanted the house to be just short of antiseptic when Roger and Constance moved in.

There were dozens of invitations she had accepted that now had to be regretted, and once the news of her move got around, she was besieged by phone calls from acquaintances who couldn't believe she was giving up "everything" to go back to Mississippi. Most were sure she would die of boredom. They all predicted she would be back by Christmas. Kirsten hoped they were wrong but wondered if they might turn out to be right. It still didn't seem possible that she and Grady would actually pull it off.

As departure time loomed, she paid a courtesy call on T.G. and Evelyn. The visit was marked by tension, discomfiture and overpoliteness on the part of all three. Kirsten thought what a shame it was that class distinction had played such a major role in their relationship. At least her in-laws spared her the sham of pretending they were sorry to see her go, though Evelyn issued a halfhearted admonishment to stay in touch. "Of course," Kirsten murmured, all the while knowing there was a very good chance they would never see or hear of each other again.

Somehow everything got done, and at last there was nothing left to do but go. While David packed the car, Kirsten took the time to personally thank each of the servants for the many kindnesses they had shown her through the years. A few of them had tears in their eyes, for they knew they now would be parceled out to other Patricks, none of whom would be as easy to work for as their mistress had been.

Once they'd filed out, Kirsten wandered through the rooms of the grand mansion, surprised at her lack of emotion. She and Travis had spent some wonderful times in it, but never once had it seemed like her house. Perhaps that was why she felt so little. And Denise's absence helped. They had already said their teary farewell on the eve of Denise's departure for England. Kirsten took one last look around, then hurried outside in time to see David close the trunk.

"That's it," he called. "Are you ready?"

"I guess so." As ready as she'd ever be. Now she supposed she would have to start believing it was going to happen.

LESS THAN AN HOUR after Kirsten and David had driven away, Roger Patrick returned home from his extended business trip. He was all but waylaid at the door by Constance, who was so eager to tell him about the conversation she had overheard between Grady and David that the words came out in a rush, tumbling over one another. Roger finally had to interrupt her.

"Slow down, dear. I can't understand a word you're saying. Let me change while you have someone fix us drinks. I'll join you in the study in fifteen minutes. Then you can tell me your story. I'm sure it's...fascinating."

Constance loathed her husband's often condescending manner toward her, but it was a loathing she kept strictly to herself. She could endure any of his character faults, suffer any slights at his hand in return for the privilege of being a Patrick. She had been long on lineage but short of cash when Roger had come into her life, and their subsequent marriage had been a dream come true. Both of them had acquired exactly what they wanted. Roger had a wife his father approved of, and Constance had money and a husband who assured her a comfortable place on Long Island's closed social list. She never asked herself if she loved her husband or even if she liked him very much. What difference did that make? He was a Patrick, and he had made her one. Constance was, if nothing else, everlastingly grateful.

Roger fully expected to hear the usual kind of insignificant gossip that his wife and her friends thrived on. Most of what interested Constance bored him senseless. That afternoon, however, her story was interesting...very interesting. Yet, Roger was his father's son—thorough and precise. Even as he listened, he wondered how much of what Constance told him she actually had heard and how much was what she hoped she'd heard. He'd never really understood his wife's hatred of Kirsten. He hadn't approved of his older brother's wife for the same reason his father hadn't: she wasn't their kind. Traditionally, Patrick men chose their wives with the same care they devoted to choosing breeding stock for their Kentucky Thoroughbred farm. Travis had offended the family's sensibilities by marrying a woman from the working class. But Constance's dislike of Kirsten was a more personal thing. Therefore, Roger wondered how much credence could be given to his wife's story.

But there had to be a kernel of truth to it; Constance wasn't that inventive. So he agreed with her on one thing: T.G. needed to hear about this. A phone call to his father resulted in an invitation to "come right over." And once he and Constance were in T.G.'s august presence, Roger let his wife do the talking.

Constance's account of the overheard conversation was fairly accurate, with one slight difference. Like most people, she wasn't gifted with total recall, and she quoted Grady as having said, "The divorce was my idea. It gave you and your mom a chance for this kind of life." With a few words omitted, the meaning had changed considerably.

When Constance finished speaking, T.G. remained silent for a minute or two. His eyes narrowed suspiciously; otherwise, his expression did not alter. Finally, he cleared his throat. "Collusion?" he suggested. "Perhaps the husband was in the picture all along. When Travis became so enchanted with Kirsten, she and her hubby might have cooked up a scheme. A quickie divorce, pass herself off as a widow, marry poor, besotted Travis, perhaps get a healthy divorce settlement in the future."

Roger was fascinated. "Maybe they've been meeting secretly all these years. Maybe she's been siphoning off her allowance money and giving it to her ex."

T.G. rubbed his chin thoughtfully. "Maybe. But one thing bothers me about this supposition. Kirsten stayed with Travis until 'death do us part.'"

"I don't see anything so unusual about that," Constance chimed in. "Maybe she got used to this way of life. There are plenty of women who would put up with anything for Patrick money."

"Really, dear? How interesting." Sarcasm dripped from Roger's voice.

"Well...I mean, nobody in our crowd, of course, but someone from Kirsten's background...." Constance decided it was time to shut up.

T.G. wasn't paying attention to them. He was too deep in thought. After a few minutes of ponderous silence, he shook himself out of his reverie. "Well, whether there was collusion or not, it's evident that Kirsten went into the marriage under false pretenses. All right, you two, this doesn't leave the room until I say otherwise. I don't want Evelyn troubled with it, or Aunt Judith or any of the others. And I certainly don't want a whisper of it to reach Denise's ears."

"Right," Roger and Constance chorused.

"I'll do whatever I decide needs to be done. In the meantime, forget it." He looked at his son. "Don't leave the house without speaking to your mother." Thus dismissing them, he stalked out of the room, leaving Roger and Constance to stare after him dejectedly. They had expected a dramatic outburst of indignation. T.G., it seemed to them, had been disappointingly uninterested.

Nothing could have been further from the truth. T.G. was far more intrigued by Constance's story than he would have let anyone know...yet. True gentlemen of class and means, he staunchly believed, never showed their emotions outside the bedroom. But inside he felt outraged. If what he had just heard proved to be true, they had been duped by a beautiful, clever schemer.

Many years ago, at his father's knee, he had learned that with his wealth and contacts, he could easily arrange for life to spring no surprises on him. This afternoon he had been surprised, and he was furious.

But he cautioned himself against haste. First he wanted solid, damning evidence. A man in his position couldn't be too careful or too discreet. The Patricks despised publicity that they themselves didn't control. He wouldn't make accusations or ask questions until he already knew the answers.

In the privacy of the paneled study that no one entered without his invitation, T.G. picked up the telephone and dialed. A minute passed, then a masculine voice came on the other end of the line.

"This is Isaac Irving."

"Isaac," T.G. said crisply, "get over here right away. There's something I want you to do for me. Find out what I want to know this time, and I'll let you make out your check yourself."

ISAAC IRVING WAS fifty years old, of medium height, weight and build. Average described him to a tee—he had light brown hair cut conservatively, gray-green eyes, no distinguishing features and no scars or birthmarks. He didn't wear eyeglasses, jewelry or fine clothes. He invariably dressed in off-the-rack suits of neutral colors and always wore white shirts. He wasn't the sort of man who stood out in a crowd, not even in a crowd of two. He wasn't a man one remembered.

Which was exactly the way he wanted it. That helped him do his job well. He looked like Everyman. Except Isaac was a private investigator who specialized in finding people who didn't want to be found, and he was so successful at it that he owned a plush home in Westchester, three automobiles, a pleasure boat and a twin-engine Cessna. His working credo was missing persons weren't really missing at all; if they were never found, it was because no one wanted to find them. He had proved that true time and time again.

The secret of his successful track record, he readily told anyone who asked, was the exhaustive background checks he ran on his subjects. He boasted that by the time he was ready to actually begin searching for a person, he knew more about his subject than the subject did. His procedure, he claimed, was infallible, although he naturally refused to divulge the precise methods, techniques, and tricks of the trade that enabled him to command top dollar from his invariably wealthy clients.

T.G. had, for one reason or another, employed Isaac many times in the past. The Patrick patriarch didn't care how the man did what he did, only that he could do it. After he explained to the investigator just who it was he wanted investigated, he said, "Finding Kirsten will be child's play for you, m'boy. She's going to Mississippi. Probably Jackson, but maybe not. She isn't hiding from anyone, so you won't have any trouble on that score. But locating her can be done later. What I'm interested in is that background check you do.'' Reaching into his desk drawer, he withdrew a photograph, which he shoved across the desk to Isaac. "I'm curiously lacking any recent photographs of my daughter-in-law. That was taken the day she and Travis were married. She's fifteen years older now, but all in all, she hasn't changed much.''

Isaac stared at the image of the beautiful, dark-haired young woman, then placed it in his briefcase.

"I want you to find out everything about her from birth right up to the day that picture was taken,'' T.G. said.

"Suppose you tell me what you knew about her when the picture was taken.''

"Not nearly as much as I should have, I can see now. She was born and raised in Jackson, Mississippi. Sometime in 1974, she accepted a job at Bayshore Inn near Biloxi, a resort the family owned in those days. Travis was spending the winter there. She was a widow with a young son . . . or so we were told. We now have reason to believe that wasn't the truth. In fact, it may turn out that little of what we were told about Kirsten was the truth.''

Isaac knew the Patricks and their kind—the old, moneyed families who invariably married within their exclusive circle. The oldest scion's marriage to a working girl, he imagined, had sent shock waves rippling all along the North Shore. "Why didn't you have a background check run on her then?''

"Doubtless I would have if I had known about Kirsten before the deed was done, but not a word about the relationship had reached my ears. They had been very discreet, and one day, without telling a soul, they simply went to the courthouse in Biloxi and got married. It was days later before I learned about it. The shock was tremendous, as you can imagine. A much younger woman of the working class! However, I doubt that Travis would have divorced her even if we'd learned she had just been released from prison. He was absolutely insane about her. To have tried to force an end to the marriage..." T.G. shrugged. "That might have caused a rift in the family, unwanted notoriety—who knows? It was best to do nothing and just try to accept it."

Isaac nodded noncommittally, withdrew a pen from his shirt pocket and began to write. "Normally I start with the past and work toward the present. In this case, I'll do just the opposite. Full name?"

"Kirsten Janice Marshall O'Connor Patrick."

"Age?"

T.G. frowned. "Forty...two, I think. Next month."

"Height and weight?"

"Hell, I don't know. About five-five, I guess. Trim."

"Make and model of car."

"An '89 metallic-blue Cadillac Eldorado."

"License plate?"

"I have no idea. New York, that's all I know."

"I'll find it. Charge accounts, credit cards?"

"Of course. Dozens. All of them."

"Does she have any unusual hobbies or belong to any special-interest groups or organizations?"

"What does that have to do with anything?"

"Mr. Patrick, people with common interests usually get to be pretty friendly, at least during their meetings. And special interests are often acquired fairly early in life. You never can tell what anecdotes from her past your daughter-in-law might have related to other members of these organizations."

"Oh . . . well, let me think. . . ."

Isaac asked questions for more than an hour. When the session ended, T.G. felt he'd been of little help. He really hadn't paid that much attention to Kirsten or had much close contact with her. He knew that Isaac could find out much more about his subject if he could talk to Denise, but T.G. wouldn't allow that. For now, only he and Isaac were to know that Kirsten was being investigated. Besides, he doubted Denise would have told the investigator a thing. She had always seemed overly protective of Kirsten.

If T.G. was disappointed, Isaac wasn't. When he left the Patrick estate that afternoon, he was armed with a wealth of information about Kirsten Janice Marshall O'Connor Patrick.

THEIR TRIP TO MISSISSIPPI turned out to be something of an adventure for Kirsten and David. They took their time, never driving more than three hundred miles a day, sometimes less. They headed west through southern Pennsylvania, south through Virginia, then all the way across Tennessee, spending the last night on the road in Memphis. During it all, they had searched out small restaurants and quaint inns, shunning the new and glitzy in favor of local color. They stopped to buy souvenirs and handcrafted objects of art throughout the Appalachians. When road signs pointed to something they thought might be interesting, they detoured to see it firsthand. Kirsten had jetted all over North America, Europe and Japan, but she'd never made a trip like this one. She didn't know when she had enjoyed anything more.

Nor had she ever enjoyed such blissful freedom. It was wonderful to get out of bed every morning, throw on whatever was comfortable, not fuss much with her hair and makeup and know that every single minute of the upcoming day was her own. Not once would she have to employ the poses and practices she had so carefully learned as a member of Long Island society. No one cared how she looked, what she said, at which table she was seated. Finally she was granted the privacy and anonymity she had so often craved when being a Patrick had just been too much for her. She was smug in her contentment.

It wasn't until they drove under the brick arch of the Hamilton House compound that the first wave of panic seized her. What in hell had gotten into her? What was she going to do all day every day? Grady had his work. David already had announced his intention of appointing himself Ramon's apprentice. Great for them, but she had to fill her days, too. She hadn't cooked a meal or done a dab of housework since David was a child. She had no hobbies. Many times during the past ten days she had fleetingly questioned whether this move was the wisest thing she could have done. Now it seemed downright idiotic.

Then they approached Grady's house and saw him standing on the front porch. They had telephoned him every night during the trip to give him progress reports, so he'd known approximately what time to expect them. He stood there in his starched khakis, his arms akimbo, and the grin on his face was heartwarming, welcoming. He bounded down the steps when the car pulled to a stop, jerked open the passenger door and held out his hand to Kirsten.

"These have been the longest ten days of my life," he said. "Maybe in a minute I'll let myself believe the two of you are really here."

As soon as he opened his mouth, Kirsten felt better. She had no idea what the outcome of this peculiar arrangement would be, but Grady genuinely wanted them there, and that in itself was reassuring. It was nice to be wanted. Too many times since Travis's death she had felt anything but wanted.

Grady embraced her fiercely, and when David came around from the driver's side, Grady embraced him, too. "Welcome home," he said in an emotion-filled voice.

It was going to be all right, Kirsten decided. She might not be prepared to think of this as home yet— maybe she never would—but everything would be fine. She felt so comfortable when she was with Grady. And not being here meant being very alone back in New York. This probably was the best place for her at this stage of her life. She'd find something to do.

IT WAS THE ODDEST THING in the world, Kirsten reflected: the three of them sitting around the dinner table, just as though they had done it every night for years. Then getting up to rinse dishes and put them in the dishwasher, talking about the things she and David had seen and done on their trip, wondering aloud what was on television that night and planning tomorrow's activities. One minute it all seemed so natural; then Kirsten would remember that it actually was completely unnatural. Perhaps Grady and David belonged together—they certainly seemed to think they did—but she had no idea where her place was.

When Grady didn't know he was being watched, she studied him and tried to envision doing what he claimed to want—living with him permanently, the three of them being a family. But it was useless. True, he was an attractive, appealing man, and he could tug at her heartstrings, but it was far too soon to know if the pull stemmed from something deeper than surface attractiveness. And she had to remember that later Grady could very well suffer some mind changing of his own.

As they were finishing up in the kitchen, David mentioned wanting to telephone Mona Cuellar to tell her he was back. When Kirsten and Grady went into the living room a few minutes later, he was hanging up the phone. He asked, "Is it okay if I use your car, Mom? Mona says she'd like to go out for a soda. I won't be gone long. Tomorrow's a workday for her."

"Sure," Kirsten said, "that's fine."

"I guess I remember how to find her house. I wasn't driving the last time I was there, so I didn't pay a lot of attention."

Grady refreshed his memory, and in a minute David was on his way out the front door, twirling the car keys and whistling softly. Kirsten stared after him, shaking her head slightly. "Mona certainly made an impression on him."

"You sound as though that bothers you," Grady commented.

"It's not that. I'm more surprised than anything. David was never girl crazy, not the way some of his pals were. He always seemed to have to get to know a girl well before any serious dating began."

"I don't call going out for a soda serious dating. Don't worry about Mona. She's got a good head on her shoulders, and she comes from a very straight-arrow family. David could do a lot worse, and Mona will help him get acquainted. Most of the young people their age are off at school, but there's usually a gang of them around on the weekends.''

"I'm not worried. At least, I don't think I am.'' Heaving a weary sigh, Kirsten sat down on the sofa. She was beginning to feel the effects of the long trip, and she was experiencing something of a letdown. Their "adventure" was behind them; now came the serious business of getting acclimated to a new place, new circumstances. She had thought she was ready for a change, but perhaps the change should have been less drastic than this.

"You sure look worried about something,'' Grady said. He sat down beside her, very close, and took her hand in his.

"It's just that everything feels so...strange,'' she admitted. "I guess you don't understand.''

"Oh, I think I do. This isn't exactly an orthodox arrangement.'' The smile he gave her was sympathetic and encouraging. "I'm hoping you'll be able to relax and not try too hard. It's bound to take some time to discover what it is you want. I'll do my best to make it easy for you.''

Kirsten smiled weakly. If he really wanted to make it easy for her, she thought, he wouldn't be sitting so close to her or holding her hand so warmly. He was such a wonderful man, charming and reassuring, and she had been lonely this past year. That was a dangerous combination. She would have to be constantly on guard, making sure her head, not her emotions, governed her decision.

"For instance,'' Grady went on, "these are bachelor quarters, pretty cramped for three people. This past week I've given some thought to adding on another bedroom and bath.''

"Oh, Grady, not for us. Please don't do anything so permanent and expensive for us. David will be going off to school, and I..." She faltered.

"And you, of course, don't know what you'll be doing."

"Well, no. How could I? I just got here. Everything's so uncertain. Besides, would you want to go to all that expense with Dallas hanging over your head?"

Grady laughed lightly and shook his head. "Why is it so easy for me to forget all about Dallas?"

Kirsten looked at him thoughtfully. "How do you really feel about that promotion? Do you want it?"

"I don't know. I honest to God don't know. It seems like I should want it, if you know what I mean. I'm flattered as hell that Vanessa would even consider me, but I'm not a big-city type. I'm not a coat-and-tie man, either, and I'm sure you remember how easily I get that penned-up feeling. I've always been content with what I have here, and I'm even more so now that you and David are in the picture."

"Could you turn it down?"

"I suppose I could."

"Would you?"

Again the little laugh and shake of his head. "I don't know. Talk about indecisiveness."

"Grady," Kirsten said softly, "will you promise me something?"

"If I can."

"Promise me that if the time comes for a decision, you won't let me or David influence it a bit."

He looked at her in astonishment. "How can I promise that, Kirsten? You know what I want. I've been completely honest about that. I want the three of

us to be a family. How could I not let my family influence that big a decision?''

"Oh, Grady, I . . ." Her shoulders rose and fell. "I
just wish—''

"And I just wish you would let tomorrow take care
of itself. I'm not going to pressure you, and I'm not
going to pounce." He grinned in his irresistible way.
"Unless you call kissing pouncing. I seriously doubt
that I'll be able to keep from kissing you." As if to
punctuate that remark, he leaned forward and did just
that—kissed her soundly and deeply.

It was only the fusion of two pairs of lips, Kirsten
reminded herself, but when Grady kissed her, the action seemed brand-new and magical, something that
only they had discovered. For a minute she reveled in
the desire that the sensible side of her nature normally would deny her. When Grady broke the kiss, she
opened her eyes. His own, she saw, reflected a mix-
ture of lust and merriment. "You only confuse me
more with that kind of carrying-on," she confessed.

"The confusion won't last long, Kirsten. When it
clears up, I'm banking on your feeling the way I do—
that we belong together, that it was a mistake to ever
let it end. But I take full blame for that."

"I don't think you're nearly as sure about us as you
want me to believe. I don't see how you can be.
There's not much of the old me left. Sometimes I'm a
stranger even to myself." She got to her feet. "It's
been a long day, and I'm very tired. Would you mind
terribly if I toddle off to bed?"

Grady stood, too. "No, you really do look tired.
Sleep in tomorrow if you feel like it. I'll wait up for
David."

Kirsten smiled. "It's been some time since anyone waited up for David."

"Well, he'll have to humor me. I'm new at this parenting business."

"You'll do all right. Good night, Grady."

"Good night."

For a long time after Kirsten had left the room, Grady sat on the sofa, hands clasped on his knees, thinking. She had forced his thoughts back to Vanessa and Dallas. He had played the ostrich too long.

There was more to consider than merely a change of locale and a new job description. The promotion would mean an entirely different way of life, and not one that was compatible with his basic nature. He recalled the Vanessa he had first met—when she had been younger. She had been a whirlwind of energy and channeled that energy in so many directions that Grady had often wondered how she remembered where she was supposed to be at any given minute. Hamilton House received the lion's share, of course, but there had always been enough left over for civic, charitable and political activism. Several prominent politicians owed her their careers; one prestigious museum owed her its existence. Once Grady had jokingly asked Vanessa if her secretary had had to schedule her private times with Stuart, and he had been astonished when she had seriously answered, "Just about. If we had left them to chance, they probably wouldn't have happened."

What a way to live, had been his immediate thought, and his opinion hadn't changed appreciably through the years. As much as he admired the Hamiltons, as much as he owed them, he never once had even fleetingly experienced the desire to be like them.

Now there was a one in three chance that that kind of life would be offered to him. Anyone else would have been thrilled; he was just uncertain.

He wondered why he didn't simply call Vanessa, thank her from the bottom of his heart, then ask her to please remove him from consideration. This couldn't have come at a worse time. In another year or two he might be more receptive, but right now his main goal in life, his main challenge, was to convince Kirsten she should be with him. And he was beginning to realize it might take a heap more convincing than he'd imagined.

Odd, he thought. Kirsten would be perfect in Dallas. It was a life she could slip into as easily as she put on a new dress. And Grady had been around enough corporate wives to know there were many who assumed responsibility for all the extracurricular pursuits that came with their husbands' jobs, freeing the man to concentrate on business. Such an arrangement was a team effort, with each partner having a realm of responsibility. Kirsten would be a real asset in a situation like that. She could run interference and keep him from making a total ass out of himself on occasion.

Grady chuckled under his breath and rubbed his eyes. Kirsten had been back nine hours, and he already had them in Dallas, her a civic leader and himself the C.E.O. of Hamilton House. He'd best back up and take some of his own advice—let tomorrow take care of itself.

And fervently hope that Vanessa would chose either Matt or Paula. That would be the easy way to solve his dilemma. Let someone else solve it for him. What a cop-out.

CHAPTER ELEVEN

THE NEXT DAY Kirsten suffered an anxiety attack, although she wouldn't have thought to call it that. She woke feeling nervous and shaky, unable to eat, and she was overcome with the need to cry buckets of tears. Though she managed to keep the tears in check, her head throbbed painfully. She told Grady she thought she'd picked up a bug during the trip, but he knew better. Burning bridges could be a traumatic experience. He was completely understanding.

"Stay in bed and rest today," he suggested. "I'll make you some weak tea and toast, and we'll see how your stomach tolerates that."

She slept the better part of two days, rousing herself only now and then to nibble on something bland. But on the third morning she woke feeling curiously refreshed. She dressed hurriedly and went into the kitchen, where Grady and David were having a delicious-smelling breakfast of ham and waffles.

"In case anyone's interested," she announced, "I think I'm going to live."

"Hungry?" Grady asked.

"Only starved."

She ate ravenously while Grady looked on. He was so relieved that he felt a little shaky himself. He had feared Kirsten's spell with the blues, or whatever it had been, would send her running back to New York before he'd even had a chance to work some magic. Long after David had gone to join Ramon in the fields, he stayed with her, talking to her until he had satisfied himself that the blues truly were gone, that she really did feel as pert and chipper as she assured him she did. It was the last time he would have cause to worry about her state of mind.

The days came and went, one after another, and Kirsten spent them doing exactly as she wished. The weather was not so hot now, so the mornings were wonderful for taking long walks, sometimes with David's Walkman plugged in her ear, sometimes with only her own thoughts for company. She read everything she had been meaning to and then some, and she took up cooking. On the days when Grady made his rounds in town, she always accompanied him, delighting in how easily one could get acquainted in a place like Culver. Sometimes on Friday nights they attended high school football games, and often on Saturdays they drove to Jackson for shopping and dinner. Most evenings they simply sat and talked. Grady had a burning desire to know everything about David's life from birth on, so Kirsten, to the best of her ability, tried to recall all the little details.

It was the simplest sort of life, and the best part of it all was that no one cared that her name was Patrick. What did that mean in Culver, Mississippi? Here people only cared that she was Grady's "lady friend," a woman from his past who spoke with a Yankee accent. At last she was free of the stultifying restraints that being a Long Island society matron had imposed on her. Most of all, she no longer, neither consciously nor subconsciously, sought anyone's approval. She no longer made "appropriate" conversation. She could simply be herself, and herself, she decided, wasn't a bad person to be.

Gradually, her former life became something that seemed to have happened in the dim, distant past. She certainly didn't miss it. Only a long, enthusiastic letter from Denise put her back in touch with it, but the letter had come from England and was full of London and Raymond Billingsley, so Kirsten's thoughts when she finished reading it were more on her good friend than on "home."

Most of all, she delighted in the changes she saw in David. She didn't think she had ever seen him so contented. With time to consider exactly what their lives had been like thus far, she realized that this was the first time her son had not been striving to be the best at something—sailing, polo, track...whatever. In high school, he had been driven to be at the top of his class so he would be accepted by Harvard. Apparently once he'd gotten there, the whole nerve-frazzling process had started all over again.

Once, when they were alone, Kirsten had asked him just what there was about the life in Culver that appealed to him so. She was curious.

"I don't know, Mom. I can't even describe the feeling I have when I get out of bed in the morning. It's...just great. You're looking better than I've ever seen you, and that makes me feel good. Getting to know Dad and, more importantly, getting to like him has been..." David shrugged, at a loss for words.

"And, of course, Mona Cuellar has nothing to do with it," Kirsten said with a knowing smile. For a split second she would have sworn David actually blushed.

"She's the first female friend I've ever had. I don't know why we get along so well, but she's not like any other girl I've ever known. She's just so...nice. No pretense. And she knows how to talk about something other than what she's going to wear Saturday night.''

''Grady says her father's very strict with her.''

David's brow furrowed. ''That's the understatement of the year.''

''How does he feel about your blossoming friendship?''

''Hard to say. But Ramon likes me, I can tell that much. Maybe when Mona and I go off to school, we can get to know each other better. I hope so. Dad tells me to be patient and it'll happen.''

David's early infatuation with Grady hadn't been a fluke. Father and son grew closer every day. It often amazed Kirsten that the three of them—she, Grady and David—had so easily established this pleasant, compatible coexistence. They lived in rather close quarters but never got in one another's way. It seemed to her that it should have been more difficult, what with different temperaments to be accepted, various likes and dislikes accommodated and personality quirks adjusted to. Maybe Grady had done all the adjusting. For her it had been so easy. It was like playing house.

So, of course, it couldn't last. Changes would have to come. She and Grady would either have to expand their relationship or let it wither on the vine. She often caught him looking at her in a way that made her heart pound, and there was a lot of gentle touching and light kissing. This, she understood, was their courtship period, and Grady conducted it masterfully. He never pressured for more than platonic cohabitation, though every look, every touch clearly told Kirsten he wanted much more. She sensed he was poised, just waiting for her to give him a sign.

What she didn't understand was why she didn't go on and give him that sign. She hadn't been in his house more than a week when she realized that Grady touched her on some deep emotional level that hadn't been touched before. Many times she actually felt something passing between them, a kind of charged energy, and she spent many sleepless hours in bed at night, thinking about him and wondering. She'd never been one for fantasizing, but she easily fantasized about him. He was so appealing, so easy to be with, so patient, and there did seem to be something potent there.

Then she would turn around and worry that her newfound sense of well-being, of freedom, might be clouding her judgment. Maybe the true bond was David, and if that was the case, would it last once he was gone? Was there enough between them this time to prevent them from separating? Perhaps she should give the arrangement a few months, then go back to New York, see old friends and old places, and make her decision from there.

But each morning, she would wake, dress and go into the kitchen, where she always found Grady in his fresh, starched khakis, making coffee. He would turn and smile as soon as he heard her. She would smile back and reach into the refrigerator for the pitcher of orange juice. The day would begin much the way the day before had, and nothing at all would be resolved in her mind.

Theirs was anything but a conventional relationship, all the more reason to marvel that it made her so happy. What was there about living under the same roof with Grady that made her feel refreshed, revived and vital? And was it fair of her to take so much happiness and give nothing in return?

After weeks and weeks of this sort of ruminating, Kirsten asked herself some point-blank questions.

Did she want to leave?

No.

Was it Grady or the place, the atmosphere?

It was Grady. Their rapport grew daily. She looked forward to seeing him at the end of the day. Being with him had become as natural as drawing her next breath. If he was to leave, she would be miserable. There was no getting around it—she had fallen for him all over again.

How strange, she thought. She had imagined that when her decision came it would be the result of a sudden flash of insight, a burst of realization, a moment of truth. Or perhaps there would be a passionate outpouring that neither of them could stem. Instead, it had come on insidiously, without her even knowing it was happening. He had done what he set out to do. She loved him again.

Once she accepted that, she began looking at him with new eyes. Everything he said to her took an intimate turn. His movements, she now noticed, were blatantly sexy. Those nighttime fantasies of hers became decidedly erotic.

So what was she waiting for?

IT WAS Friday afternoon. David returned to the house much earlier than usual, far ahead of Grady, and announced he had been invited to the Cuellars' house for dinner; afterward he and Mona were going to a movie. Something clicked in Kirsten's head. That night she and Grady would, for the first time, have considerably more than an hour or two alone. The thought sunk in, took hold and wouldn't let go. Perhaps this was what she had been waiting for—time. Enough time to turn an evening into an occasion, to create a certain mood . . . to just see what could happen.

While David got dressed for his evening out, Kirsten decided what she would prepare for dinner. She still was something of a novice in the kitchen, so she stuck with simple things—salad, chicken breasts, rice and some of those tiny green beans David had brought in from the field yesterday. Having decided on the menu, she went into her room to change before Grady arrived.

It was odd how little clothes had come to mean to her, she mused as she riffled through her closet. Mostly she dressed for comfort—in jeans, slacks and such—and she'd half forgotten she owned some of the things she saw hanging there. Several items were considered and dismissed. Finally, she chose a silky white blouse and a border-print skirt and began getting dressed.

At six o'clock David stuck his head in the door to tell her he was leaving. "Hmm, you look nice. Are you and Dad going out?"

"No. Isn't he home yet?"

"Nope."

"Well, have a nice time."

"I ought to be home shortly after midnight. That's Mona's curfew." He went off whistling, and a minute later Kirsten heard the front door open and close.

More minutes ticked by. She was giving herself a misting of cologne when she heard the door again. "Kirsten?" Grady called.

"I'll be right there," she called back, then scrutinized her image one last time in the mirror and stepped out into the hall. When she entered the living room, Grady was standing in the center of it, reading the front page of a newspaper. He glanced up and smiled, then did a double take.

"Uh-oh," he said sheepishly. "Did I forget something?"

"Forget something?"

"Are we supposed to go somewhere tonight?"

Kirsten chuckled. "Can't a woman put on a skirt without everyone thinking it's a grand occasion?"

He looked her over, up and down. "You look great, Kirsten. Maybe I should take you somewhere."

"I don't want to go anywhere. I already have dinner planned." With a grin she added, "And you know how we serious cooks hate having our plans changed."

Grady folded the paper and laid it on the coffee table. "All right, we'll stay home. Where's David?"

"He'll . . . be gone all evening. Dinner and a movie with Mona. He'll be home shortly after midnight." Without making eye contact with him, she left the room and went into the kitchen.

Grady stared after her. He felt as though he'd been hit in the chest with a sledgehammer. Was it wishful thinking on his part, or were signals being sent? David was going to be gone all evening. Kirsten had gotten all prettied up and didn't want to go anywhere. His heart began to pound like crazy.

Then reason intervened, and he cautioned himself. He could be reading a hell of a lot more into this than existed. Kirsten might simply have felt like putting on a skirt for a change. There hadn't been much occasion for her to dress up since coming here; maybe she missed that sort of thing. As for not wanting to go anywhere, Culver wasn't exactly bursting with scintillating nightlife.

But just in case... Grady cleared his throat. "Ah...do I have time for a shower?"

"Of course," Kirsten called. "There's no hurry about dinner, or anything else, for that matter. We have all evening."

"So we do," he muttered under his breath as he all but sprinted down the hall to his room. The shower was just what he needed, and tonight he kept the water a few degrees cooler than he normally liked it. *Control, my good man. Don't build yourself up for a big letdown.*

Yet, he'd noticed some subtle changes in Kirsten during the past few weeks, a certain mellowing. She had adapted to life here far better than he would have dared hope. She seemed to actually enjoy Culver, and he didn't think that stemmed merely from the novelty of "slumming." Unless he completely misread her, she was genuinely glad to see him at the end of every day. It probably was crazy to say, but she seemed to be seeing him through new eyes.

His gut instincts were working overtime. There had been a look in her eyes—not seductive, exactly, not a come-hither type of thing. That wouldn't be Kirsten's style. It had been...receptive? He allowed himself the hope that tonight they'd finally get this frustrating relationship off the ground. They'd move backward, forward, something.

If he did say so, he'd been magnificent... as well as gracious, gallant and smooth. Grady grinned as the adjectives tripped through his mind and the water's stinging spray pummeled his body. But, for heaven's sake, how long could a man stay damned near saintly? Especially when the beautiful woman he adored was always around, filling up the house with her presence, her scent, her violet eyes and soft, sweet smile. He honestly didn't know how he had kept his hands off her. No Lochinvar on a white steed, no slayer of dragons could have pulled off the courtly routine better than he had, but enough was enough. It was time for a change.

He shaved, splashed himself with after-shave, then put on tailored trousers and a polo shirt. By the time he stepped out into the hall, he was wishing for the moon and prepared for anything.

Kirsten had set the table with a cloth instead of place mats, with matching napkins instead of paper ones. She was seated on one of the stools at the breakfast bar, legs crossed, sipping a glass of wine. Her eyes brightened when he appeared. "Hmm, you look nice."

"Thanks."

"Can I get you a drink?"

"I'll do it."

Once he'd mixed a Scotch and water, Grady carried it to the bar, straddled the stool next to Kirsten and simply looked at her for a minute, his expression both pleased and speculative. The air between them was charged with... what? Not tension. She looked completely relaxed, bemused, slightly pensive, and if he wasn't exactly relaxed, he certainly wasn't tense. He guessed what he felt was a kind of pleasant expectation.

"You're staring," Kirsten finally said.

"I'm a man. It's hard not to stare at you, Kirsten."

"But didn't your mother ever tell you . . ." Her eyes fell in dismay. "Oh, God, Grady, I'm sorry."

"Hey, don't be." He reached to touch her arm. "That kind of thing just rolls off my back. I'm an orphan. I've always been an orphan. I can say it with no more trouble than I can say I have hazel eyes. I promise, my hang-ups have all been laid to rest."

"Still, it was thoughtless of me." Flustered, Kirsten took a minute to recover. "So . . . how was your day?"

"Unremarkable. Yours?"

"The same, and the more unremarkable my days are, the better I like them."

"You don't miss . . . the other place?" Grady studiously avoided ever referring to Long Island as Kirsten's home. The next time she mentioned home, he earnestly hoped she would mean here.

"No," she said simply.

"Sure?"

"Of course I'm sure."

It occurred to Grady that he hadn't touched his drink. He took two quick swallows, then faced her again. "So tell me . . . have you been reasonably happy here? Reasonably content?"

Kirsten had lifted her glass to her lips. Now she smiled at him over its rim. "Much more than reasonably so. The time I've spent here has been wonderfully rejuvenating."

Hope swelled inside Grady. "Would you say it's been better than you thought it would be?"

"Much better . . . and easier. I expected to find living with you difficult. It isn't."

"Have I been a good boy?"

Kirsten laughed lightly. "You've been marvelous."

"Has my conduct been exemplary?"

"Yes, I think exemplary describes it perfectly."

"And you have no reason to fault me on any score?"

"Not one that I can think of."

"Doesn't that kind of behavior deserve a reward?"

"I'm sure it does." She glanced down at the amber liquid in the glass she held. When she lifted her head again and her eyes met his, her smile was almost elfin. "So I suppose the only thing left to determine is just what form the reward should take."

Oh, boy! Grady took another hefty swallow of his drink. A man would have to be incredibly dense not to feel that something momentous was about to occur. He set his drink down and turned to her. She was smiling at him in a most beguiling way.

"Grady, you seem terribly agitated about something."

"I am. Well, not agitated, exactly. Excited. Kirsten, look at me."

"I am looking at you."

"These vibes I'm getting. Are they...real?"

"Absolutely."

He swallowed hard. "When...did it happen?"

"Does it matter?"

"Not a bit." Grady reached across the small space that separated them, took her free hand and deftly pulled her off her stool and onto his lap. She almost spilled her wine all over both of them. Removing the glass from her grasp, he set it beside his on the bar. Then he settled her into the cradle of his lap with arms made for her and began to shower light kisses along her jawline and the underside of her chin.

"If it's been easy for you, it's been damned difficult for me," he murmured between nibbles. "Having you here all the time and not having you at all. Just waiting for you to make some kind of move, give me a sign. Once or twice I even considered bribing David to take a powder so we could be alone."

Little bubbles of pleasure rippled in Kirsten's throat. "Why didn't you?"

"Oh . . . I guess I questioned the propriety of all but telling him I wanted to make love to his mother."

Grady's mouth captured hers in a searing kiss. And he couldn't stop kissing her. Each time they drew breaths he had to kiss her again. The arm around her shoulders pulled her more tightly against him. His other hand moved along the length of her, from the side of her breast to her waist and down the lustrous fabric of her skirt, feeling the shape of her thigh underneath. The stool swiveled, and he began rocking her, back and forth, back and forth, lulling her into a state of mindless euphoria. Then he lifted his head and smiled down at her half-closed eyes, her tiny purrs of contentment. "I love you, Kirsten, just like before. I was pretty sure I did, but after weeks of living in this house with you, now I'm damned sure of it."

"You knew this would happen, didn't you?" she murmured without opening her eyes. "You knew if you got me here, this would happen."

"Let's just say I hoped. I thought there was a chance. I felt there was something still there."

Kirsten nestled her head deeper into the curve of his neck and sighed. "I don't want to leave this place. I don't want to leave you."

"I don't think I could let you go if you did." He continued rocking back and forth, kissing her softly, rubbing and petting, waiting. She was so soft and warm, and he was becoming uncomfortably heated.

Though desire simmered just beneath the surface, Kirsten at that moment felt nothing but pure bliss. She wiggled deeper in his lap, unwittingly eliciting an elemental response in Grady that caused him to feel strangled. "If you thought it might happen, even would happen, I confess I didn't. I didn't see how it was possible for two people to come together after so many years and feel so much for each other," she confessed dreamily. "It seemed pretty farfetched. I told myself I was only taking the haven you offered, but . . . I love you, Grady. Just like before."

The knot in the pit of Grady's stomach tightened. "Do you remember 'before' now?"

"Quite a bit, yes."

"It was magic, wasn't it?"

"I seem to recall that . . . yes, it was magic."

He stood up, keeping her cradled in his arms. "Let's see what we can do about finding some of that magic now."

She linked her arms around his neck and sighed shakily. "I'm in your hands."

My, God, Grady thought. *At last! At last it's going to happen!* He wondered if he could actually put one foot in front of the other and propel them forward. Somehow he managed, pausing for a second when he came to the door of his room, then carrying her into it.

As he set her on her feet, his arms went around her with a need that bordered on desperation. There were few words, almost no preliminaries. Grady had thought of this moment a hundred times, had lived and relived it in his mind a hundred different ways.

Now that it was upon him, he thought he would burst with anticipation. He quickly stripped off her clothes, then his, and took her in his arms again. Her body was still taut, her breasts high and firm, and her skin felt very warm and velvety. He led her to the bed and guided her down onto a thick comforter that billowed around her naked body. The heat that had threatened to consume him earlier subsided somewhat. Now that she was his, he had to explore every perfect inch of her, which he did with agonizing slowness.

Kirsten lay back and allowed him the luxury of caressing her. Grady's mouth and fingers continued their exquisite torture until Kirsten felt she could no longer breathe. When she was sure she couldn't endure the delight another minute, she reached for him and crushed him to her. She felt him shudder and heard him take a deep, quivering breath, then all control vanished. She arched, wrapped her legs around him and forced him to enter her. Kissing, biting, nipping, fondling, they ached for release but fought it, neither wanting the delicious sensations to end, and through it all, Grady remained eager and hard inside her. Only when their passion had carried them to the edge of exhaustion did they let go. It was a great, surging rush, exploding from him in ecstatic bursts, from her in pulsating waves. When it was over, Grady knew the greatest peace of his life.

Kirsten did not know how long they lay entwined in each other's arms, neither saying a word. Her skin tingled, and her bloodstream sizzled with life. Now she remembered. She had been loved this way before, during the few short months they had been together prior to his leaving for the war. It was so unlike anything she had experienced with Travis. She closed her eyes and cast her mind back as far as she could, back to the night she'd first seen Grady at that dance. Amazingly, she began to relive every single minute they had spent together before he'd left. She smiled against his chest; in fact, even her bones seemed to be smiling. She felt wonderful.

She also felt hungry. Stirring, she raised herself up on one elbow so she could look down at Grady. He was smiling, too. "I'm starved," she announced. "And I haven't done the first thing about dinner."

"Just whip up something," he said drowsily.

"I don't know how. I either have to do something really simple that no one could screw up, or I have to follow a recipe verbatim."

"Then I'll whip up something. I'm hungry, too—hungrier than I've been in a very long time."

LESS THAN HALF AN HOUR later, Kirsten was devouring a dish of uncertain composition that had to be the most delicious thing she had ever eaten. "You amaze me," she told Grady. "You just throw these things in a skillet, and it comes out tasting like this. It's terribly distressing that the man of the house can cook so much better than the lady of the house."

Grady reached out to tuck an errant strand of hair behind her ear. "Are you going to be the lady of the house on a permanent basis . . . or were you only after a roll in the hay?"

She shot him a look of mock indignation. "Do I look to you like a woman who would only be after a roll in the hay?"

"Does that mean yes?"

"Of course it means yes. When you carried me down that hall, I knew I was making a commitment."

Grady swallowed hard. "I love you."

"I love you, too, Grady. I really do."

They talked the night away. Grady was due in Dallas the week after next. When he returned, they would make arrangements to get married within a few days. Until then, it was agreed that, with David in the house, they would keep to separate bedrooms. A modern nineteen-year-old would, they guessed, be fairly blasé about sex, but perhaps not so when his mother was involved. "I'll just have to start coming home for lunch," Grady told her with a wicked grin. They talked and laughed and hugged until almost midnight, then shared a lingering kiss in the hallway before going off to sleep in their respective beds. Just before drifting off into sound slumber, Kirsten heard David come in and bound up the steps to the loft. Tomorrow, she thought sleepily, her son was going to be a very happy young man.

But at some point during the night, long before sunrise, she woke to the feel of Grady's hands sliding across her skin. At first she though it was a dream, another of the wildly erotic fantasies she had been having of late, and she gloried in the out-of-mind feel of what he was doing to her. What wonders would her mind conjure up this time? Stretching, she snaked her body into a curve and waited for the sensations to come.

Then she felt his lips on hers, felt the slight scratch of stubble against her chin and knew it was no dream. What dream kiss included stubble? His arms reached under her, and she felt her nightgown being pulled over her head. His legs wrapped around her. She purred with pleasure as he entered her. There was time for nothing but responding and reacting, which she did ardently. She was the most fortunate of women, she fully realized, to be able to relive the once-in-a-lifetime madness of first love.

Of course a certain amount of decorum would be called for. They would have to be discreet because of David, but there would be moments. She and Grady had been handed that rarest of all gifts, a second chance. And this time around they were going to have that beautiful life they had been robbed of before.

She could not have dreamed that, many miles away, there were forces at work designed to destroy her idyll.

CHAPTER TWELVE

ISAAC IRVING normally conducted his investigations in a totally detached manner, never knowing or caring why his clients wanted the information he gathered. But in the case of Kirsten Janice Marshall O'Connor Patrick, he was intrigued, first because it was T. G. Patrick himself who wanted her checked out, and second, because he couldn't figure why old T.G. would be so interested in someone with such an unremarkable background. Kirsten, it seemed to Isaac, was about as average as they came. Which was why the investigator burned some midnight oil in his Jackson motel room, poring over the information he had thus far obtained.

Kirsten Marshall's had been the typical middle-class upbringing of an only child with a widowed, working mother. All through school she had been well liked and a good student, though not an exceptional one. Like legions of other young women who couldn't afford college, she had gone to business school after high school and later had taken a secretarial position with a large company. Then had come marriage to an Air Force pilot and six months of living with him at Barksdale Air Force Base in Louisiana. When his squadron was sent to Vietnam, she returned to her mother's, in Jackson, where she bore a son. Once the baby was a little older, she rented an apartment for the two of them and returned to work for her former employer, leaving the baby with his grandmother during the day.

At that point the account became sketchy, mostly because the people who could have helped with the investigation weren't available. Apparently Kirsten had not become close to any of her co-workers during her second tenure of employment. The apartment house where she and her son lived had been razed long ago. Her mother was no longer alive, and most of the people who had lived in their old neighborhood were also gone. Isaac managed to find one woman who had known the Marshalls casually, and she seemed to remember that something awful had happened to Kirsten's husband, but she couldn't remember what it was. A subsequent check of the county court records revealed, not a death as Isaac had expected, but Kirsten's divorce from Grady O'Connor in the fall of 1974, just about the time she had gone to work for the resort where she had met Travis Patrick.

Isaac suspected the divorce was the one piece of information that would interest T.G. above all. Still, he wasn't entirely satisfied with his investigation. There was more than a three-year gap when almost no information about his subject was available, and Isaac didn't like gaps. For instance, what had the husband been doing from the time his squadron was due to return from the war until the divorce? The investigator decided to retrace his steps the following morning.

His second visit to the neighborhood where Kirsten had grown up unearthed a real find—an elderly woman named Eve Bishop. Not only had Eve known the Marshalls well, she was willing to talk about them. It was she who informed Isaac that Grady O'Connor had been a POW, which helped close the three-year gap, but that wasn't the information that so arrested the investigator's attention. Eve, as most people were wont to do, continued to talk long after he'd stopped asking questions. She had, she told him, encountered Kirsten, her son and O'Connor less than two months earlier. "Right here," she said. "Right on this street. They came by to look at the house Kirsten grew up in. Oh, they looked so marvelous! It was good to see them together again. I always thought the divorce was a mistake. They should have given it more time."

"So Mr. O'Connor still lives here in Jackson?" Isaac probed.

"No, he works in a place called Culver, less than an hour's drive from here. He's done very well. Are you familiar with the Hamilton House restaurants? That's who he's with. Something of a big shot, I take it."

Isaac was certain he now had all the information T.G. wanted, but something compelled him to pursue the matter one step further. Grady O'Connor was alive and well, and instinct told the investigator that Kirsten Patrick now was with him. That might prove to be interesting, the icing on the cake. All that was left was to visit the place called Culver. It shouldn't be difficult to find out about a "big shot" in a small town. Experience had taught Isaac that small town residents loved to talk about their fellow citizens. What else did they have to do for entertainment?

"I'M TELLING YOU, Grady," Rosemary said, "nobody famous has ever come from around here. As far as I can tell, nobody famous has even driven through Culver. And I checked with a couple of entertainment booking agencies. Anybody big enough to draw a

crowd is not going to do a show in Culver. Even if
someone would, it would be too expensive to be...
What's it called? Cost-effective? So we can scratch all
those grand plans about making a bundle with a
show."

Grady and Kirsten had stopped in at Slick's for
coffee and, as usual, had fallen into conversation with
Rosemary and Loretta. "Well, Rosie, that's too bad,"
Grady said. "I guess we'll just have to keep on keep-
in' on, doing what we've been doing. The interest
rate's pretty good now, so the money we've already
made is making some more. We'll get enough one of
these days."

"Yeah," Loretta chimed in, "but the people who've
already donated are beginning to grumble about seeing
something for their money."

"Then I guess it's time to run another announcement in the paper, reminding the good citizens how
much we need and how much we've collected." Grady
looked at Kirsten, who had been unusually quiet during the conversation. "What are you so deep in
thought about, sweetheart?"

She snapped out of her daydreaming. "Oh...sorry,
don't mind me. I was just thinking...about nothing
in particular. It's a shame about the show."

Rosemary propped her elbows on the table and
cupped her chin in her hands. "So, when are you guys
getting married?"

"I have to go to Dallas next week," Grady told her.
"When I get back, we'll do it. We'll just hunt up a
justice of the peace and do it."

"Oh, you can't do that!" Rosemary cried in dismay. "The town will expect you to be wed in a blaze
of glory."

"Rosie, this is our second time around," Grady reminded her. "We have a grown son. A big fuss wouldn't be in good taste."

"At least let us give you a party afterward," Loretta suggested, looking at Kirsten. "Bonnie out at the golf club knows how to put on a really nice to-do. Rosie and I will do the whole thing. All you two have to do is show up after you've made it legal."

Grady glanced at Kirsten uncertainly. "I don't know...."

"That's an awful lot of trouble, Rosemary," Kirsten hedged, not knowing how Grady really felt about the suggestion.

"Nothing's too much trouble for Grady," Rosemary said. "Kirsten, you don't know how important this almost husband of yours has been to this town. Fourteen years ago, it seemed like Culver was just going to die on the vine, but now we have what they call a solid economy—"

"Rosie," Grady interrupted gently, "I didn't do any of that. Hamilton House did."

"Whatever."

The tinkling of the bell over the door heralded the arrival of a customer, so Loretta hurried away. Two men at the counter got up and walked to the cash register, which brought Rosemary to her feet. "I've got to get back to work. You guys let us know about the party, hear?"

"Sure, Rosie. See you around." Grady checked his watch. "Speaking of getting back to work, are you about ready to leave, Kirsten?"

"Anytime you are."

"How do you really feel about having a party? We'll have to let the ladies know right away."

"I didn't particularly want a party, but Rosemary and Loretta seem to want to give us one so badly."

"Yeah. Well, we'll sleep on it a couple of days."

Grady pushed his chair back to get to his feet, but at that moment a stranger approached their table. "Mr. O'Connor?" the man asked.

Grady remained seated. "Yes?"

"My name is Ned Evans, and I wonder if I may have a word with you."

"Sure, Mr. Evans. What can I do for you?"

Isaac Irving reached into his breast pocket and withdrew a business card, which he handed to Grady. The investigator had dozens of different cards printed with various names, occupations and addresses, but most of the time when he used an alias, he was Ned Evans from Philadelphia. The name was ordinary enough to be virtually untraceable, and Philadelphia accounted for his accent—his one distinguishing characteristic. His luck, which had served him in such good stead on so many occasions, was holding. Small town cafés were usually good sources of information about local citizens, but to have stumbled onto this one and his quarry in one fell swoop was too good to be true.

"Mr. O'Connor, I'm with ZY Supply Company in Philadelphia, and I'm in the process of scouting desirable locations for my firm's planned expansion. This seems like an energetic community. I made some inquiries of that charming waitress over there, and she suggested I talk to you."

Ever community-minded, Grady got to his feet, stuck out his hand and flashed a welcoming smile. "Grady O'Connor, Mr. Evans. And this is Kirsten Patrick."

Isaac could see that T.G. had been right—she hadn't changed much. He nodded in her direction. "How do you do, ma'am?"

"Have a seat," Grady said, "and tell me how I can help you."

Isaac pulled out a chair and sat down. "I understand you're with Hamilton House."

"That's right."

"And the company is this town's largest employer?"

"The area's largest employer," Grady corrected. "We have six surrounding communities to draw our labor force from." He glanced at the man's business card. "Surgical supplies?"

"Right. The business has grown tremendously in the past ten years. Expansion is a must, but frankly, the cost of expanding in a huge metropolitan area has become prohibitive. We're looking for a place where the cost of doing business is less and the quality of life is better. In particular, we're scouting small, progressive communities located near medium-size cities. I was on my way from Memphis to Jackson when I saw the Hamilton House plant. It occurred to me that this area must have something to offer if a company the size of Hamilton House would invest so heavily here."

Grady was thinking of all the people—the members of the Chamber of Commerce, the bankers, the realtors—who would go into a collective swoon over this. "Well, Mr. Evans, you couldn't do better than Culver. Our local officials are supportive, and so are the residents. I can give you the names of several people who can come up with the facts and figures on the business climate here."

"What about family life?" Isaac asked. "Are you a family man, Mr. O'Connor? Have you raised children here?"

"No. I have a grown son, but he wasn't raised here."

Isaac directed his attention to Kirsten. "What about you, ma'am? Have you raised children here?"

Kirsten laughed lightly. "Almost no one takes me for a Culverite," she said. "Not after I open my mouth."

"You do sound more like my neck of the woods. Are you from the East?"

Kirsten nodded. "New York, although I was raised in Jackson. But I've been gone a number of years. However—" she glanced at Grady briefly "—I'm back to stay now."

"Did business bring you back?"

"No, the gentleman on my right brought me back."

"Kirsten and I are getting married soon," Grady explained.

"Oh? How nice. Congratulations. Now, Mr. O'Connor, let me ask about taxes..."

Grady and "Ned Evans" continued talking for another ten minutes or so. When the stranger finally left, he was armed with the names of Culver's community leaders, as well as with Grady's business card and an invitation to call him anytime he had questions. Isaac also was armed with his icing on the cake, one last bit of information that ought to tie up the loose ends. He blessed his instincts and his incredible good luck. They never seemed to fail him. No wonder he was the best in the business.

ALMOST DAILY NOW, David and Mona had lunch together in the employees' dining room, and then usually took a walk until it was time for Mona to go back to work. There were many benches strategically located around the compound to accommodate strollers, and today, after wandering aimlessly for a few minutes, they sat down on one and lapsed into a companionable silence. One of the things David liked best about Mona was that she didn't feel the need for nonstop conversation. At the moment, however, she had something on her mind.

"Dad had a talk with me last night."

"Oh? What about?"

"You."

David's head jerked toward her. "Me?"

She looked at him with a somber expression. "Uh-huh. He's worried that we're seeing too much of each other. He doesn't want me to take you too seriously."

"What's that supposed to mean?"

Mona looked down at the ground. "He says you're a Harvard man, a sophisticate, a man of the world who's been places I'll never do more than read about. He says that while he's sure you like me, he doesn't want me to start thinking you'll always be around, always be my friend, because chances are you won't. He says right now you're in a new place and don't know many people, but once you're used to being here and you get acquainted, you'll... Well, he says you'll gravitate toward your own kind."

David felt affronted. "My own kind? What's my 'own kind,' for Pete's sake? I can't believe Ramon would say those things to you."

Normally, Mona took the offense where her father was concerned—he was too restrictive, too possessive, too old-fashioned, almost old-world in his thinking. Now, however, she defended him. "Oh, I guess he has my best interests at heart. You don't talk much about your life before you came here, but you've said enough for me to have a broad picture of it. Doesn't much resemble anything I've ever known. The Cuellars are working stiffs, all of us. Probably none of us will ever be anything else, unless my brother actually does go to medical school, which I doubt. We really don't have much in common, you and I. We're from different worlds and all that."

David was all but speechless. Never before, not once, had Mona said or done anything to indicate she thought there were differences between them, and it bothered him tremendously that she apparently did now. "I don't believe I'm hearing what I'm hearing! Class distinction, Mona? That's what you're talking about, you know. Well, believe me, I'm the last guy who'd ever be guilty of practicing that. I had to deal with far too much of that garbage when I was growing up. Please don't let your father's concern ruin things for us."

When Mona didn't say anything, he grew more alarmed. Giving her shoulder a nudge, he forced her to turn to face him. "You're right, I don't talk about my life before here, because to tell you the truth, it wasn't all that great. But now I want to tell you a little story...."

He gave her a capsulized account of growing up in the mansion on Long Island. "You don't know how lucky you are, Mona—that big, close-knit family, all those aunts and uncles and cousins who get together at the drop of a hat. I never belonged, never. Neither did Mom, although she pulled it off better than most people could. We had to be tolerated because of my stepfather's last name, but we never belonged. I always knew that when I was old enough, I would go somewhere else, do something else. Finding Dad—and now he and Mom are going to remarry—well, it's just the best thing that ever happened to me.'' His voice became impassioned. ''And as for just using you to bide my time until I meet other people, that's ridiculous. I wouldn't do that. You're the nicest friend I've ever had. The prettiest, too.''

Mona looked at him shyly. ''Do you mean that?''

''Of course I mean it. I don't say things I don't mean.'' David paused. ''At least I don't anymore. I guess while I was growing up I said plenty of things I didn't mean. Things like, 'It's nice to see you, Mr. Patrick.' It was never nice to see the old goat.''

A small sound came from Mona; David turned to see her giggling. ''Oh, David, I hope you mean it. I've never known many guys, just my brothers and cousins, who don't count. Getting to really know you has been...great. You're the first male best friend I've ever had. I don't know how I would bear it if you left.'' The admission seemed to embarrass her, and she looked away.

David smiled affectionately at her averted head. There was a certain shyness about Mona that appealed to his masculine instincts. ''I'm not going anywhere, except to school, and then we'll be together more than we are now.''

''That's something nice to look forward to.'' Quickly Mona jumped to her feet. ''I've got to get back to work. Don't bother coming with me. I'm going to have to run to hit that clock on time. And, David...please don't tell anyone what I said about

Dad's talk with me. I'm afraid it sounded like I was fishing for reassurances from you.''

"I don't tell anyone the things you and I talk about. I trust you won't tell anyone all that poor-little-rich-kid drivel I was spouting."

"Nobody. See you later."

"Right." David watched her spring off. Talk about a misfit, he thought disgustedly. He hadn't been good enough for the Patricks, but he was too good for the Cuellars. What a load of nonsense. He hated that kind of thing.

It bothered him that Ramon worried about his relationship with Mona, but he didn't know what he could do about it. He guessed they would just have to wait and prove the man wrong. David had never been anything but completely honest with Mona. Knowing her was one of the nicest things about being in Mississippi.

His mom and dad were another. Every time he thought about them getting married again, he got all choked up. And relieved. From day one he had worried that his mom would end up going back to New York, leaving him pulled in two directions. Now that wouldn't happen. The marriage meant she would stay here. David smiled with satisfaction. It also meant that the Patricks would never again intrude on their lives.

T.G. FOUND IT ODD to be studying his daughter-in-law's life in such minute detail. Not that it had been a remarkable life—far from it. The most extraordinary thing, to the patriarch's mind, was that such an ordinary woman could have captivated Travis so.

Isaac's report was thorough, the kind of work one would expect from a high-priced investigator, but it was nothing but so much dry data until T.G. reached the part concerning Kirsten's divorce from Grady O'Connor. His stomach muscles constricted over that one. So they had been duped, after all. While waiting for the results of the investigation, the elderly man had almost convinced himself it couldn't be. The Patricks, on the whole, were far too astute and skilled in both social and business strategies to be taken in by a nobody from the backwoods, no matter how beautiful and clever she was. Kirsten, he'd decided, wouldn't have been able to fool many of them for long. Now, he could see, he had been wrong.

The worst, however, was yet to come. The report's conclusion left T.G. shaking with disbelief and rage. "I was told," Isaac had written, "by O'Connor himself, that he and the subject are getting married soon."

It took some time for T.G. to recover. When he did, he was overcome by a desire for revenge, immediate retaliation. Kirsten could not be allowed to get away with this. He reached for the telephone. When Roger's voice came over the line, he growled, "Get over here right away."

"Of course" was his son's instant reply.

While he waited, T.G. reread the report, not once but twice, scribbling notes in the margins as he did so. He was livid, but in a curious way, learning about Kirsten's duplicity eased the elderly man's mind on one score. For years he had pondered the whys and wherefores of his older son's impetuous marriage. Why, he would ask himself, had Travis mocked the family tradition of marrying only quality and breeding? Had it been a deliberate attempt to cause turmoil within the Patricks' inner circle? Travis, he recalled, had never strictly toed the party line the way Roger so willingly did. Had Travis derived some sort of malicious pleasure out of introducing a peasant into their midst?

In the end, having no clear answer to his questions, the patriarch had simply accepted Travis's obvious obsession with his young wife as the only reasonable excuse. Now he had a better answer. His son, in middle age, had been taken in by an extremely cunning and alluring female. It had happened to better men. For some reason that made T.G. feel better. Masculine frailties were far, far easier for him to understand than blind passion and devoted love.

Less than fifteen minutes passed between the phone call and Roger's appearance in his father's ultra-private inner sanctum. "Something's wrong," he said. It wasn't a question.

"In spades. Sit down and read this."

Roger read Isaac's report with a passive expression. When he finished it, he tossed it onto T.G.'s desk, sat back and rubbed a forefinger over his mouth, seeming deep in thought. Then suddenly, surprisingly, he began to laugh . . . and laugh.

T.G. glowered at him. "I fail to see anything humorous about this."

Roger wiped his eyes as his laughter trickled down to a chuckle. "It's funny, Dad, but I don't mean amusing. It's absurd, incredible. The outsider, the embarrassment, Travis's slap in our collective face managed to pull the wool over all our eyes but good. Where's your sense of the ridiculous? I find it ironic that she was able to do it at all . . . much less for years and years."

"Try to pull yourself together, will you? We need to decide what we're going to do about this."

Roger looked mildly surprised. "Do about it, Dad? What can we possibly 'do' about it? Kirsten's marriage to Travis is fact. She stayed married to him until he died, also fact. She inherited his share of the estate, all very legal. I don't see what we can do about that. If she remarries, we have to buy back her percentage, but we can live with that. Personally, I suppose we should be relieved she apparently intends marrying soon. That will effectively rid us of her once and for all."

"But do you have any idea what her percentage is worth, how much money we'd have to give her in a lump sum?"

Roger frowned his irritation. "I happen to know what the family is worth."

"Do you think I want that money enriching the life of some...fish farmer?" T.G. sputtered.

"I repeat, I don't see what we can do about that. The inheritance is legally hers. If you wanted to contest the will, you should have done it right after Travis died, not now."

"Maybe, but if the marriage was entered into fraudulently, there might be means..." T.G. sat back in his chair and folded his hands across his middle. "Play the devil's advocate for me a minute. Let's explore the collusion theory once more. I'm thinking back to the conversation Constance overheard. The O'Connor fellow said he'd suggested the divorce, that it gave Kirsten and David a chance for 'this kind of life.'"

"That's what Constance said she heard. Who remembers a conversation perfectly? Besides—" Roger indicated the report lying on the desk "—where's any evidence of collusion? From all indications, Kirsten didn't meet Travis until after her divorce.''

''I wouldn't be too sure. According to Isaac's report, she had to go to the resort to be interviewed several times before getting that job. She could have met him then. He liked to brag that he fell for her the first time he set eyes on her. Maybe she knew that and mentioned it to her husband, then they hatched their scheme. Kirsten and O'Connor might have been meeting secretly for years,'' T.G. suggested.

''Again, where's the evidence?''

''Certainly she could have been channeling money in his direction for years. She had her own account, and Travis would never have questioned how she spent it. He also gave her a very handsome allowance.''

''Dad, all of us give our wives very handsome allowances.''

''Yes, but in Evelyn's case, and in Constance's, proof of how they spend theirs is evident everywhere, mostly on their backs. But it seemed to me that Kirsten lived frugally by our standards.''

''What you call frugal others might term sensible.''

T.G. lapsed into silence for a minute, then said, ''She lied about the divorce. That much we know.''

''I doubt a judge would get any more excited about that than if she had lied about her age.''

''She's marrying O'Connor again. That fact bothers me more than anything else. I have this gut feeling that they never lost contact with each other, that they were just biding their time. Statistics considered, Kirsten could have been expected to be a relatively young widow someday.''

''Then why did she and O'Connor wait a year after Travis's death to rendezvous?''

"To squirrel away as much money as she could. For the sake of appearances, to keep us from having suspicions, any number of reasons."

"That's pretty thin, Dad." Actually, Roger was impatient with playing devil's advocate. He, as much as his father, possibly a bit less than Constance but certainly more than his mother, considered Kirsten an affront that his brother had inflicted on the family. Nothing would have pleased him more than seeing her become just a regrettable part of the Patrick legacy, one of those family skeletons nobody ever mentioned. "If you don't mind my abandoning my role, I must say I agree with you right down the line. Something stinks to high heaven. But I still don't think we have a prayer of stripping a widow of her legal inheritance, not without some nasty publicity. You'll never be able to keep it quiet, not if Kirsten chooses to talk. Remember Denise's divorce?"

T.G. visibly shuddered. "That regrettable episode taught me a lesson, dear boy. We jump the gun on her, make it impossible for anything she might say to be news. As for stripping her of her inheritance, that platoon of fancy lawyers we keep on the payroll could strip Peter of his sainthood if they set their minds to it. However, I don't think it will come to that. I doubt that Kirsten would want to become embroiled in a lengthy court battle. I'm hoping that with family consensus behind us, we can simply confront her with what we know, and she'll agree to anything we suggest. Then this whole sorry mess will be behind us."

Roger thought that was hoping for quite a lot. For all of Kirsten's malleable ways, for all her hunger for acceptance and eagerness to please, she possessed a

certain feistiness that she'd never been able to entirely
squelch.

T.G. was all-business. "Muster the troops, Roger.
The first order of business is a family meeting. I want
others' ideas about this. Do we run a background
check on Grady O'Connor? Do we investigate Kirsten's finances while she was married to Travis? I want
everyone here, every last one of them, down to the
cousins. They'll be far-flung, so it'll take some time.
Let's say next Friday. The institute's boardroom at
2:00 p.m."

"Does that include Denise?"

T.G. thought a minute. His daughter was a strange
one. Always had been, even as a child. Though his
sons, particularly Roger, had been fairly predictable,
he'd never known what Denise was apt to do in any
given situation. Her friendship with Kirsten, in the
face of solid family disapproval, was typical. Sometimes T.G. was incensed by her behavior, other times
merely mystified. Always he suspected her of taking
delight in rowing against the current. Obviously, Denise's obstinate uncomformity was a throwback to
some of Evelyn's more undesirable ancestors.

Yet, she was family, a Patrick. "Yes," he said.
"Denise, too. This has to be unanimous, a show of
solidarity. I think even Denise will be taken aback by
her dear friend's skulduggery." The old man smiled
maliciously. "Definitely include Denise."

CHAPTER THIRTEEN

ON MONDAY AFTERNOON, Kirsten regretfully said goodbye to Grady. "I wish you didn't have to go," she said. "Three days will seem forever."

"I wish I didn't have to, either, sweetheart, but duty calls. I'll be coming back on the flight I always take, so that means I'll drive through the front gate just about five o'clock Thursday afternoon."

"It'll be another reunion all over again."

"We'll have a party, just the two of us," Grady said with a wink as he draped an arm around her and kissed her soundly.

Kirsten slipped her arms around his waist. "I'll miss you."

He kissed her again. "I'll miss you, too, sweetheart. I'll try to call tomorrow night, but don't get concerned if you don't hear from me. I never know what Vanessa has in store for me. Take care of yourself. I love you."

"I love you, too."

She sighed sadly as she watched the Cherokee disappear from sight. The rest of the day dragged interminably, as did the evening, and Tuesday was more of the same until Grady called just as she and David were finishing their evening meal. "I can't talk long," he told her. "I'm having dinner with some company people, and I still have to get dressed."

"How are things going?" Kirsten asked.

"I'm one tired soul. The pace here is incredible. The home office is a busy, busy place. Anything new there?"

She chuckled. "What would be new?"

"Nothing, and that's just the way I like it. By the way, it looks like I might not get back until Friday."

"Oh, great," Kirsten muttered.

"Vanessa thinks I ought to visit our operation in the Rio Grande Valley, and she's probably right. I haven't been there in some time. So I won't be flying straight home from Dallas, and I have no idea what the schedules are. I'll do my best to cut it short, but you probably won't hear from me, and there's no way you can reach me down there. It's strictly the boondocks. I guess you'll just have to look for me when you see me coming. It won't be later than Friday, though, promise."

"Well, I'm disappointed, but I guess it can't be helped. As you said, duty calls. Has Vanessa said anything more about . . . you know?"

"Not a word. I guess we really will have to wait for her birthday."

They talked for fifteen minutes, until Grady declared he positively had to start getting ready for his dinner date. After hanging up, Kirsten went into the kitchen and found the dishwasher whirring and David wiping off very clean counters. "What a nice surprise," she said appreciatively.

"It's the least I can do in return for the kind of meals that are served in this place. You're turning into a pretty fair cook, Mom."

"I try, but I'm afraid your father will always be the best cook in the family."

"That was Dad on the phone, wasn't it? What'd he have to say?"

"Not much. He's very busy and might not be home until Friday. He sends his love." Kirsten opened the pantry and took out a jar of instant coffee. "I think I'll have a cup. Want one?"

"No thanks. I sorta promised Mona I'd come over tonight. Are you afraid to stay here alone?"

"Not a bit. There's a night watchman on duty, and the processing plant works around the clock. I don't feel at all isolated."

"Well...if you're sure."

"I'm sure. Go on and have a good time."

Once David had left the house, Kirsten checked to see if there was anything remotely interesting on television, but there wasn't, so she picked up the novel she had been reading. After fifteen minutes she gave that up, too. Her thoughts, she realized, were all on Grady and, unfortunately, on Dallas. Every time it was mentioned, she got a peculiar feeling in the pit of her stomach.

Things were so nice the way they were—peaceful, relaxing. She and Grady had plenty of time to spend together. But everything would change if he got that promotion. The tempo of their lives would accelerate dramatically. She would be forced to spend more than an occasional night or two alone, and when Grady was home, there would be obligations—a lot of them. She wasn't in the least worried that she couldn't handle them with aplomb, but she hoped she wouldn't have to. That kind of life had been left behind in New York, and she didn't miss it at all.

Kirsten did worry about Grady, however. His very nature was at odds with that kind of existence. She couldn't picture him dashing through the door of their bedroom, as Travis often had, peeling off his clothes on the way to the shower and calling over his shoulder, "Formal or informal tonight?" There had been a time when three or four black-tie affairs a week had been the norm. Some people thrived on that kind of life, but she had often found it grueling, and she imagined Grady certainly would. And it definitely robbed a husband and wife of a lot of quality time together.

Kirsten would have cut out her tongue before saying as much to Grady, but she often caught herself wishing that Vanessa Hamilton would give the job to someone else. Perhaps that was selfish, even unconscionable. It wasn't right of her to wish Grady wouldn't get something he obviously deserved, but she couldn't help it. She didn't want to go to Dallas. It was as simple as that.

THE FOLLOWING MORNING Kirsten went into town to do some shopping. When she returned to the house just before noon, the phone was ringing. Dumping her purchases onto the sofa, she answered it.

"Hello."

"Thank God," the voice on the other end of the line said. "I've been calling every fifteen minutes for an hour."

"Denise! How wonderful to hear from you. Where are you?"

"New York, which isn't where I planned to be at all. I was supposed to go to Paris with Raymond today, but I was summoned home by imperial command. *C'est la vie.* Kirsten, are you sitting down?"

Frowning, Kirsten sank into the nearest chair. "I am now. What's wrong?"

"Everything. It has hit the fan, sweetie. The family has found out about Grady."

Kirsten sucked in her breath. "How?"

"I have no idea how they found out in the first place, but Dad hired a private detective and confirmed it. They know he's alive, where he is, and they know you're with him. They also know the two of you are going to marry soon. By the way, congratulations."

"I...I can't even imagine how..." Kirsten rubbed her suddenly throbbing temple, then sighed resignedly. "Well, if they know, they know. There's nothing I can do about it, and it really doesn't make any difference any longer."

"That's what you think. I haven't told you the half of it. When Roger phoned me in London to tell me to get home right away, he was very mysterious. There was no reason given. But Roger came over after I got in last night, and my darling brother couldn't resist gloating. He told me plenty. First of all, they think you lied to Travis about being a widow. Second, they suspect you and Grady of all sorts of evil doings—collusion, for one."

"I...I don't understand. Collusion? Grady and me? In what way?"

"Oh, Kirsten, their imaginations are really working overtime. They're suggesting you and Grady cooked up a quickie divorce so you could marry Travis for his money. I asked Roger if they had proof of that, but all he said was 'It fits.'"

Kirsten gasped. "That's so ridiculous! I hadn't even met Travis when Grady and I split up."

"There's more. They're suggesting you might have been giving Grady money all these years. Again, no proof, but they're considering the possibility of investigating your finances while you and Travis were married."

Kirsten was sputtering. "Let them investigate all they damn well please. I've never heard anything so absurd in my life. If it hadn't been for David, I never would have seen Grady again."

"I know, but I didn't dare defend you. I played dumb as hell because I didn't know what you would want me to tell them. You and Travis both swore me to secrecy, remember?"

"Yes, yes, I remember. But tell them the truth now. Tell them the lie was Travis's idea, tell them the whole story." Kirsten was genuinely upset. She would have sworn she didn't give a flip what the Patricks thought about anything, but she did. It bothered her enormously that they would think her capable of such shenanigans.

"Kirsten, listen to me. Dad and Roger want to believe what they're believing. It's always annoyed Dad that you shared the family wealth equally with Roger and me. Now he thinks he has good cause to do something about it, and Roger is encouraging him every step of the way."

"You've lost me, Denise. What are you talking about?"

Kirsten heard Denise take a deep breath. "Dad's called a family meeting at the institute's boardroom Friday afternoon. Patricks have been summoned from the four corners of the world. Relatives I'd forgotten existed are checking in. Dad wants to be sure everyone is on his side before he makes his next move.

There'll be one dissenting vote, of course—mine. Other than that, I don't know."

Kirsten shook her head in confusion. "Vote? Vote on what? I don't understand."

"A vote to strip you of your inheritance."

Kirsten's mouth dropped. "Is that legal? Can they do it?"

"I don't know," Denise said sadly. "When Dad sets his mind to something, I sure wouldn't bet he couldn't do it, particularly if he has all the Patricks backing him up. His lawyers are awfully smart, and Dad pays them a hell of a lot of money. If there's a way, they'll find it. Dad says your marriage to Travis was entered into fraudulently. It's all I can do to keep my mouth shut."

"It's not fair. Travis wanted me to have that money, and to tell you the truth . . . I was counting on it."

"Really? That surprises me. Knowing you, I half expected you to tell them to take the money and shove it."

Maybe I should, Kirsten thought. *Maybe that would be the smart thing to do. Go out in a flurry of bravado.* "Are you at your house?" she asked.

"Yes," Denise said.

"Will you be there awhile?"

"As far as I know, I'll be here all afternoon."

"I'm going to have to think about this. My brain doesn't seem to be functioning very well at the moment. Let me call you back within the hour."

"Sure. I'll be waiting. Kirsten, I'm awfully sorry about this, and Travis would be horrified. My family gives me such a pain in the butt sometimes."

"Thanks for the call, friend. If it hadn't been for you, I wouldn't have known anything about this until after the fact. Right now, I have some heavy thinking to do."

After she'd hung up, Kirsten sat staring at the phone a few minutes, her thoughts a confused jumble. Gradually, however, they began to sort themselves out. She was a very affluent woman. Would losing the inheritance be that big a deal? True, she'd had some plans for the money, but no one knew about them, not even Grady, so she wouldn't disappoint anyone if she did nothing. Trying to fight the Patricks probably was folly, anyway. Singly, they were powerful; collectively, they might be able to topple parliaments.

Good Lord, T.G. had gone to a lot of trouble to get what he believed to be the goods on her. A private detective, yet! She doubtless had been the easiest case of the investigator's career, since she and Grady had done nothing to conceal their whereabouts or the nature of their relationship. Still, it was unsettling to know that at some time during the past weeks, she had been followed, observed, inquired about. She couldn't imagine who a detective could talk to who would know much about her. She was really acquainted with only a handful of local citizens. But then, everybody knew Grady, and Kirsten imagined they had been the objects of endless gossip.

Sighing, she got to her feet, picked up her packages and carried them to her room. What a time for Grady to be gone, and she had no idea how to reach him. It would have been comforting to hear his thoughts on all this. What to do, what to do?

Give it up, Kirsten, her inner voice said. *There's no way you alone can fight the Patricks, and if you try, you'll just come across as mercenary.*

Maybe, but it didn't seem right not to put up a show of protest, at least. It wasn't the money, although it was rightfully hers. She had been a loving, faithful wife to Travis for a lot of years, and he'd often declared it was his intention to leave her financially beholden to no one. Still, it wasn't the money.

Unfortunately, it wasn't the money for the Patricks, either, she was sure of that. Her thirteen percent was nothing to them. They merely wanted to ram home a point: outsiders were not acceptable and never would be; outsiders had no right to their wealth. Damn them all.

Suddenly Kirsten was aware of hunger pangs. She went into the kitchen to see what was available for lunch, and while she was putting together a sandwich, the phone rang. When she answered it, a masculine voice identified himself.

"Hello, Kirsten, this is Al Daniels with the Chamber of Commerce. Grady introduced us a few weeks ago."

"Oh, yes, Al. How are you?"

"Fine, thanks. I called Grady's office and was told he is out of town."

"Yes, I expect him back no later than Friday."

"And I'm leaving for a chamber convention tomorrow, so will you give him a message for me?"

"Of course."

"Grady called me a few days ago about a fellow named Ned Evans who's scouting locations for his company...ZY Supply in Philadelphia."

Kirsten's mind went blank for a minute, then she recalled the encounter in Slick's. "Yes?"

"Naturally I wanted to follow up on it. That kind of thing would be a real boon to a community like this.

Tell Grady the number he gave me is a nonworking one. You can also tell him that directory assistance couldn't find a ZY Supply Company in the Philadelphia area. Ask him to recheck his information and give me a call sometime late next week. I'd sure hate to see a thing like this slip through our fingers.''

"I'll make a note, Al, and see that Grady gets it the minute he returns.''

"Appreciate it. And while I have you on the phone, I hear that congratulations are in order. That's great.''

"Thanks, Al. That's nice of you.''

Kirsten scribbled the note and placed it near the phone. Then she went back to her sandwich. She hadn't taken more than two bites of it, however, when something went *ping!* inside her head. That nondescript little man in Slick's Café, the one who had engaged Grady in a lengthy conversation about a company that now couldn't be located... Was her imagination getting the best of her or could he possibly have been...?

He must have been! If anyone had been asking around about her and Grady, they would have heard about it. The detective hadn't needed to ask about them; they had told him everything he'd wanted to know.

What had they told him? Kirsten searched her brain and recalled nothing particularly noteworthy. She had told him she was from New York, and Grady had told him they were getting married. That man, Ned Evans or whoever, and Grady had talked for twenty minutes or so, and during that time she probably hadn't uttered more than four or five sentences, but maybe she had told him a lot. Then the Patricks had put two and two together and come up with ten.

Kirsten shuddered. Something in her raged against the invasion of privacy; she not only felt invaded, she felt violated. That the Patricks could have gotten so close to her, could have used an innocent conversation to incriminate her when she had done nothing wrong, infuriated her.

All at once she knew what she was going to do, what she had to do if she ever wanted to look at herself in a mirror again. Her sandwich forgotten, she resolutely marched back to the phone and placed a call to Denise. When her friend came on the line, Kirsten didn't waste time on preliminaries.

"I'm not going to make it easy for them, Denise. Get me a reservation at the Plaza for tomorrow night. What time is the meeting Friday?"

"Two o'clock."

"Better make reservations for Friday night, too."

"Oh, boy!" Denise exclaimed. "This ought to be something."

"It'll be something, all right. I have no intention of rolling over and playing dead. If nothing else, I hope to make that meeting the most uncomfortable one any of them have ever sat through. If you happen to talk to Roger again, just keep playing dumb. I'll call when I get in tomorrow. Will you come to the hotel?"

"You better believe it! I'm anxious to see you again."

"It'll be good to see you, too, Denise. I want to hear all about Raymond and London and everything. I just wish we were meeting under different circumstances."

"Yeah, me, too."

"See you tomorrow. Right now, I have a lot to do."

The first thing Kirsten had to do was make reservations out of Jackson the following morning. Then she had to decide what to take with her. Her image when she walked into that boardroom Friday afternoon was of paramount importance. She cursed Grady's absence, hating that she wouldn't be able to talk to him before she left and wondering what he would think of this action of hers. Even if he was appalled by it, surely he would come to understand in time.

Silently she cursed the Patricks, each and every one of them—except Denise. For years she had bent over backward to please them, to accommodate them, to adapt to their snobbish and antiquated ways. Her thanks was this attempt to rob her of her inheritance. They might succeed, too. She might not be able to do one thing about that, but she planned to make her presence felt. They didn't accept her, but they were going to have to deal with her.

Later that afternoon, when David came home and found her packing, her son was aghast to learn her plans. "Forget it, Mom. Tell the Patricks 'up yours' and forget it. Why do you care about the money, anyway?"

"It's difficult to explain, David. I'm afraid you wouldn't understand."

"I'll bet you've got that right. And I don't think Dad will, either."

"Yes, he will...eventually. If I could get in touch with him, I would, but I can't. So tell him I'll explain everything just as soon as I can."

"How long will you be gone?"

"I don't know. It depends on what happens at that meeting. As things stand now, I have reservations at the Plaza for tomorrow night and Friday."

"I can't believe their filthy old money means so much to you," David fumed.

"It's not just the money, David. There are principles involved here. And there are certain misconceptions I want to straighten out."

"I wish you would drop it."

"I can't."

David wondered just how far she would be willing to pursue this. "Let's say they're able to take away the inheritance. What are you going to do then?"

Kirsten stopped her packing long enough to give it some thought. "I'm not sure. I haven't thought much beyond Friday afternoon. I might fight them. I'd have to talk to an attorney, but if it seems there's a chance of winning, I just might fight them."

"That could take years!" David exclaimed. "What about the wedding?"

Kirsten rubbed her eyes tiredly. "David, please, one thing at a time. I'm very upset and angry right now. Let's deal with each thing in its turn."

David was frightened. To him, everything depended on his mother and father remarrying. That would bring order and stability to their lives. It would keep them together and keep him here. But if his mother went back to New York and got involved in a court fight, there was no telling what would happen to all of them. He shoved his hands into his pockets and shook his head. "I've got a bad feeling about this, Mom. I don't like it one bit. I sure wish we could get hold of Dad," he said worriedly.

PALM TREES, blooming bougainvillea, exotic birds and citrus groves did not fit the popular image of Texas for the average person, but in the Rio Grande

Valley, they could be found in abundance—along with thousands of recreational vehicles and mobile homes sporting license plates from places like Indiana, Illinois, Minnesota and Michigan. The "winter Texans" had begun arriving for their annual stay in the balmy valley. The locals' easy-going friendliness, mañana attitude and the nightlife and shopping in Mexico, across the river, combined to create a haven for midwesterners. Grady loved it. Next to Mississippi, the valley was his favorite spot on earth. And this time it was like an antidote, a welcome relief from the hustle and bustle of Dallas.

He didn't know why the big city had gotten him down so much this time. Normally he flew in, took care of business, then flew out without paying much attention to his surroundings. To him, Dallas meant DFW International Airport, the Anatole hotel and the Hamilton House Building, period. This time, however, as his taxi had pulled out of the airport and headed down the freeway for the hotel, he'd taken a careful look around. *Frenzied* was the adjective that first popped into his head. It reminded him of nothing so much as a stirred-up anthill. Envisioning living and working there had actually depressed him. Kirsten, accustomed to New York, would easily adapt, but he wondered if he ever could. The city's effect on him had been so pronounced that he had come within a whisker of confessing his true feelings to Vanessa and asking her to remove him from consideration.

He hadn't, though, and now that he was in the valley, far removed from the unbelievable traffic and the scurrying throngs of people, he tried to view the promotion from a more detached perspective. It would be an honor, of course, and it would bring him more wealth and clout than he ever would have dreamed of possessing. Plus, there were times when it rather amused him to think of "the farmer" rising to the very apex of the corporation. There were plenty of people within the Hamilton House organization who would be stunned to their toes if the presidential plum was offered to Grady O'Connor.

But that kind of thinking was nothing but whimsical. When he was serious, his thoughts took an entirely different turn. He wasn't the big city type and never would be. He didn't want his days and nights to be filled to the brim with obligations. Everything he truly wanted he already had.

He wished he had more insight to Kirsten's true thoughts about the promotion, about moving to Dallas, about everything. The few times they had talked about Dallas, she had only said, "Wherever you are, Grady, is where I want to be." It was a nice thing to say, the perfect thing, but would she really enjoy that big a change in their lives? She seemed happy and content with their present arrangement. And moving would complicate matters some where David was concerned. Their son was so certain that his future was in Mississippi. Grady guessed what it all boiled down to was he liked things exactly the way they were now.

And he was anxious to return to them. As much as he enjoyed visiting the valley, this time he suffered an acute attack of homesickness. On Wednesday afternoon, several of the company officials gave him the grand tour of Hamilton House's holdings, from McAllen to Harlingen to Brownsville. Wednesday night, nothing would do but they all go across the river to drink tequila and feast on platters of spicy food, which didn't exactly leave Grady at his sparkling best

Thursday morning. By midafternoon he decided he'd seen enough. A company man flew him to San Antonio in his private plane. From there Grady made the quick flight back to Dallas, where—without a minute to spare—he caught a flight to Jackson.

And somewhere high over Louisiana, he made his decision. When he got home, he was going to tell Kirsten they weren't going anywhere. And first thing tomorrow morning, he would call Vanessa and tell her the same thing. It wasn't worth it. Leave the power and wealth to someone else. Either Matt or Paula would enjoy it more and handle it better than he would. All he wanted was Kirsten, David and home.

CHAPTER FOURTEEN

ONCE KIRSTEN REACHED the privacy of her room at the Plaza, she spent the remainder of the afternoon in hibernation. It was a shame, she thought, to be on Fifth Avenue, within walking distance of the finest shopping in the world, and not be able to take advantage of it, but for the time being, it was best not to run the risk of encountering a bunch of Patricks. The Plaza was exactly the kind of place the out of towners would stay, and Bergdorf Goodman was exactly the kind of store they would patronize. She reminded herself that this was anything but a pleasure trip. Accordingly, when Denise got to the hotel, the two women had cocktails in Kirsten's room until it was time to go to dinner.

"You look wonderful, Kirsten," Denise commented. "Like a bundle of fresh air and sunshine."

"I've had plenty of both. And I feel wonderful, too." Her brow furrowed. "At least I did. Before you called, I didn't have a care in the world. Being with Grady again and seeing David looking so fit and happy has been wonderful for me. But this business with the family really has upset me."

"I can imagine—it's upset me, too. And I've got a fresh piece of news for you. From the minute I first learned about the reason for the meeting, my one burning question has been how did it all get started?

Who found out about Grady in the first place? That had never been answered. Then Roger came to see me again. I shamelessly plied him with liquor, and he finally spilled the beans. Dear Constance is behind every bit of this."

"Constance? But how?"

"Remember the Saturday morning that Grady was at your house? Apparently when he and David took a walk they sat down on one of the benches to rest. Constance was on the other side of the hedge. She heard enough to know that Grady is David's dad, and that was enough to call in the private investigator."

Kirsten's eyes closed briefly. "Constance, of all people. It's all beginning to fit. She came to see me that afternoon, which was something that happens once in a blue moon. I had the strangest feeling she was looking for something. Now I know. She was looking for Grady. Oh, I'll bet she's getting the most enormous kick out of all this. I never could understand why she disliked me so much, but there's no denying she did...does."

"Come on, Kirsten. It was jealousy, pure and simple. Travis brought in a wife who was younger and prettier than she was, thereby switching the spotlight off her. I'm afraid she's just dying to be present at your downfall."

"How sad" was all Kirsten could think of to say.

"Sad but true. Now, you're going to need all the ammunition you can get, so I think we ought to go over tomorrow's esteemed gathering one by one. Maybe I can give you some idea what to expect from them. First, Aunt Judith..."

The women talked for more than two hours. Denise had done a fantastic amount of homework. Kirsten couldn't imagine how she had accumulated so much information about so many relatives, many of whom Denise hadn't seen in years. She listened carefully, knowing she couldn't possibly remember everything, hoping she would remember what was important. It was daunting to realize she would be walking into a gathering of mostly strangers, none of whom owed her any allegiance at all. She could feel her resolve crumbling.

"The only nonfamily person present tomorrow will be Nelson Harding," Denise was saying. "That's a plus for you."

Kirsten nodded uncertainly. Nelson was the senior partner of the law firm that handled the Patricks' legal affairs. But more than that, he and Travis had been the closest of personal friends since childhood. Kirsten had always enjoyed a warm social relationship with Nelson and his wife, but she wondered if his loyalty to Travis extended to her. It had not been tested since Travis's death.

"Do you notice anything unusual about the group?" Denise asked when she'd finished her rundown.

Kirsten pursed her lips. "Other than the majority sharing a common last name, no."

"There are twelve widows in the bunch, Kirsten. Count 'em—an even dozen. If we're smart, we might be able to do something with that."

"I can't imagine what," Kirsten said wearily. "My mind is spinning, and I'm starving to death. Enough of this. Maybe after a night's sleep, my brain will start working again. Right now, it's numb." She got to her feet. "I can't take any more of this room. Let's go get something to eat."

"SHE WHAT?" Grady roared. It was after nine o'clock when he at last walked through his front door, bone weary but alive with the anticipation of being greeted by Kirsten. Instead, there was only David...and some startling news.

"She left this morning," David told him. "I've never seen her so mad. I thought after she'd slept on it, she might calm down a little, but I was wrong. I'm not kidding, Dad. She was furious."

Grady couldn't believe it. "Because of the money? It means that much to her?"

His dad looked every bit as distraught as David felt. "I don't understand it, either, and I'll swear she was talking in riddles half the time. She said that principles were involved, that certain misconceptions had to be straightened out. I don't have any idea what she was talking about. All I know is she got a phone call from Aunt Denise. There's a family meeting tomorrow afternoon, and old Mr. Patrick is going to ask everyone to vote to take Mom's inheritance away from her."

"Why didn't she tell all of them to kindly go to hell? She's got plenty of money. She doesn't need that interest check every month."

"I guess Mom didn't tell you. If she remarries, the family is supposed to buy back her percentage from her. I don't know what it would come to. A bunch, I guess. Enough to make Mr. Patrick break out in a rash if he had to fork over that much money to her."

Grady shook his head in dismay. "How did they know she's getting married? That last I heard, Kirsten hadn't even told Denise yet."

"I don't know, Dad. I wish I did. I all but begged her not to go, to wait until you got home before she did anything, but she said she had to be at that meeting tomorrow afternoon.''

"She's going to walk into it alone?"

"That's what she said, and except for Aunt Denise, I can't think of one friend she'll have there."

"Did she say anything else I should know?" Grady asked, almost fearing the answer.

"Well, let's see . . . I asked her what she was going to do if they did take that inheritance away from her, and she said she might fight it. I told her it could take years, but she just blew that off."

Wearily Grady sank to the sofa and put his head in his hands. "The money must be awfully important to her, and I wouldn't have thought it would be. To just pack up and race off to New York like that . . . I can't believe Kirsten would do it. I honestly thought nothing back there was important to her anymore."

David felt more helpless than he ever had in his life. He'd never seen his father upset, and now that he had, the sight did odd things to his insides. "I did everything I could," he said apologetically.

"I'm sure you did, son. Did she say when she would be back?"

"No, just that she had reservations at the Plaza for tonight and tomorrow night." David waited, but Grady only continued holding his head in his hands. "What are you going to do?" he finally asked.

"I'm not sure I can do anything. This is Kirsten's ball game. She didn't ask for my advice or opinion or anything."

"But all this just happened yesterday, and we didn't know how to reach you. Mom said she would have if she'd known how. It seems like we ought to do something."

"Like what?"

"Couldn't you call her?"

Grady gave that some thought, then he got to his feet and crossed the room to the phone. "I guess a call can't hurt. Where did you say she's staying?"

"At the Plaza."

Grady got the number and placed the call. However, there was no answer from Kirsten's room, and he didn't want her paged. For all he knew, she didn't want anyone knowing she was there. He thought of leaving a message, then decided against it. She'd contact him when she was ready.

He didn't think he'd ever felt so lousy. What bothered him more than anything was not her running off to New York, it was her running after Patrick money. She'd always declared that the things she'd enjoyed as a Long Island socialite had little meaning for her. Apparently, finding herself in dire danger of losing a great chunk of her wealth, she'd changed her mind. What else would she change her mind about?

"No answer," he told David as he replaced the receiver.

"She and Aunt Denise have probably gone to dinner."

"At this hour? It's after ten in New York."

"Hey, New York's New York. They don't roll up the sidewalks at ten the way they do here."

For the longest time, Grady simply stood with his hand on the phone, staring off into space. Finally, with a growl, he reached into the desk drawer and took out an address book.

"What are you doing?" David asked anxiously.

"Calling the airlines," he answered tiredly. "Another plane, another trip. Damned if I'm not going to apply for the frequent flyer discount."

David relaxed somewhat. He didn't know what his dad could do, but just knowing Grady was going after his mother made him feel better. Maybe his dad could talk some sense into her, get her back here. Hopefully then everything would get back to normal.

Once Grady had the reservationist on the line, he glanced over his shoulder. "Want to come along, son?"

"To New York?" David shook his head. "No, thanks. I didn't lose a thing there."

KIRSTEN AND DENISE opted for an out-of-the-way Italian restaurant that none of the Patricks would be caught dead in. It was the perfect place to linger over food and wine and more talk, this time about pleasant subjects. Kirsten heard all about London and Raymond Billingsley, and she in turn regaled Denise with tales of small town life. It was ten-thirty when they left the restaurant, and Kirsten was in her room by eleven, where she intended staying until she put in her surprise appearance at tomorrow's meeting. She briefly considered phoning David to see if he'd heard from Grady, then remembered how unhappy her son had been with her this morning. She wasn't much in the mood to listen to more of that. She'd hold off calling until after the meeting, when, hopefully, the business with the Patricks would be resolved once and for all.

Kirsten slept as late as she could the following morning, then ordered a room service breakfast and dawdled away the hours reading the *Times* from the front page to the classified section and watching television. Naturally the hours dragged, but finally she could begin getting dressed to face the ordeal.

She once had heard or read that a monochromatic color scheme encouraged others to look at one's face and concentrate on what one was saying, rather than be distracted by complicated lines or patterns. For that reason, she had brought along a cranberry wool chemise of superb tailoring and simple lines, its severity softened only by two strands of perfect pearls at the neckline. Once she was dressed, she looked in the mirror and saw no signs of the turmoil that raged and boiled inside her. Satisfied, she left the room and went downstairs to hail a cab for the short ride to the institute.

Only when she stepped out of the taxi and looked at the imposing entrance doors of the institute's brick building did Kirsten experience a moment of panic. Recalling all the rejections and denials of previous years, she wondered if she actually could confront T.G. and Roger and those other Patricks. They were movers and shakers, while she, especially now, was without influence or power. But even while the panic assailed her, she knew she had to do it. Those very rejections and denials demanded it. Squaring her shoulders, she pushed through the glass double doors and walked purposely to the elevators.

The boardroom of the Patrick Institute was a spacious, beautifully decorated seat of power that testified to the great wealth of the Patrick empire. Done in a rich rust-and-blue color scheme, its paneled walls were adorned with many valuable paintings, all of them from the Patricks' private collections. The focal point of the room was a long polished oak table, and at its head, in a thronelike chair, sat the patriarch of the family.

And quite a family it was, judging from the crush of people who had gathered together that afternoon. The usual members of the board were seated in their customary places around the table. Others sat where they could. Most stood or mixed and mingled. The cacophony of voices and laughter did not subside appreciably when Kirsten entered the room. Many of those present either didn't notice her entrance or didn't have any idea who she was. But those family members who were acquainted with her and knew the purpose of today's meeting looked at her in absolute shock, none more so than T.G. and Roger. As soon as he recovered sufficiently to move, Roger hurried to her side.

"This is a private family meeting," he hissed.

"No, it's not," Kirsten said coolly. "It's a lynching. And since I happen to be the lynchee, I think I have every right to be here."

"I suppose this is Denise's doing."

"If you're wondering how I came to know about this little get-together, I have my sources. I'm not entirely without friends." She hoped that would plant the tiniest seed of doubt in Roger's mind that Denise was her only ally.

Nonplussed, Roger opened his mouth to say something, then changed his mind. Pivoting, he hurried to the head of the table and to T.G.

"What in hell is she doing here?" the elderly man muttered under his breath.

"She says that since this meeting concerns her, she has every right to be here."

"How in the devil did she know about it? She's supposed to be in Mississippi. Who brought her here?"

"My guess would be Denise, but who knows? There are a lot of people here. I suppose it's not inconceivable that some of them are Kirsten's friends."

"Get rid of her."

Straightening, his face flushed, Roger went back to Kirsten and cupped a hand under her elbow, exerting slight pressure. "My father wants you to leave," he said.

She jerked free of him. "Then tell your father he'd best find someone who's willing to bodily remove me from this room."

Mouth agape, Roger stared at her a minute, then walked back to his father's chair. "She says we're going to have to bodily remove her."

Fuming, T.G. considered the impact that sight might have on the assemblage and decided against employing such strong-arm tactics. "All right, goddammit, let her stay."

Few people in the room were aware that anything unusual was taking place. They were much too busy visiting relatives they seldom saw. When it became apparent to Kirsten that no one was going to forcibly remove her from the gathering, she searched the room for Denise. Finding her, she threaded her way through the throng to her friend's side.

"Nervous?" Denise whispered.

For an answer, Kirsten grasped her hand and squeezed tightly. Denise patted it reassuringly. "It'll be over soon. If you want to feel better, just take a look at Constance. She looks like a mouse just crawled inside her blouse."

Kirsten cast a quick glance in Constance's direction. The woman visibly blanched as their eyes met. Kirsten smiled enigmatically, then turned her head. She looked around the room, trying to identify friends and foes. Evelyn, would of course, vote the way T.G. wanted her to vote, so Kirsten dismissed her mother-in-law without another thought and settled her glance on Aunt Judith, who looked very stylish in her soft wool suit and beautifully coiffed silver hair. Judith, the widow of T.G.'s long-deceased younger brother, was a bright, capable woman of sixty-five, whom Kirsten had always considered a friend. However, from Travis's accounts of the various board meetings, she knew that Judith invariably rubber-stamped all of T.G.'s suggestions. Until she proved otherwise, Judith would have to be considered opposition.

In fact, Kirsten noted ruefully as her gaze moved around the room, with the exception of Denise, she couldn't count on any of these people. What was she doing here? What had she possibly thought she would accomplish?

T.G. was having some trouble bringing the meeting to order. After repeated tries, the milling gradually subsided, and when T.G. called for silence, the talking stopped, too. All eyes focused on him. He cleared his throat.

"First of all, I want to thank all of you for coming. I realize that this meeting was organized on short notice and involved travel for a lot of you. I would not have asked you to interrupt your busy schedules if I did not think this was important."

Suddenly, an air of curiosity filled the room. Kirsten guessed that most of the younger members were feeling flattered that the head of the family had included them in something "important." Others seemed to be filled with expectation. Still others, the handful in the room who knew exactly what was coming, merely looked uncomfortable.

Slowly the preposterous story began to unfold. Not even T.G.'s sonorous voice could prevent the tale from sounding like one of those newspaper accounts of what had taken place on a soap opera the previous week. Had Kirsten not been involved, she would have thought it funny, and she wondered why the others weren't laughing uproariously. They had come to the meeting expecting to hear something momentous, perhaps something of great import, and what they were getting was pulp fiction. It was all she could do to keep quiet.

But keep quiet she did, until she was sure T.G. was finished. There was a nervous rustling sound as those in the room realized what was being asked of them. Furtive glances were exchanged. Kirsten happened to make eye contact with Judith at that moment, and she thought she saw sympathy in the older woman's eyes, but perhaps that was only wishful thinking. One thing was certain, however; not many of the gathering realized that the subject herself was present. Steadying herself as best she could, Kirsten got to her feet.

"I'd like to say something, if I may."

"I don't think that's necessary," T.G. said, not looking at her.

"Oh, but it is. Since I'm the person under discussion, I have a right to defend myself. That's the democratic process."

Gasps could be heard throughout the room. T.G. looked furious. "This is unorthodox," he snapped.

"This entire proceeding is unorthodox," Kirsten countered. "I have some things I want to say."

A masculine voice in the back of the room spoke up. "Good Lord, let the lady talk." Other assenting voices and nods followed.

A moment of silence followed. Then, giving up, T.G. said, "Very well. Have your say."

All eyes in the room turned to Kirsten. "I'm sure all of you thoroughly enjoyed the story you just heard. I thought it was highly entertaining, but please take it for what it was—entertainment. There wasn't a word of truth in it."

Challenged, T.G. turned red-faced. "Did you or did you not lie to my son about being a widow?"

"I did not. Travis knew from our first date that I was divorced and had a son. However, he chose to lie to you because he thought being a widow would make me more acceptable to the family. How wrong he was."

Roger spoke up. "We have only your word against Travis's on that, and, sadly, he isn't here to corroborate or deny it."

"No, but I am." Denise got to her feet. "I knew all along that Kirsten was divorced. Travis told me as much not long after he and Kirsten got married, when it became obvious that I was going to be her one friend in the family. He thought it would be nice for her to have someone to talk to about it."

T.G. glared at his daughter, incensed that she was up to her old tricks. "Again, that's your word against a dead man's."

"Friends, lister to me and believe what I say. This meeting is a ludicrous farce," Denise said. "I would like to remind everyone here that this whole sorry mess is the result of an overheard conversation. Are all of you willing to believe that Constance has such total recall that she can remember a conversation verbatim?'' She paused long enough to shoot a scathing look in Constance's direction. ''Besides, what difference does it make whether Kirsten was divorced or widowed? The fact is, she was single when she met and married Travis, and she was a wonderful wife to him for a lot of years. Who cares about Kirsten's life before she met Travis? Nobody, I'll wager. Not even my father nor my darling brother, who claim to. Kirsten's greatest sin, in their eyes, was in being born poor, then having the temerity to marry a man who wasn't.'' That said, Denise sat down.

Kirsten was enormously grateful to her. It wasn't so much what Denise had said, it was that she'd said anything at all. As a full-fledged Patrick, she carried weight, even if she was at loggerheads with her father half the time. Slightly encouraged, Kirsten surveyed the crowd. ''And that brings us to what I did after my first marriage. There seems to be a lot of speculation about that. I've been accused of collusion with my ex-husband during the time I was married to Travis, and that is absurd—pure fabrication. Until two months ago, I had not seen or heard from Grady O'Connor since 1974, and there's not one word in that private investigator's report that suggests otherwise. I challenge anyone in this room to read that report and point out even a word that hints at collusion. You can't because there is none. The alleged collusion is simply the product of some overactive imaginations.''

T.G. looked around the room and tried to gauge the collective reception to all this. ''Remember, this woman is remarrying her ex-husband, a man she claims she accidentally stumbled across only two months ago.''

Kirsten took a deep breath. ''Ah, yes. My marrying my ex-husband seems to be proof positive that I've been guilty of all sorts of dastardly deeds. Well, there was nothing 'accidental' about meeting Grady again. My son set out determinedly and methodically to find his natural father, and he succeeded. Had it not been for that, Grady and I doubtless would have never seen each other again.''

T.G. was impatient. He had expected to come to this meeting and dictate what would happen. He was unnerved that it didn't seem to be happening. ''All right, all right, you've heard both sides of the issue. I will say that the marriage was entered into fraudulently, and Kirsten is not entitled to the great sum of money my son left her. I further maintain that the thirteen percent in question is rightfully the family's, that no money should change hands. However, I want to be fair. I realize that Kirsten has become accustomed to a certain standard of living over the years, so I suggest that she be given a monthly allowance for a year— say ten thousand dollars. That should . . . er, ease the transition somewhat.'' He looked at Kirsten expectantly.

She merely looked at him, a mirthless half smile on her face. ''No, thanks,'' she said. ''I'm in no danger of being destitute. I merely insist on what's rightfully mine. I want my husband's will to be carried out to the letter. If it isn't, I'll take it to court.''

''My dear Kirsten,'' T.G. said, fighting for control, ''with the legal resources we have at our disposal, there's no way you can win.''

''We'll see.''

A shroud of silence fell over the assemblage as the two adversaries stared at each other, both unrelenting. T.G. stirred first. "All right, then I think it's time for a vote. It will make the participants less uncomfortable if you will wait outside, Kirsten. And this time I won't hesitate to have you bodily removed should it be necessary."

"It won't. Thank you for your time, ladies and gentlemen."

There was quite a distance to cover between her chair and the door. Kirsten was aware that every eye in the room followed her progress. When she reached the door, she grasped the knob, paused and turned. "There's just one more thing," she said.

"What is it?" T.G. asked irritably.

Kirsten's eyes roamed over the assemblage. She took care not to look at T.G., Roger, Evelyn or Constance, while trying to make direct eye contact with most of the rest. Everyone's rapt attention was fastened on her. Most were fascinated, for it was the first time any of them could recall seeing T.G.'s authority even mildly questioned. "You gentlemen present might wonder if it's worth the trouble and expense of having an attorney draw up your will if Mr. Patrick can so easily invalidate any portion of it he doesn't like. Of course, if you're very careful to marry only women of 'class and breeding,' that shouldn't be too much of a problem." The last was said mainly for the benefit of the young people present who would live most of their lives in the twenty-first century and might reasonably be expected to balk at the elder Patricks' caste system. Kirsten spoke in a clever, steady voice that betrayed none of her nervousness. "Also, there are a lot of widows here today, and, unfortunately, through the years your ranks grow. Ask yourselves what kind of precedent you want to establish with this vote. Are each of you absolutely sure you've never at any time in your life done something that Mr. Patrick or Roger or some future director might not approve of?'' Opening the door, she left the room.

Outside in the deserted hallway, her reserve slipped, then crumbled. Leaning against the wall beside the door, she put a hand to her left breast, as if that would somehow still her heart's frantic beating. Dear God, she didn't want a court fight. Dear God, she didn't want any of this!

CHAPTER FIFTEEN

GRADY WONDERED how long he could hang around the lobby of a posh place like the Plaza Hotel before being arrested for loitering. He looked at his watch for the umpteenth time. He'd been there more than an hour, trying to look purposeful and important while reading the same newspaper four times and keeping a watchful eye on the entrance. He didn't dare go get a drink or a bite to eat for fear of missing Kirsten. She was still registered at the hotel, so she'd be back. It might not be for hours, but sooner or later she would be back.

He was beat. He'd been operating at a dead run since getting out of bed this morning, and it was beginning to tell on him. He felt terrible, but he knew that stemmed from more than the day's frantic pace. Kirsten's hurried trip back to New York to try to salvage her inheritance had him tied in knots. He was, he admitted to himself, scared to death.

Since the minute she'd reentered his life, he had felt himself growing more and more emotionally dependent on her. He hadn't experienced even one minute's reluctance about making a total commitment to her, and he'd thought—hoped—it had been the same for her. Unfortunately, right now she seemed more committed to maintaining her wealthy status. What else could account for her dropping everything and racing back to confront the in-laws she claimed she was gladly rid of? Today he was going to find out which was more important to her: their future or that blasted money. And he was going to do it if he had to wait in the damned lobby until midnight.

Grady stood up to stretch his legs, and as he did so, he caught sight of her sailing through the entrance. Kirsten reached the elevators before he caught up with her. Grabbing her by an arm, he swung her around, almost knocking her off balance. Her startled expression immediately gave way to one of astonishment.

"Grady! What on earth are you doing here?"

"Waiting for you."

The elevator doors opened with a swoosh, and the conveyance disgorged its load of passengers. Kirsten and Grady were swept up with the group that surged forward to take its place. It wasn't until they reached Kirsten's floor that she was able to say anything to him. By that time she had recovered from her surprise and was overcome with delight and curiosity. They reached her room, and she slipped one arm around his waist to squeeze him before unlocking the door. "I'm so glad to see you. I thought you'd just now be on your way home from Texas."

They stepped into the room, and Grady closed the door. "No, I cut the trip short. I had something important to tell you. I got in last night only to find you gone."

"And you got on another plane today?" she asked in surprise. "How wonderful! Did David come with you?"

"No."

Kirsten tossed her handbag onto the dresser and turned to lock her hands behind his neck and kiss him soundly. In her joy at unexpectedly having him with her, she failed to notice that he stood woodenly, accepting the kiss but not returning it. "Do you mean that you and I are actually alone together in New York? How absolutely delightful!"

"Kirsten, I want to talk to you."

She stepped back, now aware of the harshness of his voice, the hardness of his expression. She realized that he didn't seem as glad to see her as she was to see him. "What's wrong?"

"I want to know the meaning of this," he said, his hand slicing through the air to indicate . . . what?

"Are you talking about this hotel room?" she asked in bewilderment. "I always stay at the Plaza when I need a room in the city. I certainly don't think I'm welcome to use the Park Avenue apartment any longer."

"I'm not talking about the room, for heaven's sake! I'm talking about the reason for this sudden trip of yours."

"Didn't David tell you?"

"He said you got a call from Denise telling you that the Patricks wanted to take your inheritance away from you. You got panic-stricken and ran back here."

That struck the first spark of indignation in her. She stepped back to prop her hip against the dresser. Crossing her arms at her waist, she pursed her lips and regarded him levelly. "I wasn't panic-stricken. I was furious. There's a big difference."

"Does their goddam money really mean that much to you?"

Kirsten sucked in her breath as she slowly realized what she was being accused of. "Listen," she said between clenched teeth, "I've had my integrity, my motives, even my morals questioned enough for one day, thanks. I'm sure not going to take the same treatment for you." Pushing herself forward, she went to sit on the edge of the bed. Her chest heaved in agitation. "It wasn't merely the money."

"Yeah, I know. Principles were involved."

"Sarcasm doesn't become you, Grady. You're damned right principles were involved. It was time somebody let T. G. Patrick know that he is not yet in charge of the universe."

Sighing, Grady loosened his tie and pulled it off. He also shed his suit coat and tossed it onto a nearby chair. Then he went to sit beside Kirsten on the bed. A minute of ponderous silence ensued. Once again, he thought ruefully, he probably hadn't handled things very well.

Finally Kirsten turned to him. "They were accusing us of all sorts of terrible things—being in cahoots, planning our divorce so I could marry Travis and channel money back to you—all sorts of things."

"And you let that bother you? Let them say whatever the hell they like," Grady fumed.

"They had a private detective investigate me. That really ticked me off."

"A detective? What for?"

"To catch me dead to rights, without a leg to stand on, of course. To bring all my evil scheming to light. I think the detective was that man who talked to you in Slick's last week, the one who supposedly worked for a company that was expanding."

"What on earth makes you think that?"

"Right after Denise told me about the detective, your friend at the Chamber of Commerce called. He said the phone number on that man's business card was a nonworking one, and directory assistance couldn't find a company by that name in the Philadelphia area. Peculiar, huh? That started me thinking. It's unlikely that anyone could have asked around about either of us without our hearing about it—not in Culver. The detective didn't have to ask around because he talked directly to us."

Grady tried to think what they had said to the man in the café. Not much that he could recall. "Kirsten, so what?"

"So I don't like the idea of having a detective trailing me, that's so what. I don't like having innocent remarks used against me. Because of that investigator, the Patricks found out that you and I are getting married again. To them that's proof positive that we were playing footsie all the time I was married to Travis."

"Oh, God." Grady rubbed his eyes tiredly. "I don't care what they think, and it upsets me tremendously that you apparently do."

"Of course I care," she cried, "and I'll bet you would, too, if you were in my shoes. And I'll tell you something else that upsets me. You, too, seem to be accusing me of greed and avarice. That upsets me more than what the Patricks are doing."

"What was I to think?" he asked miserably. "I came home to find you gone—"

"You might have given me the benefit of the doubt. You might have thought I had my reasons and waited to hear what they were before assuming I was a money-grubbing little monster." She reached up to flick at a tear with her finger.

She was right. Grady felt like a heel. His self-disgust knew no limits. He slid an arm around her shoulders and moved closer to her. "I'm sorry, sweetheart. You're right—that's exactly what I should have done. It just scared me so much."

"Scared you? I...don't understand. What were you afraid of?"

"Oh...maybe I worried that if that kind of money meant so much to you, you could never be happy with what I could give you. Or I might have been afraid of your getting involved in a lengthy court battle, spending so much time here you would forget about home."

Kirsten truly was shocked. "Grady! Forget about you and David? You two are my life now. Did you even for a minute honestly think I could do that?"

"I guess I probably wasn't thinking."

"True."

"I behaved horribly."

"Also true."

"Am I forgiven?"

He looked so contrite, like a naughty little boy, that Kirsten couldn't hold back a smile. "Yes, you're forgiven. And just for the record, no matter what had happened here today, I would have been home tomorrow. I could hardly wait to get back. In fact, the first thing I planned to do when I got to the hotel was call the airlines and find out the earliest possible flight."

"Thank God."

"But now, that's the last thing I want to do. We seem to have acquired ourselves an interlude." She smiled at him adoringly. "You know, having you chase me all the way from Mississippi to New York is rather touching. Romantic, even."

Grady grinned. "I gotta tell you, when I left home, I was good and steamed."

"You're not steamed anymore, are you?"

"No, not at all."

"That's nice." With her manicured forefinger she traced his jawline and studied it with the interest and precision of a plastic surgeon. Then, as if approving of what she saw, she showered his face with a series of tiny, light kisses. At the same time, she kicked off her shoes and crawled into his lap. Grady cradled her as she continued her nipping and kissing. She deftly unbuttoned his shirt midway to his waist and slipped her hand inside to feel the satisfying warmth of his skin. Then her head rolled back against his shoulder, and she looked up at him. "Aren't you even slightly interested in what happened at the meeting?"

"Not particularly. I'm far more interested in what's happening here."

"I'd really like to tell you."

"All right—what happened at the meeting?"

Kirsten shot him a smile of mild triumph. "Denise told me the whole story afterward. It never got put to a vote. First of all, once I'd left the room, Nelson Harding—he's an attorney—told the gathering that what they actually were talking about was reversing a will, and he reminded them that they would have to go through proper legal channels. Of course, that could take forever, as everyone there surely was aware. Then...I guess my parting shot to the crowd made an impact."

"Parting shot?"

"I simply suggested to all the widows there—and there were a lot of them—that they might very well be in my position someday. It must have been a good defense. Denise said that after the discussion following Nelson's statement, sentiment seemed to be running in favor of just forgetting the whole business. A few people suggested—out of earshot, I'm sure—that Mr. Patrick might be getting addled in his old age. Maybe he and Roger figured it was easier to leave things as they were and be rid of me.''

Grady tensed. ''So you'll get the money.''

''Yes, I'll get the money.''

Damn! Was he being disloyal to her by wishing she wouldn't? He wanted her coming to him free of any vestiges of her marriage to Travis Patrick. But he loved Kirsten unreservedly. If the money was important to her, it should be important to him, too. ''Well, sweetheart,'' he said lightly, ''it looks as though you're destined to be Culver's wealthiest citizen.''

Pulling back slightly, she looked at him questioningly. ''I didn't tell you, did I? Grady, I don't want that money for me.''

''You don't? Who do you want it for?''

''Nobody. Oh, I'll probably put a little of it in David's trust, but—''

''Wait a minute. You lost me.''

''I want it for the birthing center, of course. The way things are going now, the place might get built in 2012. Last week it suddenly dawned on me that I was due to come into a hunk of cash soon. I certainly don't need it, but it could do so much good. That's why it infuriated me to think of the Patricks taking it away from me. I was counting on it for the center.''

For a minute Grady was too overcome to speak. And to think he'd once, if only briefly, suspected her of greed. She was the most selfless person he'd ever known. ''I guess you're going to be a real heroine to the town.''

Kirsten looked horrified. "Oh, God, no! That money is going to be donated anonymously. Do you hear me, Grady? I want you to promise me that no one will ever know where it came from. Only you and me and—well, maybe a lawyer or somebody to see it's done right—are ever to know. Promise?"

"You'll miss a shot at fame and glory, you know. No brass plaque with your name emblazoned on it."

"Promise?"

"Okay, I promise."

Kirsten relaxed and settled back in the comfort of his lap and enveloping arms. "What do you think of the room?"

Grady looked around. "Pretty swanky."

"Mmm-hmm. Although something in my basic nature cringes at the thought of spending over four hundred dollars a night for a place to lay my head."

"Is that what it costs to spend a night in this joint?"

"You can spend a lot less . . . and a whole lot more. But the Plaza is the Plaza, and New York is New York, and tonight they're both ours." She kissed him soundly then, slipping her tongue between his teeth. Her hand inside his shirt moved in sensuous circles; his own hand slid along her hip and thigh, rubbing and petting her. She heard him sigh contentedly. Breaking the kiss, she ran the tip of her tongue along the seam of his lips. "Are you thinking about the same thing I am?" she cooed.

"I'm thinking about dinner," he said teasingly.

"Bet you aren't."

"You won't be able to take me just anywhere, you know. This suit and a change into something comfortable for the flight home are all the clothes I brought with me."

Kirsten set her feet on the floor and stood. "Then you'd best take your suit off and hang it up, don't you think? We don't want to muss it. And since this dress is the nicest thing I brought, I guess I should hang it, too." She pulled him to his feet. "Let me undress you."

With movements that were like caresses, she stripped him down to his undershorts and carefully hung up his clothes, retrieving his coat from the chair. "Warm the bed for me," she said. "I'll be right with you."

Snuggled in the warmth and comfort of the bed covers, Grady propped himself on one elbow and watched her undress. He marveled at the seeming ease with which she pulled down the long back zipper of her dress. First her hands went to her nape, and she inched the fastener down as far as she could. Then her arms swooped down and came up behind her back in a movement he wasn't sure he could have duplicated. "How do you do that?"

"It takes years of practice," she said, "and it helps if you're a contortionist." Stepping out of the chemise, she hung it beside his clothes, and as she made her way to the bed, she discarded her lingerie piece by piece, leaving a trail of wispy silk on the carpet. Smiling seductively, she slithered beneath the covers to join him.

"You smell absolutely divine," Grady whispered as he gathered her close and felt her soft body go limp against his. "I've never even asked you the name of the perfume you wear."

"Juliana," she murmured. "Shamefully expensive."

"It's worth it. Whatever it costs, it's worth it. Don't ever run out of the stuff." He kissed the pulse point at the base of her throat that she had dabbed with the perfume hours earlier. The aroma filled his nostrils. "I am madly, wildly, insanely crazy about you. You own my heart. No one else has ever touched it."

"Grady...darling...I want to ask you a question."

"What a time for questions."

"When are we going to get married?"

"Monday we'll take care of the preliminaries. By this time next week, you'll be Mrs. O'Connor again. It's about damned time, too."

"That's good. Tonight will be the first time we've been able to sleep together all night long. Going back to the old arrangement is going to be very hard." Under the covers, her seeking hands found him. "Speaking of which..."

Their bodies entwined like interlocking fingers. By now Kirsten knew exactly how to fit herself against him. She stroked the length of his leg with her foot and kneaded his hard buttocks with her fingers. She knew every inch of him, and yet each time they were together, it was like embarking on a voyage of discovery. Amazingly, she could honestly say that every time they made love was the best it had ever been.

Her mouth and hands were never still. She gloried in his strong, muscular body and the things it could do to her, just as she gloried in his attractiveness and quiet charm during less passionate times. Now that they'd been given this gift of a full evening together, she was determined to raise him to new heights of desire, and she succeeded. She kept up her sensuous ministrations mercilessly until Grady was panting and fully aroused. Stroking him, she smiled, pleased with her abilities and wishing their coupling would never end.

But, of course, it had to. All of a sudden Kirsten felt the rush of heat in her body's core, a heavy congestion between her thighs. Moaning against his chest, she said, "I had planned to make this last and last and last, but it's not possible. Darling, I'm afraid you're going to have to take me now."

"Thank God," Grady groaned as he moved over her. "I'm about to explode."

And an explosion it was—wild, uninhibited and mind shattering. They also allowed themselves something that wouldn't have been possible in the little house where their son also lived—a most vocal climax.

But in some ways, what followed was the most thrilling of all: long, long minutes of lying wrapped around each other, while their bodies cooled and their breathing returned to normal. They savored the new experience and later, when they finally released each other, Kirsten turned, dovetailed her body into his and fell instantly, contentedly, soundly asleep.

"SWEETHEART, IT'S SIX O'CLOCK. Are you going to sleep forever?"

Grady's voice came to Kirsten out of a sleep-induced fog. He coaxed her awake with a flurry of kisses until she stretched and purred like a kitten. "This is heaven," she cooed. "Heaven, I tell you." She sat up and propped a pillow against the headboard. Leaning back, she pulled the sheet up over her breasts. "This morning when I woke up in this bed, I couldn't have imagined the day would turn out so delightfully."

Returned Grady, "This morning all I could think of was getting up here, finding you and getting you home as quickly as possible. Somehow I feel insecure when you're outside the state line." He threw back the covers, stood and crossed the room. "I left in such a hurry I forgot to pack a robe. I hope the towels are big."

"This isn't a cheap motel darling," Kirsten said. "The hotel furnishes terry robes. Help yourself."

"Class," he murmured appreciatively. "Pure class." Then he disappeared into the bathroom.

Kirsten pulled her legs up under the sheet and hugged her knees. From the bathroom came the sounds of water splashing and Grady whistling. She laid her cheek on her raised knees and waited for him to reappear. Only a few minutes passed before he did. As soon as he stepped into the room, she patted the edge of the bed. "Come over here."

He walked to the bed, sat and studied her with a faint smile. "What's on your mind?"

"Earlier you said you hurried home yesterday because you had something important to tell me. What was it?"

Grady scratched his chin. "I thought it was important at the time. It no longer is."

"But what was it?"

"I was going to tell you that I planned to call Vanessa and tell her I didn't want the job."

For a split second Kirsten's breath seemed to catch in her throat. "Oh?"

"But that was yesterday. This morning I changed my mind. Hell, I can't do that. I don't have any idea why Vanessa is considering me—she said something about liking my 'style,' whatever that is—but the point is, I'm on her list. If she offers me the job, I'll have to take it. I don't see how I can do anything else."

Kirsten expelled her pent-up breath. She would analyze her true feelings about this later. "That's good," she said softly.

"Is it, sweetheart? Is it really? I know you've never come right out and said you don't want to go to Dallas, but that's more or less the impression I got."

"No," she lied. "I'm sorry if I haven't been more enthusiastic about the prospect, but so much has happened to me in such a short time. I haven't reacted to anything predictably. Whatever happens, I know things will turn out wonderfully well for us."

Grady shoved himself off the bed and began slowly pacing the room. "I hope you're right. I'd be lying through my teeth if I said I wasn't flattered to be under consideration. And if the promotion is offered to me, my male vanity will almost demand that I strut and gloat for a few days. But then hard reality will set in, and that's when my confidence will likely turn to mush. There are so many things I have to think about. I'd hate to see our lives—yours, mine and David's—undergo any major changes right now. I worry about keeping up the pace the new job would demand. I worry about having my days filled with obligations, and I worry about not seeing nearly as much of you as I'd want to. But mainly I worry that you won't like it."

"Do you ever worry that you wouldn't be able to handle the job?"

"Hell, no! I know I could do it."

"Then those other worries will take care of themselves." Kirsten motioned for him to return to the bed. When he was sitting beside her once again, she took his hands in hers and squeezed them. She vowed on the spot that Grady would never, ever know how much she yearned to keep the status quo. If the promotion materialized, she knew far better than he did just how much their lives would change. First off, David would be away at school, and considering how close he and Mona had become, Kirsten doubted their son would want to fly to Dallas many weekends. Secondly, if she and Grady were lucky, they might spend a couple of nights a week snuggled on the sofa, simply talking. There would be no more mornings of coffee and gossip in a small café. They would have to entertain a lot, which would call for a certain kind of house. The list seemed endless. But Grady must never suspect that she even thought of such things.

"You wouldn't be human if you didn't have doubts, darling," she said. "Major changes are scary. I know because I've been there. When I went to Long Island as a bride, I entered a world I hadn't known existed. I was terrified for months. Virtually every experience was a new one. There seemed to be firsts every day. Adapting to a new life-style has to be done gradually, but one day you look around, and it seems you've lived that way all your life." She reached out, ran a hand up the inside of the robe's sleeve and stroked his arm. "And I'll help you. We'll conquer Dallas together."

The lady had a way with words, Grady thought. She was also the ace up his sleeve. He supposed he would never be completely free of doubts and uncertainties, not for a few years, at least. He'd have to run a few races and learn how to pace himself. But the one solid truth of his life was that he and Kirsten belonged together and always had. With her by his side, he probably could move mountains. He ought to be able to handle a little thing like running a Fortune 500 company. They would field whatever was thrown them, and they would do it together. "Come here," he said huskily, reaching for her.

Pulling her against him, he kissed her deeply, again and again. Small gurgles of pleasure sounded from Kirsten's throat. the sheet covering her fell away; she pushed his robe open, then caressed him from chest to thigh. When at last they were forced to part to gasp for breath, her head went back and her eyes gleamed. "You'll make the most marvelously handsome C.E.O.," she said with a sigh. "You'll look so distinguished sitting behind your big desk, handing down important decisions. You'll be wonderful at anything you do, Grady."

"Your confidence in me warms the cockles..." Her roving hands were merciless; they bewitched him. "Kirsten...sweetheart," he croaked. "You are driving me crazy."

"No matter what happens, no matter what the future has in store for us, I know you'll rise to the occasion...." Her hand encountered him. "Oh, darling...I'll say!"

CHAPTER SIXTEEN

HOW CAN TODAY be my eightieth birthday, Vanessa Hamilton asked herself with a smile, *when I don't feel a day over seventy?*

She sat at the desk in her upstairs bedroom suite, waiting for tonight's guests to begin arriving and vaguely wondering if she was overextending herself. It had been a busy week, and the following evening there would be yet another party, a smaller, more intimate affair hosted by longtime friends. Tonight's soiree, on the other hand, was all her doing, and it promised to be lavish. The guest list was composed mostly of her Hamilton House colleagues and their spouses. She had been planning it for months. Everything would be perfect—the food, the wines, the flower arrangements, everything; she never entertained in half measures.

Satisfied, she got to her feet and walked to a small Victorian table, where she poured herself a sherry. Carrying it to the fireplace, she stood gazing down into the flames and thought of the evening ahead. Employees from all over the country had been arriving in Dallas since early that morning, ostensibly for no other purpose than to spend an evening filled with food and drink and revelry to celebrate her birthday. Actually, tonight's guests—to their great surprise, she was certain—would witness the changing of the guard, the passing of the torch. After almost a year of studying and pondering, she was ready to make her announcement.

As she took a sip of sherry, she thought of the three contenders for the throne—Matt Logan, Paula Steele and Grady O'Connor. What a splendid trio they made. All of them were bright, capable and loyal; all of them richly deserved the presidency. Coincidentally, all of them had married during the past year— Grady as recently as seven weeks ago. Choosing among them had been difficult for her, which was unusual. Normally she was a swift decision maker. And as many times as she had studied Matt, Paula and Grady, she had wished that Hamilton House could be successfully directed by a triumvirate. However, that was not possible. Every ship needed a captain, so she had made the choice that would be announced after dinner. She hoped no one would be disappointed. Most of all, she hoped that Dolph Wade would not cause any unpleasantness.

Vanessa's expression changed, and her eyes narrowed as she thought of her once trusted executive vice president, the man who had been heir apparent for so many years. Dolph, caught red-handed in his scheming, was unaware that she knew of his disloyalty and had taken steps to circumvent it. She genuinely regretted that he had forced her to take measures to protect the future of the business she had spent fifty-five years building. Confronting him with what she knew was not something she relished doing, but nothing could happen to Hamilton House. The sacrifices she and Stuart had made on its behalf had been too many and too great.

Her thoughts were interrupted by a knock at the door. "Come in," she called, and it opened to admit the tall, distinguished figure of Christopher Nance, her banker, financial adviser, confidant and friend. Christopher alone knew of the difficult soul-searching that had accompanied her decision, for he had been with her every step of the way. Vanessa's face broke into a radiant smile of welcome.

"Christopher! Come join me in a sherry."

"How is the birthday girl?" the banker asked, crossing the room in long strides to place a fond kiss on her cheek.

"Far better than one has any right to be at eighty, I suspect."

"Eighty, Vanessa! And look at you. You are absolutely beautiful."

"You're a dear to say so. How about that sherry?"

"Is there time? The first trickle of guests has begun arriving. I thought you would want to know."

Vanessa waved that aside with a jeweled hand. "Let's give the majority of them time to get here."

Christopher smiled. "You want to make a grand entrance."

"Of course. If I merely fade into the woodwork, what's the point of throwing a bash like this?"

"You? Fade into the woodwork? That will be the day."

Vanessa poured another sherry and handed it to her friend. Taking it, Christopher asked, "Apprehensive about tonight?"

"Of course. Wouldn't you be?"

"Probably. How do you suppose the three contenders are bearing up?"

"They're an accomplished lot, Christopher. They wouldn't be my vice presidents if they weren't. I imagine they'll all handle tonight with their customary poise and grace."

As she lifted her glass to her lips, Vanessa chanced to glance at her reflection in the cheval mirror. All of her life people had told her she was beautiful, but vanity was not one of her shortcomings. She, more than most women, could judge her own appearance with an objective eye. The black silk Adolfo gown was the perfect costume for the drama that would unfold tonight, she decided. Her diamond necklace sparkled against it like stars in a midnight sky. The new style her hairdresser had suggested for her enviable silver mane was becoming. She looked exactly the way she wanted to look—dignified, a trifle austere, completely aristocratic, every inch the woman of power and means she was.

Eighty! she thought again in wonder. *Only a decade younger than the century. Good heavens!*

"TAKE A GOOD LOOK at the house, Kirsten," Grady said as he offered her his hand and helped her out of the chauffeured limousine Hamilton House had furnished them with. "You're one person who'll be able to appreciate it."

"I'm so nervous," she confessed, "and you look so at ease, the very picture of relaxation."

"Which proves how deceiving looks can be. My butterflies are reproducing like hamsters."

They moved up the flagstone walkway and were ushered into the grand house by two uniformed servants. One relieved Kirsten of her *peau de soie* cape and invited them to join the other guests in the library, where cocktails were being served. As they crossed the foyer, Grady paused to look in a mirror and adjust his black tie.

Kirsten watched him admiringly. "I'm still trying to come to grips with the sight of you in a tux," she said.

"I feel silly as hell."

"You look divine."

"I can count on my fingers the number of times in my life when I've worn one of these monkey suits, and I'm including my Air Force dress blues in that."

"Stop fidgeting. Trust me when I tell you that you look marvelous."

"Well, one nice thing—I'll look just like every other guy here."

"No, darling, believe me, you won't look like every other guy here, not unless they're an unusually handsome bunch."

Grady turned and drank in the sight of her. Earlier, while they were dressing in their hotel room, he had watched in fascination as she had transformed herself into an exotic creature who took his breath away. Her raven hair had been lifted, piled and twisted into a complicated series of swirls interlaced with pearls. Her makeup, always artfully applied, was more vivid than usual, and her electric-blue dress hugged her body's bountiful curves before cascading down to its tulip-shaped hem. Heads would turn tonight; Grady would bet on that.

Taking her arm, he leaned closer to her and spoke confidentially. "Listen, sweetheart, there are going to be a lot of people here tonight who I've met at other company functions but whose names I won't remember. If someone comes up to us and I don't mention his or her name right off the bat—"

"Got'cha. I quickly stick out my hand and introduce myself. That forces them to come up with a name. I'm way ahead of you."

"Thank God I'm here with a pro. Before the evening is over, you're sure to notice that this isn't exactly what I do best."

The library was an impressive room with floor-to-ceiling windows flanking a stone fireplace. The other walls were lined with glass-front bookcases, each crammed with books from top to bottom. Furniture placement divided the room into several separate sitting areas. In spite of its size, which bordered on being cavernous, the library managed to convey a feeling of coziness, and it made a gracious setting for cocktails and conversation. It was already quite crowded, so Kirsten and Grady made their entrance unnoticed. She braced herself. Although she was an old hand at walking into a room full of strangers and exuding poise and confidence, she had never learned to really enjoy it. Tonight was the culmination of a busy week that had included getting David off to school and readying themselves for this trip. She was beginning to droop a little.

Actually, the past *seven* weeks had been hectic, what with the wedding and the beautiful party afterward, Thanksgiving, her birthday and Christmas. Maybe after tonight the pace would slow. Maybe. Hopefully.

Slipping her hand into the curve of Grady's elbow, she pasted on her best party smile.

There were many rooms in Vanessa's house that Grady had not seen, and this was one of them. "I've always wondered how many books a room had to have before it could be called a library," he commented. "I think this one qualifies."

His scrutiny continued. Suddenly Kirsten felt him tense. "Uh-oh," he muttered.

Her head came around. "Uh-oh, what?"

"Look over there to the left of the fireplace. See the man in the gray suit?"

"Uh-huh."

"That's Dolph Wade. I wondered if he would be here tonight."

"Is he the one who's fallen from grace?"

Grady nodded. "With a resounding thud. The evening, my pet, may get very interesting."

"This is lots better than going to a movie."

Grinning, Grady once again scanned the crowd. Spotting a very familiar face, he motioned to Kirsten with a jerk of his head. "Come on. I'll introduce you to half of my competition."

Their quarry was a tall, dark-haired man who was standing slightly apart from the mainstream, deep in conversation with a stunning red-haired woman. Grady walked up to him and lightly slapped him on the back. "Matt?"

Matt Logan turned. His face lighted up in recognition, and he stuck out his hand. "Grady! Good to see you. How've you been?"

"Can't complain about a thing. I want you to meet my wife, Kirsten."

"Delighted. And you've never met Lesley."

Introductions were made all around, and the usual party pleasantries were exchanged. For the first time, it occurred to Grady that he, Matt and Paula had more in common than simply competing for the same job. All three of them had married since they had last seen one another. Matt's wife was a real looker, maybe even in Kirsten's league, which was saying a lot.

"How's Carol?" he asked, referring to Matt's daughter.

"She's fine, thanks."

"Still in hot pursuit of an Olympic medal?"

Matt's expression sobered. "No, Carol hurt her knee quite badly last spring. I'm afraid competitive skating is a thing of the past."

"What a shame," Grady said, genuinely sorry to hear the news. "From what I've heard, she had a real shot at it."

"It could be worse," Lesley Logan put in. "She's opening a skating clinic next month, and her partner in the venture is the young man she's had a crush on half her life. All we get out of Carol these days are smiles." She turned to Kirsten. "You know how it is when you're nineteen."

"Sort of," Kirsten said. "Grady and I have a son who's nineteen, and I think he's experiencing his first serious crush."

That meant nothing to Lesley Logan, but Matt, who was aware that Grady and Kirsten had only been married a couple of months, looked startled. Grady chuckled. "It's a long story, pal. I'll explain later."

At that moment their little group was joined by a beautiful brown-haired woman with a radiant smile.

Judging from the reception she received from both Grady and Matt, Kirsten correctly guessed that she was Paula Steele, the rest of the competition. She would make a beautiful president, Kirsten thought; poised and self-confident, the kind of person who would remain unruffled even if walls were collapsing all around her. Again introductions had to be made and pleasantries exchanged.

"Okay, Paula, where's the new husband?" Grady asked. "Matt and I want to give him the once-over, see if we approve."

Paula looked at her watch. "Right now Dane is getting ready to go onstage in Kansas City. When you're married to a performer, you get used to attending parties solo."

"What's your married name?" Matt asked. "Everyone still calls you Paula Steele."

"It's Markham, but I'm keeping Steele for business purposes. I've simply been around too long for people to get used to a new name."

Soon they were joined by other guests; there were more handshakes, more practiced smiles. Kirsten was bombarded with names from all sides. She was grateful when Grady took advantage of the confusion to spirit her away.

"Did you see the look on Matt's face when you said we have a son who's nineteen?" Grady asked with a laugh.

"That just popped out. Sorry."

"Why? I thought it was funny. There must be a bar around here somewhere. Let's get a drink. Booze makes these affairs less tiresome."

"You have an attitude problem, my love," Kirsten admonished.

With Grady in the lead, they threaded their way through the throng and found the bar. They had just placed their order when there was some sort of commotion at the threshold. An air of anticipation seemed to fall over the room. Grady looked out over the sea of heads, then bent slightly to whisper to Kirsten. "The grande dame herself is making her entrance."

Eagerly, Kirsten stood on tiptoe and strained for a glimpse of the human dynamo she had heard so much about. When she finally saw Vanessa Hamilton for the first time, she gasped. "That woman can't be eighty!"

"Isn't she something? A living legend. Watch her work the room."

Vanessa had pushed into the crowd with the enthusiasm of a young girl. She shook hands with everyone, smiling all the while, accepting and acknowledging introductions to spouses she had not met. Unlike most of the people there, she would remember the names long after tonight's party, for she had mastered the art of data storage before computers were invented. Not a soul would leave at the end of the evening without having been on the receiving end of a personal word from the great lady herself. By merely entering the room, Vanessa had captured the spotlight and placed it directly over her head. The guests all seemed to surge forward, like concertgoers eager for a glimpse of their idol.

It was a spectacular entrance. Kirsten couldn't take her eyes off their hostess, and when it became obvious that she and Grady were next in line to be greeted, she was partly mesmerized, partly intimidated and wholly fascinated.

DINNER HAD BEEN in progress for some time. The great dining room—Kirsten thought dining hall would have described it more accurately—was resplendent with starched linen, flowers, gleaming china and crystal and silver. Eight tables had been set up to accommodate the dinner guests. Usually Kirsten cursed whatever carved-in-stone law dictated that husbands and wives could not be seated at the same table, but tonight her dinner companions were charming and interesting. There was, she noticed appreciatively, an amazing lack of shoptalk.

Naturally, everything about the meal was a study in perfection. Each course was more delicious than the last, each wine more excellent than the one preceeding it. Matt Logan sat on Kirsten's right and kept her highly entertained with tales of his daughter's skating career. And it was Kirsten, not Grady, who explained to Matt just how two people who had been married less than two months came to have a nineteen-year-old son.

"Now there's a story Lesley would lap up," Matt said. "We, too, first met many years ago, then happened on each other again quite by chance. I truly believe it's a shame that youth must be wasted on the young. I hope this time everything works out splendidly for you and Grady."

"It will," Kirsten said confidently. Glancing over her shoulder, she sought out Grady's table. Making eye contact with him, she winked. He winked back.

Kirsten seems to be having a good time, Grady thought. But then, she was good at this sort of thing. His own tastes ran more to backyard barbecues and Slick's fried chicken. His mind kept wandering, and he was having a damnably hard time keeping track of the conversation going on around him—not that he thought he was missing anything. Across from him sat Sharon Carpenter, the Midwest Division vice president. Grady liked Sharon, but she was a consummate company person. He suspected Hamilton House was her life. She rarely discussed anything but business. The gentleman on Sharon's left, a man from accounting whose name Grady had already forgotten, was of like mind, so the two of them pretty well dominated the conversation. The other two women at the table were company wives who seemed terrified of saying a word lest they say the wrong one. Rounding out the group was Dolph Wade. Dolph, Grady noticed, was three sheets to the wind and listing badly. If they didn't take away the wine pretty soon and serve the coffee, there was no predicting what might happen when Vanessa made that blasted announcement.

At last dessert was served and consumed. Then rustling noises filled the air as plates were pushed aside, glasses emptied and chairs pushed back slightly. At the table nearest the fireplace, Vanessa stood and clapped her hands. "All right, everyone, let's adjourn to the library for coffee. I have something to tell you that I think everyone will find very interesting." She led the way in a swirl of black silk, her steps sure and lively.

Curious glances were exchanged, and there were mutterings and whisperings as the diners stood and slowly filed out of the room. Thank God, Grady thought. Finally Vanessa was getting the show on the road. He quickly caught up with Kirsten, who slipped an arm around his waist.

"Wasn't the food delicious?" she commented.

"I didn't notice."

"Oh, Grady!" She laughed in exasperation. "How could you not notice food like that?"

In the library, people scattered around finding seats while servants served coffee and mints. No one seemed to notice that Vanessa had quietly gone to sit at the far end of the large room, behind a long mahogany table that served as a reading desk. The table's location was important. When she called for attention, all eyes in the room would be directed toward her.

She waited a minute for the servants to finish their duties. Looking out over the people gathered in the room, she realized that, with the exception of Christopher and one or two others, all of them were indebted to Hamilton House and, therefore, to her. Who would have thought when she and Stuart opened that little café in south Dallas that one day so many people would depend on her for their livelihood? Where had they found the time to do what had been done? Where had they found the sheer energy?

As with many successful people, Vanessa had always been too busy working to sit back and reflect on her accomplishments. Now she did just that, and she was pleased. It made her determination to do all she could to protect the future of what she had built seem even more right than before.

The noise level in the room was subsiding somewhat. She got to her feet, and that effectively brought on instant silence. All eyes turned expectantly in her direction. "I want to thank all of you tonight. It's made my birthday a particularly memorable one. From now on, I fully expect to receive a standing ovation everytime I celebrate another."

Little titters of laughter followed that remark. Vanessa waited for it to die before continuing. "But eighty is eighty, after all, and one cannot reasonably hope for many more productive years. For that reason, I've spent a great part of the past year thinking about the disposition of my estate. However, my estate is only composed of possessions, things that are easy enough to give away without too much thought to what will become of them. Hamilton House, Incorporated, on the other hand, is something else entirely." She paused.

People shifted in their seats, dresses rustled, and cups clinked in saucers. "I've been fortunate over the years to have been surrounded by intelligent, capable employees who were, above all, loyal to me and the company. That is why Hamilton House has grown, through the efforts of all of us, not just one or two people. And I'll confess that for too many years I trusted that it would continue to do so after I was gone. Then something occurred that made me realize how naive I was. Sadly, there are people who have a price, and once that price is met, values are forgotten, loyalty in particular." Vanessa paused again and looked pointedly at Dolph. Her contempt was obvious. The man visibly blanched.

Oh, boy, Grady thought, *she's going for the jugular.*

Vanessa continued. "I'm sure all of you heard about the buy-out offer from Barrington International. I never considered it for a minute, of course, but it became clear to me that someone else had, that someone else surely would do business with Barrington if I wasn't around. Hamilton House would no longer be the same, and I couldn't allow that. Therefore, I have chosen my successor, someone I can trust to keep the company intact and guide it into the next century. Furthermore, I want that successor to assume the duties of president immediately and not wait until I'm in my grave."

For the vast majority of the people gathered in the room, the news was a thunderbolt. Stunned shock rippled through the crowd. Vanessa was stepping down? How could that be? She was indestructible. Only Grady and Kirsten, Matt and Lesley and Paula sat silently. But Kirsten's stomach was churning, and she was sure the others' were, too. She reached for Grady's hand; his palm was clammy. This had better not take much longer. He couldn't take much more, and she didn't think she could, either.

"I've considered several people," Vanessa said, "any one of whom would make an excellent president. Frankly, this decision was the most difficult one of my life, but it had to be made. Commencing no later than May 1, I will kick myself upstairs to become chairman of the board and turn the reins of the presidency over to...Paula Steele."

Grady was assaulted with a dozen different emotions and impressions. First, relief flooded him, and he felt Kirsten go absolutely limp against him, reinforcing his suspicion that she had hoped they wouldn't

be coming to Dallas. And when Paula's name was announced, he had chanced to be looking directly at
Matt, who was seated across from him. Grady
couldn't read a thing in his colleague's expression, but
one would have had to be dense indeed to miss Lesley
Logan's reaction to the news. She patted her husband's arm, and the look on her face was like a kid's
on Christmas morning.

"Thank God," he heard Kirsten whisper.

"Amen," he answered.

"Back to our nest."

"You'd better believe it."

Then he glanced toward the fireplace, where Dolph
Wade was standing. The man's alcoholic flush was
gone. His face was positively ashen. How the mighty
had fallen, all because of greed and disloyalty.

Vanessa had something else to say. "I'm sure Paula
will receive the same cooperation and excellent level of
endeavor from all of you that I've always enjoyed. Of
course, she will choose whoever she wants to serve as
her executive vice president."

A hush fell over the crowd. A choked sound came
from the man by the fireplace. Most of those present
were too embarrassed for Dolph to look in his direction. "Now wait a minute, Vanessa!" Dolph cried, his
voice almost apoplectic.

"No, you wait a minute," Vanessa said coldly. "I'll
speak to you later." Dismissing him with an imperious glance, she turned back to the rest of the guests.
"The company will change hands with scarcely a rip-
ple, which is as it should be. Now, for those of you
who want, liqueurs will be served. Please have a good
time. And thank you again for coming."

What could only be described as subdued chaos ensued as everyone tried to crowd close to Paula and congratulate her. Grady felt too limp to move for a minute, so he was one of the few who saw Vanessa sweep grandly out of the room, followed by a stunned and chastened Dolph. Then he felt Kirsten pat his knee in silent communion. Motioning to her that he would be right back, he made straight for Matt.

"Well, that's that," he said. "How do you feel?"

Matt smiled. "Relieved that it's over, that's for sure. I've known about this for almost a year, and I'll confess something to you, Grady. There were times when I wanted the job and just as many times when I didn't."

Grady nodded. "I know the feeling. And I'll bet if we ask Paula, she'll say she felt the same way."

"She's going to make a fine C.E.O."

"Agreed. Let's go congratulate her."

"We'll have to stand in line," Matt said, indicating the crush of people who were mobbing Paula.

Kirsten came up to stand beside Grady just then. He looped an arm around her shoulders and smiled down at her. The three of them were soon joined by Lesley, and they waited their turn with Hamilton House's new president.

"This is Lesley's first trip to Dallas in years," Matt told them. "We're going to spend tomorrow doing some sight-seeing. Want to join us?"

"Thanks, Matt," Grady said, "but I'm sure the four of us will be in Dallas at the same time quite often in the future. Give us a rain check. Kirsten and I already have plans for tomorrow."

"We do?" Kirsten asked in surprise.

"Sure. We're going home."

A smile wreathed her face. "That's the second-best news I've heard all night."

IT WAS AFTER ELEVEN when the last of the guests departed. "Come, Christopher. Let's go into the den, watch the fire die down and have a brandy," Vanessa said as she and the banker left the library. Already the servants had begun clearing away the party debris.

"You had words with Dolph?" Christopher asked, following her down the hall to the comfortable retreat at the rear of the house.

"Yes, some very unpleasant ones, I'm afraid. It's over, thank God. This has been a difficult year."

"Paula seemed pleased, and neither of the gentlemen in question showed signs of disappointment."

"No, I think both Grady and Matt were enormously relieved. I chose well." Vanessa sank onto one of the sofas flanking the fireplace. "Please pour, Christopher dear."

Christopher unstoppered the decanter on the coffee table. "That was quite a performance tonight, Vanessa. You have a flair for drama."

"I do, don't I? If I come this way again, perhaps I will be an actress."

Christopher handed her a snifter and sat across from her. Vanessa sipped at the brandy, settled back and smoothed her gown. An involuntary sigh escaped her lips.

"Sad?" the banker asked.

"No. Paula will do a splendid job. I confess to something, Christopher. I'm tired. There are aches and pains I don't talk about."

"Admitting your mortality, my dear?"

"Simply admitting that it's time to bring down the curtain, turn the spotlight on someone younger." She lifted the glass to her lips. Over its rim she favored Christopher with her incomparable smile. "But one thing I'll tell you—while it was turned on me, the show had a hell of a good run."

HARLEQUIN *Temptation*

Lovers Apart

FOUR CONTROVERSIAL STORIES! FOUR DYNAMITE AUTHORS!

Don't miss the last book in the LOVERS APART miniseries, April's Temptation title #344, YOUR PLACE OR MINE by Vicki Lewis Thompson.

HARLEQUIN'S WISHBOOK
SWEEPSTAKES RULES & REGULATIONS
NO PURCHASE NECESSARY TO ENTER OR RECEIVE A PRIZE

1. To enter the Sweepstakes and join the Reader Service, affix the Four Free Books and Free Gifts sticker along with both of your Sweepstakes stickers to the Sweepstakes Entry Form. If you do not wish to take advantage of our Reader Service, but wish to enter the Sweepstakes only, do not affix the Four Free Books and Free Gifts sticker; affix only the Sweepstakes stickers to the Sweepstakes Entry Form. Incomplete and/or inaccurate entries are ineligible for that section or sections of prizes. Torstar Corp. and its affiliates are not responsible for mutilated or unreadable entries or inadvertent printing errors. Mechanically reproduced entries are null and void.

2. Whether you take advantage of this offer or not, on or about April 30, 1992 at the offices of Marden-Kane Inc., Lake Success, NY, your Sweepstakes number will be compared against a list of winning numbers generated at random by the computer. However, prizes will only be awarded to individuals who have entered the Sweepstakes. In the event that all prizes are not claimed, a random drawing will be held from all qualified entries received from March 30, 1990 to March 31, 1992, to award all unclaimed prizes. All cash prizes (Grand to Sixth) will be mailed to the winners and are payable by check in U.S. funds. Seventh prize to be shipped to winners via third-class mail. These prizes are in addition to any free, surprise or mystery gifts that might be offered. Versions of this sweepstakes with different prizes of approximate equal value may appear in other mailings or at retail outlets by Torstar Corp. and its affiliates.

3. The following prizes are awarded in this sweepstakes: ★ Grand Prize (1) $1,000,000; First Prize (1) $25,000; Second Prize (1) $10,000; Third Prize (5) $5,000; Fourth Prize (10) $1,000; Fifth Prize (100) $250; Sixth Prize (2,500) $10; ★ ★ Seventh Prize (6,000) $12.95 ARV.

   ★ This Sweepstakes contains a Grand Prize offering of a $1,000,000 annuity. Winner will receive $33,333.33 a year for 30 years without interest totalling $1,000,000.

   ★ ★ Seventh Prize: A fully illustrated hardcover book published by Torstar Corp. Approximate Retail Value of the book is $12.95.

   Entrants may cancel the Reader Service at anytime without cost or obligation to buy (see details in center insert card).

4. Extra Bonus! This presentation offers two extra bonus prizes valued at a total of $33,000 to be awarded in a random drawing from all qualified entries received by March 31, 1992. No purchase necessary to enter or receive a prize. To qualify, see instructions on the insert card. Winner will have the choice of merchandise offered or a $33,000 check payable in U.S. funds. All other published rules and regulations apply.

5. This Sweepstakes is being conducted under the supervision of Marden-Kane, Inc., an independent judging organization. By entering this Sweepstakes, each entrant accepts and agrees to be bound by these rules and the decisions of the judges, which shall be final and binding. Odds of winning in the random drawing are dependent upon the total number of entries received. Taxes, if any, are the sole responsibility of the winners. Prizes are nontransferable. All entries must be received at the address printed on the reply card and must be postmarked no later than 12:00 MIDNIGHT on March 31, 1992. The drawing for all unclaimed Sweepstakes prizes and for the Bonus Sweepstakes Prize will take place May 30, 1992, at 12:00 NOON at the offices of Marden-Kane, Inc., Lake Success, NY.

6. This offer is open to residents of the U.S., the United Kingdom, France and Canada, 18 years or older, except employees and their immediate family members of Torstar Corp., its affiliates, subsidiaries, and all other agencies and persons connected with the use, marketing or conduct of this Sweepstakes. All Federal, State, Provincial and local laws apply. Void wherever prohibited or restricted by law. Any litigation within the Province of Quebec respecting the conduct and awarding of a prize in this publicity contest must be submitted to the Régie des Loteries et Courses du Québec.

7. Winners will be notified by mail and may be required to execute an affidavit of eligibility and release, which must be returned within 14 days after notification or an alternative winner will be selected. Canadian winners will be required to correctly answer an arithmetical skill-testing question administered by mail, which must be returned within a limited time. Winners consent to the use of their names, photographs or likenesses for advertising and publicity in conjunction with this and similar promotions without additional compensation.

8. For a list of our major winners, send a stamped, self-addressed envelope to: WINNERS LIST, c/o MARDEN-KANE, INC., P.O. BOX 701, SAYREVILLE, NJ 08871. Winners Lists will be fulfilled after the May 30, 1992 drawing date.

ALTERNATE MEANS OF ENTRY: Print your name and address on a 3″ ×5″ piece of plain paper and send to:

In the U.S.	In Canada
Harlequin's WISHBOOK Sweepstakes	Harlequin's WISHBOOK Sweepstakes
3010 Walden Ave.	P.O. Box 609
P.O. Box 1867, Buffalo, NY 14269-1867	Fort Erie, Ontario L2A 5X3

LTY-H491RRD

H A R L E Q U I N
American Romance®

THE ROMANCE THAT STARTED IT ALL!

For Diane Bauer and Nick Granatelli, the walk down the aisle
was a rocky road....

Don't miss the romantic prequel to WITH THIS RING—

I THEE WED
BY ANNE McALLISTER

Harlequin American Romance #387

Let Anne McAllister take you to Cambridge, Massachusetts, to
the night when an innocent blind date brought a reluctant Diane
Bauer and Nick Granatelli together. For Diane, a smoldering
attraction like theirs had only one fate, one future—marriage.
The hard part, she learned, was convincing her intended....

Watch for Anne McAllister's I THEE WED, available *now* from
Harlequin American Romance.   ITW